The Perfect Christian

Still Divas Series Book Two

The Perfect Christian

Still Divas Series Book Two

E.N. Joy

www.urbanchristianonline.com

Urban Books, LLC
78 East Industry Court
Deer Park, NY 11729

The Perfect Christian: Still Divas Series Book Two
Copyright © 2012 E.N. Joy

ISBN 13: 978-1-60162-837-4
ISBN 10: 1-60162-837-4

First Printing July 2012
Printed in the United States of America

10 9 8 7 6 5 4 3 2 1

This is a work of fiction. Any references or similarities to actual events, real people, living, or dead, or to real locales are intended to give the novel a sense of reality. Any similarity in other names, characters, places, and incidents is entirely coincidental.

Distributed by Kensington Corp.
Submit Wholesale Orders to:
Kensington Publishing Corp.
C/O Penguin Group (USA) Inc.
Attention: Order Processing
405 Murray Hill Parkway
East Rutherford, NJ 07073-2316
Phone: 1-800-526-0275
Fax: 1-800-227-9604

Other Books by This Author

Dedication

This book is dedicated to the best mother-in-law in the entire universe: Gwendolyn Marsh of Toledo, Ohio. I know Mother Doreen was your favorite character in all the Divas books. I hope I did her justice for you in this book. And also, allow me to take this opportunity to thank you for being so supportive in what I do, which includes scheduling your vacation days around my tour dates so that you can look after the kids. And with that goes a thank you for being the best grandmother I could ever ask for my children. I love you!

Acknowledgment

I'd like to acknowledge my ghost writer. You gave me the title and the subject matter for *The Perfect Christian*. But when it was time for me to sit down and write it, my mind was blank. I had no idea in which direction the story was going to go. But there you were to just take over things and begin to tell me exactly how the story would play out. All I had to do was sit at the computer and take dictation. I can honestly say that this book would not exist if it was not for you. So I acknowledge you and thank you, ghost writer a.k.a the Holy Ghost.

Chapter One

"Mother Doreen, if you aren't just the most beautiful bride I've seen in all my life . . ." Paige's words trailed off as she choked back tears. She had never seen her church mother look so happy and so content in all the years she'd known her. It touched her heart knowing that the joy of the day was because of the Lord. The joy of the Lord, since it was not given by man, could not be taken by man. Eternal joy is what Mother Doreen would have. How could that not have brought tears to anyone's eyes?

"Oh, for Pete's sake! Are you about to start back up that crying mess?" Unique asked Paige as she stormed in between her and Mother Doreen with pressed powder in hand. "You'll get her started again too." She nodded toward Mother Doreen. "And no way is that gonna happen; not after I've been here since eight o'clock this morning . . ." She looked down at her watch. ". . . over an hour ago . . . applying this Mary Kay makeup to her face." Unique pointed the powder puff at Mother Doreen's made-up face. She then looked at a weeping Paige. "You, on the other hand, Sister Paige, get all your crying out now. Because just as soon as I'm finished touching Mother Doreen up, you're next."

"Okay, I'm sorry. I always cry at weddings." Paige wiped away her falling tears, tears that had been contagious since she arrived. Whenever she cried, for some reason, everybody else got to crying too. Unique had already touched up Mother Doreen's makeup twice thanks to Paige's domino effect.

"I know every time I start crying, Mother Doreen does too—everybody does, so I'll cut it out." Everyone gave Paige a doubting look. "I will. I promise."

Although Paige had made the statement with such conviction, it meant nothing as she stared at Unique touching up Mother Doreen's makeup. The older woman looked angelically glamorous. The beauty of the Lord is what Paige thought of the vision before her. And, of course, that thought brought back the water-works as she burst out crying again.

Every head in the church dressing room turned to Paige. Every eye shot her a look that said, "You better stop crying now, or else."

"Okay, okay. I'm sorry," Paige apologized again. "I just can't help it. Mother Doreen has been like a mother to all of us at New Day Temple of Faith. I'm just so ha-ha-happy for her," Paige cried out.

"That's it. Somebody get her out of here now," Unique ordered, pointing to the door.

"I'm so on it," Deborah offered, who had been standing in the mirror admiring the wonderful job Unique had already done on her makeup. "'Cause she's about to ruin my makeup too." Deborah ushered an emotionally torn-up Paige out of the dressing room. On any other day, the room served as the dressing room for both the dance ministry and the changing room for baptism candidates. But today, it was reserved for Mother Doreen and her female bridal party of three, all who were in attendance except for her sister, Bethany, who had yet to arrive at the church.

"Oh, leave my bridesmaid alone." Mother Doreen smiled at Unique. "The child can't help it. I spent all night and this morning doing the same thing; crying my eyes out. Ain't nothing wrong with a few tears to express one's happiness." Mother Doreen closed her eyes while Unique pulled out her eye shadow case and touched up Mother Doreen's eyes. "And if you didn't have my face all done up, I'd still probably be crying."

"And I get all that," Unique said, "and you can go back to all that sniffing and snorting just as soon as you make it down that aisle—but not a minute sooner. I need folks to see all this hard work I've done." Unique paused to hammer in her point. "Do you know how many referrals I got after the last wedding I did? Humph. Don't call me conceited. Call me convinced. I know I've been on my J-O-B today beatin' y'all's faces." She continued the touch-up.

"And a wonderful job you've done indeed, Sister Unique. And thanks again for agreeing to do the makeup for my entire bridal party for free. I couldn't have asked for a more perfect gift from you."

"Trust me," Unique said with her lips tightened, perfecting Mother Doreen's eye makeup, "I'm going to end up booking more weddings and Mary Kay parties as a result of my work here today. Folks are going to see all of you and be so wowed, they'll be hunting me down at the reception," Unique laughed.

"And I'm sure they will. I thanked you in the program and even added your business Web site," Mother Doreen winked.

"You didn't?" Unique said in shock.

"I sure did," Mother Doreen confirmed. "I mean, that's the least I can do with you doing it for no charge and all. And with the huge discount you and Sister Tamarra gave me on catering the reception, why I even listed the Web site for the catering business too."

"You're too much, woman of God. Just an angel is what you are." After making that statement, a serious look crossed Unique's face. "Speaking of Sister Tamarra, how awkward do you think it's going to be with Sister Paige and Sister Tamarra seeing each other during the reception?"

Paige and Tamarra, once the best of friends, hadn't seen each other since the day Paige handed Tamarra divorce papers—divorcing her as a best friend. Paige had been devastated to learn that Tamarra had slept with her husband on the morning Paige married him. Paige thought she'd never be able to forgive Tamarra. She forgave her, though, but made it clear that because the bond of trust had been severed, so had their friendship.

Mother Doreen thought for a moment. "I'm sure all will go well. Besides, Tamarra will pretty much just be in the kitchen. Her and Paige more than likely won't even cross each other's paths. Before I even asked you guys to cater the event, I talked to Sister Paige about it. She was honored that I even came to her for her input, considering it was my big day. She said it was my wedding day and that it wasn't about her, not one iota. She wanted me to be happy. Well, having the best cooks in Malvonia, Ohio, prepare my wedding day feast is exactly what's going to make me happy."

"Thanks, Mother Doreen. Like I said, you're an angel."

Just then, the dressing room door opened. "Okay, I got rid of crybaby," Deborah told them, closing the door behind her. "She's in that little bathroom off the kitchen waiting for you to come do her makeup, Sister Unique." Deborah looked down and patted her lilac dress. As the maid of honor, she was dressed in a gown identical in color to Sister Paige's bride's maid dress and Sister Bethany's matron of honor gown. Although the gowns were the same color, they each were of a different style and fit in order to complement the women's figures. When Deborah looked up, both Mother Doreen and Unique were staring at her with horrified looks on their faces. Deborah shrugged. "What?"

"What?" Unique said mockingly. "What do you mean *what?* Uh, *hello* . . . Sister Tamarra is catering. She's running back and forth in and out of the kitchen."

"And?" Once again, Deborah shrugged, still not understanding the dilemma.

"Oh my," was all Mother Doreen said as sweat beads started to form on her forehead.

Deborah started to sense the seriousness of the matter after noticing Mother Doreen sweating. "I still don't understand what the big deal is. So Sister Paige is in the bathroom off the kitchen, and Sister Tamarra is in the ki . . ." Both Mother Doreen and Sister Unique could see the lightbulb go off in Deborah's head. "Oh my is right, Mother Doreen," Deborah said.

"It's okay, just calm down," Unique said. "You two stay in here, and I'll go get Sister Paige and bring her back in here to do her makeup." Unique headed to the door and mumbled under her breath, "Hopefully without incident, 'cause Lord knows I don't want to get caught up in nothing and end up back in jail." Unique thought of those dreadful months she'd once spent in jail. Being charged with the death of her three children and for being a drug dealer had been devastating. Even though she was released and her name ultimately cleared of all charges, the stench of jail still rested within.

"What did you say?" Mother Doreen asked Unique with a worried look on her face.

"Oh, nothing. Nothing at all," Unique replied with a fake smile. She then looked at Deborah and swallowed hard. "Uh, Sister Deborah, do you mind coming with me?"

"Why?" Deborah asked, already feeling guilty for setting up the situation.

With a stone-cold serious look on her face, Unique replied, "Just in case I need backup."

Chapter Two

"Stop acting like a fool!" Paige scolded herself in the bathroom mirror. She was acting a ridiculous mess if she didn't say so herself. She thought she could do this. She thought she could stand up as Mother Doreen's bridesmaids without getting all emotional, but she was failing miserably.

Paige had been a basket case ever since walking into the church and seeing all the wedding décor. She'd held up during the wedding shower and the rehearsal dinner, but actually walking into the wedding-ready church had just set off something inside of her. Memories flooded her mind; memories of what could have been. No— memories of what should have been.

The memories of her own wedding day should have brought nothing but tears of joy to her eyes, but instead, they were tears of hurt and pain. "She slept with Blake on the morning of our wedding. How am I supposed to ever get over that?" Paige asked her reflection in the mirror. "I can forgive, but how do I forget what I'm forgiving?" Paige wondered why God had granted Himself a sea of forgetfulness but not man; not when it came to things so painful and hurtful anyway. Birthdays, anniversaries, doctors appointments—yeah, those were easy to forget. But what about the stuff people wanted to forget? It just didn't seem fair.

She closed her eyes and took a deep breath. "This isn't about you, Paige. Get it together." And on that note, she grabbed some tissue and began blotting away her tears, leaving bags underneath her eyes. If her skin wasn't so dark, the bags probably would have been red. That beautiful deep chocolate skin she wasn't so sure she admired as a child she was now grateful for.

Opening her eyes, she let out a deep breath and smiled at herself in the mirror. The deep pits in her cheeks referred to as dimples nearly sunk in her face. "Okay, now you're trying too hard. Just be yourself."

Paige turned on the water and wet her hands. She then wiped away some of the tissue that had gotten stuck to her face. Looking at herself one last time in the mirror, she willed herself not to cry again; that is, unless they were complete and utterly tears of happiness.

Unbeknownst to everyone else, most of the tears Paige had shed thus far had been tears of hurt and pain. Walking into the church this morning had been like walking in on her own self-given surprise pity party. She had no idea all the hurt would come flowing back like salmon down a stream. But it had, and the future was too bright—way too bright—to let the past get the best of her, especially when today was supposed to be about Mother Doreen anyway.

"God, I thank you for who you made me to be," Paige prayed. "Thank you that what I might have seen as pain and suffering I can now count it all joy. I'm so glad that you know me better than I know myself. I'm so glad that I have a Father in heaven that cares so much about me that He even knows how many hairs are upon my head. So thank you for loving me, God, and never failing me, even when man did. Hallelujah."

Feeling brand new, rejuvenated, and restored, Paige opened the bathroom door and headed through the kitchen, making her way back to the dressing room. With a smile on her face, she thanked God again for

showing up and pulling her out of her rut. Within moments, though, she'd have the devil to thank for showing up and pulling her down into a pit.

"Paige?"

Paige stopped in her tracks. She knew the voice, the
voice that had just called out her name.

"Sister Paige, there you are." Unique sounded like
she was almost out of breath. Rightfully so, considering
she'd just made a speedy beeline to the kitchen.

Figuring her mind must have been playing tricks on
her, Paige shook her head and kept walking toward the
kitchen exit. Unique stood panting in the kitchen doorway. Unique had one hand on her chest as she inhaled
and exhaled like she'd just run a marathon. Suddenly,
Deborah appeared behind Unique, nearly smashing
right into the back of Unique.

"Oh, you found her—good," Deborah exclaimed, just
as out of breath as Unique was.

Paige put her hands on her hips and looked back and
forth between the two women. "What in the world?
You two are acting like there's a fire somewhere and
you're running to go try to put it out."

Both Deborah and Unique gave each other knowing
looks. Then Unique spoke. "Uh, no fire—no fire at all."

"Thank God," Deborah mumbled under her breath
with her head down.

"Anyway," Unique said, walking over to Paige and loop-
ing her arm through Paige's, "let's go get your makeup
done." Unique began escorting Paige out of the kitchen as
if her life depended on it.

"Well, dang, I must be a tore-up, five-alarm fire with
the way y'all acting," Paige huffed.

"Oh no, it's not that," Unique assured her. "We just
want to make sure everybody's ready is all."

"Good, 'cause y'all had me worried there for a minute thinking—"

"Paige?"

Yet again, Paige stopped in her tracks. Once more, she'd heard a voice that she thought she recognized call out her name. Just like before, it had sounded like the voice was coming from behind her, but then Unique had showed up in front of her. All this had led Paige to believe that her mind was playing tricks on her. Was it? Was this entire wedding thing and thinking about the past making her go crazy? She reminded herself that God's Word said He'd given her a sound mind, so she shook her head—she shook it off—the voice. With Unique's persistent urging that consisted of the pulling of her arm, Paige continued her exit.

"Paige, is that you? It's me, Tamarra."

For the final time Paige stopped in her tracks. Deborah, who had been a step or two in front of Unique and Paige turned around. She was the first to see the owner of the voice: Tamarra. Unique didn't want to believe it was really her, not after they'd been so close to getting Paige out of that kitchen without incident. But the look on Deborah's face told her otherwise. Deborah nodding her head confirmed it even more so.

"Come on now, Sister Paige, you can catch up with old friends later. Right now, we've got to get your face all did up," Unique said as she pulled on Paige in an attempt to continue their trek to the dressing room. It was to no avail, though. Unique's little self had nothing on Paige's full-figured self.

Not too long ago Paige had gotten down to a size twelve, pushing for a ten, but the final stages of her weight loss had been drastic and unhealthy caused by stress. Once she began to put the pieces of her life back together, it included a few pieces of pizza and a couple pieces of pie as well. But knowing she had diabetes, she got back on track and was now maintaining a size fourteen, fluctuating to a size sixteen every now and then. Of course, this didn't do Unique any good. She couldn't budge Paige.

Ignoring Unique's pleas, Paige slowly turned around. There she had it—proof that her mind hadn't been playing tricks on her at all. The voice she thought she'd heard, oh, she'd heard it all right. There stood the proof right in front of her—Tamarra—her former best friend.

"You look good," Tamarra complimented Paige. "Real good."

Paige just stood there saying nothing.

"And it's good seeing you." A smile rested on Tamarra's face. She was truly being sincere. She missed her best friend; that much was evident as sadness and tears began to form in her eyes.

Still, Paige said nothing and did nothing.

"Well, I guess I better get back to setting up." Tamarra looked around the kitchen. "It feels good being back at New Day as well. Even if it is only in the kitchen instead of sitting in the sanctuary as a member of the congregation. Lots of memories though." Tamarra continued to look around. "Lots and lots of memories." She sighed, remembering the day she decided to leave the church, which had nothing to do with her incident with Paige. She had been engaged to a member of New Day. When things didn't work out with him and he got together with another member of the church, she knew she couldn't hang around for the drama.

What exactly was going through Paige's mind, nobody knew—that was, until a few words were exchanged between the two former best friends and then . . .

Try as she might, everything in Paige wanted to be like Jill Scott's character in Tyler Perry's *Why Did I Get Married?* When Jill Scott ran into the woman who used to be her former best friend but had slept with her husband, all Jill said to her was "I'm gonna pray for you." And that's all Paige wanted to say to Tamarra. But unfortunately, her actions spoke louder than words, because before anybody even had a chance to see it coming, the two women were brawling, and Paige had handfuls of Tamarra's hair in each of her fists. Paige hoped God was good at math, because if He knew how many hairs were on Tamarra's head just a second ago, He'd have to do some quick subtraction to figure out how many were left now.

Chapter Three

"As God is my witness, I did not throw the first blow," Paige declared to Mother Doreen as she sat in the dressing room covered in wedding cake.

It took a minute or two, but both Unique and Deborah had managed to separate the fighting divas, better known as Paige and Tamarra. It had been nothing but bad luck though, and timing perhaps, that when they were finally able to pull Paige off of Tamarra, the wedding cake was being carted into the kitchen by a couple of Tamarra's employees.

Unique and Deborah had been tugging and pulling on Paige, desperately trying to get her off of Tamarra, who squirmed, kicked, and fought underneath Paige on the floor. At first it had been all in vain. Paige had the strength of a madman that her friends couldn't seem to overpower.

Finally, Unique had managed to get a pretty good grip around Paige's waist. Deborah, in turn, got a grip around Unique's waist. On Unique's countdown of, "One, two, three . . ." both women pulled as if their lives depended on it. Fortunately, this had worked. In one huge pull from Unique and Deborah, Paige lost her grip on Tamarra. Unfortunately, though, upon the sudden release, the three women went flying backward in sort of a spin, slamming into the cake. Paige bore the bulk of the mess.

"Not only is God my witness, but so are Sister Deborah and Unique." Paige looked at them for support. Support was not what she was about to get though—not from those two.

"My dress," is all Deborah could say as she looked down at the streak of icing going down the front. "My beautiful dress." She then looked up at Paige. "Your dress . . . and your hair."

Paige ran one of her hands through her hair. She then looked at her hand covered with smushed lilac rose made of icing.

"Forget about your dress and her hair." Unique nodded from Deborah to Paige. She then nodded to Mother Doreen. "What about her cake?"

Mother Doreen just shook her head, and then buried her face in her hands.

"No, no, no. Don't do that!" Unique ran over to Mother Doreen and pulled her hands from her face. "You're gonna mess up your makeup."

"Oh, who cares about the makeup?" Mother Doreen threw her hands up. "This is a sign. All this." She swooshed her hands toward the three other women in the room who were wearing traces of her wedding cake. "I knew it. I knew it was trouble to marry Wallace in the first place. All this is just God's way of showing me the disasters to come if I go through with it."

"Nonsense," Deborah commented, walking over to Mother Doreen. "You know just as well as I do that this doesn't have anything to do with God . . ." She shot Paige an evil glare, ". . . and everything to do with the devil."

"So are you trying to say this is all my fault?" Paige asked. "Even worse, are you trying to call me the devil?

Because you know doggone well that Tamarra hit me first. Me pulling out her hair was just a natural instinct."

"There ain't nothing natural about that kind of instinct being in a Christian," Mother Doreen reasoned.

"Oh, well, forgive me." Paige threw up her hands and rolled her eyes sarcastically. "I guess you're just the perfect Christian," she said to Mother Doreen.

"No, honey, I'm far from it," Mother Doreen assured her, shaking her head. "But over the years, as you become transformed, those worldly instincts don't become so natural anymore."

Paige exhaled a relenting sigh. "I know you're right, Mother Doreen." Her tone was apologetic. "If Jesus had had those types of so-called natural instincts, He would have kicked some major booty on His way to Calvary with that cross. I'm sorry, Mother Doreen. I'm sorry for that uncalled for comment, and I'm sorry for ruining your day . . ." She looked down at her dress and over at Deborah's. ". . . and I'm sorry for ruining our gowns." She pointed to the kitchen and started to whine. "And for ruining your cakkkkkke."

"Oh, now, now." Mother Doreen stepped toward Paige in order to try to comfort her, but Unique put her arm out to stop Mother Doreen.

"Unless you want to walk down the aisle with smears of lilac icing roses on your dress, I suggest you allow your words to speak louder than your actions today," Unique suggested.

"Oh, I'm not walking down any aisle," Mother Doreen said. "I'd probably slip, fall, and break my neck doing it. No, siree; God ain't got to give me no more signs."

"Please don't talk like that, Mother Doreen," Paige pleaded. "What I did doesn't have anything to do with God and everything to do with the flesh of two people who call themselves a Christian but acted nothing like Christ." Paige continued. "No, I may not have thrown the first physical blow, but I sure enough threw the first verbal one."

"Yes, you did," Unique confirmed, nodding as she stood there now with her arms folded across her chest. "I mean, I probably would have swung on you too if you had called me a 'fornicating, adulterous, sleazy fake-whore who can't keep a man of your own, so your stuff must not be that good anyway.'"

Deborah eased over and whispered into Unique's ear. "Uh, did you really have to repeat all that?"

"I'm just sayin'," Unique said.

Mother Doreen had a look of shock on her face as she said to Paige, "You said *all* that to that woman?"

Unique butted in and answered for Paige. "She sure did, and that was *after* Sister Tamarra was trying to be cordial, saying nothing but nice things about Sister Paige."

Paige took a deep breath and tried to ignore Unique's interference. "Yes, I did say all that, Mother Doreen." She shot Unique a cutting look, then turned her attention back to Mother Doreen. She opened her mouth to further explain, but the voice that was heard belonged to Unique.

"I guess one could say those were fighting words Sister Paige spit out, because the next thing anybody knew, Tamarra had swung on Sister Paige and got her right upside the head," Unique said. "That's why that bun that was on top of her head is on the side now." Everyone looked at Paige's crooked bun as she attempted to adjust it. "I know Sister Paige saw stars, because there was power behind that lick. I heard the wind when Tamarra's fist was en route and the thud when it landed."

Mother Doreen looked at Paige. "And I guess you just had to hit her back. Couldn't just walk away and come get your makeup done, huh?"

"Oh, Sister Paige didn't just hit her," Unique explained. "She took her fists and locked them down on Tamarra's hair. In Paige's defense, though, it looked like she was just trying to pull Sister Tamarra off of her by her hair, not actually rip her hair out; which she ended up doing anyway once the two reversed positions and Paige ended up on top of Tamarra. But even when we did manage to separate the two, Sister Paige did try to lunge at her again but—"

"Look." Paige pointed an accusing finger in Unique's face. "I know Sister Tamarra is your boss and all, partner or whatever, but—"

"But, I'm not her," Unique spat, staring at Paige's finger, "so you might want to get that finger out of my face."

"And if I don't?" Paige placed her hands on her hips.

Unique became agitated and began pacing. "Oooh, Holy Spirit, kick in and hold me back."

"Girl, you can take that ghetto mess back to the projects from which it came," Paige seethed. "'Cause I am not about to go there with you. I wasn't trying to go there with Tamarra—"

"Oh, but like I said, I'm not Tamarra," Unique reminded Paige. "I don't care nothing about getting my hair snatched off. Matter of fact, I'll do it myself." With quickness, Unique snatched her long weave clip-on ponytail from her head. All that was left was a little nub of hair in a rubber band sitting on top of her head.

Initially everyone just stood there and looked at Unique like she was a nutcase, but then Deborah couldn't help it as laughter exploded from her throat. She could hardly contain herself as she laughed while pointing at Unique's nub of hair.

Before Paige knew it, she was chuckling too. Even Mother Doreen, as cool, calm, and collected as she'd tried to remain, couldn't help but laugh. Unique turned and caught her reflection in the mirror and couldn't even hold in her own laughter.

"Oooh, Sister Paige, you are right; this is a ghetto mess," Unique laughed.

In a matter of seconds, all four women were bent over laughing. They each knew that they had to laugh to keep from crying. This was not how Mother Doreen's wedding day was supposed to have gone.

"Oh, girl, I'm sorry for snapping off on you," Unique apologized to Paige.

"Yeah, me too." Paige returned the apology.

"And I'm sorry for not even thinking when I took Sister Paige to the kitchen," Deborah apologized.

"Well, now that we're all sorry, that still doesn't fix the fact that our dresses are a mess and Mother Doreen doesn't have a wedding cake." Paige's comment put a damper on things.

"Not to worry," Unique said, shaking a pointed finger. "Those satin dresses are so slick, between that and those little wipey things I have that I purchased from Amway, I'm sure we can clean them off."

"What about the cake?" Deborah asked. "What's a wedding with no wedding cake?"

"Not to worry about that either," Unique assured them. "That groom's cake Mother Doreen had us do up for Pastor Frey will do just fine once we add that beautiful cake topper. We even made some little individual cupcakes with the leftover batter that we thought the kids might enjoy. I'll wing it into something beautiful, I promise." Unique sounded so upbeat and convincing, she left very little room to doubt that, in spite of things, the wedding could still go off without a hitch.

Unique went over to her travel bag and purse and started pulling out things. "And we need to fix that hair of yours back up, Sister Paige, and get that icing out of it. I need to touch up y'all's makeup and do Sister Paige's face." Unique rambled on while the other women just watched her go nonstop. "Don't just stand there. Let's get busy," Unique ordered once she realized she was the only one moving about.

While Deborah and Paige hurried over to Unique and the three began their efforts of getting things back in order, they noticed Mother Doreen still hadn't budged.

"Oh my goodness, Mother Doreen. How could I forget about the bride?" Unique apologized. She walked over to Mother Doreen and took her hands into hers. "Is there anything I can do for you?"

Mother Doreen gave off a half smile and a nod. "Yes, as a matter of fact, you can. You can go out there and tell everybody that the wedding is off."

Chapter Four

It was an hour after the time of eleven A.M. in which the wedding was supposed to officially start, but at last, with a whole lot of praying and reasoning, Mother Doreen was ready to proceed. After Unique, Paige, and Deborah sat with her, cried with her, and prayed with her, Mother Doreen realized she was being anything but godly in thinking God was making bad things occur to keep her from getting married.

"Would God really have to go through all that?" Unique had asked. "I mean, if He didn't want you to marry that man, aren't you and God cool enough where He would just come out and say it?"

"Yeah, I agree," Paige had cosigned. "I've heard of God placing a ram in the bush, but I've never known Him to be one to beat around the bush."

"Oh yes, good point," Unique nodded.

Mother Doreen took in their words, and then said with a nod, "I guess when you put it like that . . ."

"You mean you guess when we make it plain," Unique questioned, "like God does?"

"Yes," Mother Doreen smiled. "Exactly how God does. And if God didn't want me getting married, He would have made it plain and just said so. But He didn't."

"And since He didn't, what does that mean?" Deborah waited with baited breath along with the other women before Mother Doreen finally replied.

"It means . . ." Mother Doreen stood up from the chair she'd been sitting in and waved her ring finger, "I's getting married."

All the women stood up and cheered. They hugged and planted kisses on Mother Doreen's cheek as a sign of their support.

At that moment, all set well with her spirit, and there was peace in her decision to move forth with the wedding.

In all actuality, the wedding could have started half an hour ago, but thirty minutes ago, Bethany still hadn't made it in from Kentucky. As it had been planned, Bethany would have spent the last couple of nights with Mother Doreen in preparation for her forthcoming nuptials, but she'd had a spell with her diabetes and had been hospitalized just three days prior to when she was to head out for Malvonia. Bethany had missed the rehearsal dinner, but had proclaimed that no devil in hell could keep her from her sister's wedding. The doctor reluctantly, and with caution, released her from the hospital that morning. Her husband, Uriah, loaded her up and their two kids, Hudson and Sadie, and hit the road. Bethany made it just in time to come in on the tail end of all the prayers and reasoning the other women were doing with Mother Doreen in efforts to convince her to go ahead with the wedding.

"I'm here!" Bethany had exclaimed once she'd entered the dressing room. "Sorry I'm late. Did I miss anything?"

All the women could do was shoot each other looks, and then burst out laughing.

"What? What's so funny?" a confused Bethany had asked before the women began to fill her in on the day's events.

It was Bethany's final input that had confirmed in Mother Doreen's spirit that God did not want her to leave her future husband at the altar. "God wants the best for His best," Bethany had told her older sister.

As Mother Doreen now prepared to go down the aisle, being escorted by one of the older deacons of the church, she thanked God for both her biological sister and her sisters in Christ. They were true friends indeed. They were caring friends as well. To Mother Doreen's surprise, so was that young girl, Unique. Mother Doreen had misjudged the child. With all that makeup peddling and some of Unique's antics, Mother Doreen had recalled back when she herself used to run the Single's Ministry, she didn't think the girl had any Word in her. But in that dressing room, Unique had quoted scripture that not even Mother Doreen knew was in the pages of the Bible. And boy, oh boy, could that little thing pray. By the time Unique sent up a word regarding Mother Doreen's nuptials and life with her soon-to-be-husband, everybody in the room needed their makeup done over . . . again.

All was well now. The dresses had been cleaned up. Hair had been fixed. Makeup was done to perfection. Unique had worked a miracle with the groom's cake and the cupcakes, transforming them into a beautiful wedding cake to replace the one that had been destroyed. It was so spectacular, that no one would be the wiser that it wasn't the original three-tier cake that had been demolished.

Yes, all was well, and Mother Doreen was just minutes away from becoming Mrs. Wallace Frey. The twinkle in her eyes and the permanent smile on her face was even further confirmation that all was well.

The song in which the flower girl, Sakaya, who was the daughter of the leader of the New Day's Tape and

Sound Booth Ministry, walked down the aisle came to an end. There was a moment of silence. As Mother Doreen stared at the closed double doors leading inside the sanctuary, she knew the time was now at hand. In two seconds, the audience would be asked to stand in order to receive the bride. Two seconds after that, "Here Comes the Bride" would begin to play. Two seconds after that, the doors would open, and two seconds after that, Mother Doreen would begin her trek to the man God had for her.

Two, four, six, eight—Mother Doreen took her first step into the sanctuary. Unique was going to kill her, because, by the third step, tears were streaming down her face, smearing her makeup. She had no idea she would be so overcome with emotion. She also had no idea it would look and feel as if she was living out a fairy tale. After all, she was almost seventy years old. Most would assume her life was pretty much over, yet the God she served said that was not so. The God she served said there was no age limit on what He could do in a saint's life. Look at Sarah from the Bible; she laughed when God said He'd give her new life in the form of Isaac in her womb. She laughed because she was so up in age she thought it was impossible. Unlike Sarah, though, Mother Doreen hadn't laughed. She cried.

There were many nights, unbeknownst to anyone around her, in which Mother Doreen had longed for the companionship of a man. True companionship, not like it had been with her deceased former husband, Willie, God rest his soul. Staying with Willie had been more so out of debt, that how Mother Doreen saw it, rather than out of love. She'd felt indebted to him.

Oh, she'd loved old Willie; yes, indeed, with all her heart she loved every ounce of that man. But she hadn't been in love with him. Not at the end. Not af-

ter so many disappointing and devastating things had
taken place in their marriage. But she stayed faithful
and loyal, never leaving or forsaking Willie in all of his
shortcomings, such as the gambling, cheating, drinking, lying, and so on. But when all was said and done,
Willie never left nor had he forsaken Mother Doreen.
Sure, her shortcomings in the marriage could never
measure up in number to all of Willie's. Mother Doreen
had been what most would have considered to be the
perfect wife. But most didn't know about that one huge
mistake Mother Doreen had made that would change
her and Willie's marriage—her and Willie's lives—forever.

But that was the past. That one mistake had gotten
Mother Doreen caught up in a nightmare. Today, she
was living out a dream come true. Today, God was doing for her what He'd done for Sarah. He was giving
her a new life; a new life to share with Wallace. Who
says almost being seventy years old means it has to
be the end? Mother Doreen was living proof that seventy could be the beginning. Age had nothing to do
with what God could and would do for a person. And
Mother Doreen sure was glad about what God was doing for her.

She took the tissue Unique had forced her to carry
cupped in her hand around the stem of the bouquet
and wiped her eyes. Correction, she'd dabbed her eyes
just as Unique had showed her how to do. Small dabs
would prevent her makeup from smearing. Unique,
who stood on the end of a pew smiling, winked at
Mother Doreen, giving her a sign that she'd correctly
managed to wipe away her tears without wiping away
and messing up her makeup.

While all eyes were on the bride and the double doors
were still open, Unique snuck out of the sanctuary to

go prepare for the reception. Needless to say, Tamarra had left the church after her fight with Paige, leaving the serving duties for Unique and the other workers.

By the time Mother Doreen made it down to the altar, her cheeks and jaws were aching from smiling so hard and so much. She'd managed to dab away all her tears, but when she saw Wallace crying a river, and being the debonair man that he was trying to fight them back, she started crying all over again. The two were a bawling mess down there, but it was beautiful—beautiful indeed.

They both managed to keep it together long enough for Pastor Margie to remind them and the entire sanctuary why they were all gathered there today. Mother Doreen and Wallace just stood there, facing each other, holding hands, crying tears of joy together. They were so engrossed in the spiritual connection that tied them that when Pastor Margie asked if there was anyone in attendance that had just cause why the two should not be joined in holy matrimony, they almost didn't hear the man in the back of the church stand up and say, "I do. I have a very good reason why no man in his right mind should marry that woman."

Chapter Five

Who was that man? Mother Doreen pondered. Now that Mother Doreen thought about it, she recalled that man's face. The man who'd just stood up, interrupting her wedding ceremony with claims that he had just cause why Mother Doreen and Wallace shouldn't be married—Mother Doreen recognized him. She didn't recognize him from a previous encounter or from the grocery store or anything like that. She recognized his face from only minutes ago. Just minutes ago was the first time Mother Doreen had ever laid eyes on the man; of that she was sure.

Out of all the hundred fifty or so guests in attendance, that man's face had stood out to Mother Doreen. Ironically enough, the man stood out because Mother Doreen hadn't recognized him at all. It was that and the fact that all the other hundred forty-nine guests were smiling, but this man wasn't. Why hadn't he been smiling? Mother Doreen had briefly wondered as she'd been making her way down the aisle. Was it because Mother Doreen had ruined her makeup with tears and now folks weren't going to be able to get a decent picture of her coming down the aisle? Yes, that could have been it. After all, like many of the others, the man had had his cell phone out snapping pictures. Or had it been a digital camera? Or even a disposable one? At the moment, Mother Doreen couldn't recall. And why was she worried about something so trivial anyway? What she needed to be

concerned with was why had this man—this man who
Mother Doreen knew to be a complete stranger—want
to interrupt her wedding.

Perhaps it was just all a joke. Perhaps the man was
some crazy distant cousin of Wallace's playing some
kind of untimely joke. They'd probably played jokes on
each other all the time as kids and this was the ultimate
payback. It was possible. Wallace had cousins, lots of
them; from all over. Mother Doreen's mind was scrambling for answers. But it was Pastor Margie who had
the good sense to quickly just come right out and ask
the man just what everyone in the sanctuary wanted to
know.

"Who are you?" Pastor Margie asked. She tried not to
sound so badgering, but she was somewhat upset. Who
would have the audacity to try to ruin one of the best
days of one of her best member's life? And on top of
that, Pastor Margie considered Mother Doreen a good
friend. Why, the two had even been temporary room-
mates once upon a time. Why was this man doing this
to her friend? Pastor Margie would ask that question
too. "And why are you speaking out?"

One could hear a church mouse go tinkle on a cotton
ball it was so quiet. Everyone waited in anticipation for
the man to respond.

"Right now, who I am isn't as important as why
I'm speaking out." The man, looking to be in his for-
ties, sounded and looked like a very studious man. He
stood about five feet ten. His light skin complexion was
smooth as he glared over the rim of his dark framed
eyeglasses. He had a tight haircut and was dressed in
what looked to be a very snazzy suit. When he stepped
out from the pew to the middle of the aisle, his shiny
dress shoes twinkled like a star in a midnight sky.
When he spoke those few little words, he annunciated

every single sound of every single letter to perfection. He commanded attention, and not just because he'd spoken out during the middle of a wedding ceremony, but because he just had this certain aura about him.

"Then why are you speaking out?" Pastor Margie asked again.

"You asked if there was anyone in attendance that had just cause why the two should not be joined in holy matrimony. Well, I have just cause; and that, Pastor, is my reason for speaking out."

Pastor Margie swallowed, almost afraid to ask her next question, but knew she had to in order to move forward with the wedding nuptials. "And what might that cause be?"

"She knows." He pointed and stared accusingly at Mother Doreen, who stood shocked and confused. "Please don't add insult to injury by standing up there like the perfect little bride acting as if you have no idea whatsoever why this man shouldn't marry you." He looked at Wallace. "If I were you, I'd get out of here right now, run, and never look back." His attention turned back to Mother Doreen, but he was still speaking to Wallace. "She'll ruin your life and go on with her own as if she didn't have a care in the world."

His evil stare caused Mother Doreen to look away. She felt as though she were staring evil right in the face. It didn't matter how dressed up, smart, and handsome this man looked, he meant harm . . . and she appeared to be his target. But why? She'd never met this man before in her life. Therefore, there was no way he knew her. This had to have been some mistake. For a minute there, Mother Doreen had allowed her mind to wander down the same thought path as earlier—that God was trying to give her a sign that she should not wed Wallace. But she'd come too far. She'd come all the way down that church aisle. No way He would have brought her this far . . . only to leave her here . . . alone . . . without a husband.

Frustrated as frustrated could be at this point, Mother Doreen spoke up. "Look, sir, I have no idea who you are, and you surely don't know me. Maybe I have the same name as someone you thought you knew," Mother Doreen tried to reason. "I don't know what your deal is." She threw her hands up and let them drop to her side. "All I know is that this wedding is already almost two hours late in getting started." She looked at Wallace. "And if I have to wait even one more minute to marry this wonderful man, then I'm going to lose my mind."

"How fitting you should say that," the man chuckled, "lose your mind. Considering that's exactly what happened to my mother thanks to you."

Still, Mother Doreen was very confused, and it showed on her exasperated face. "Child, I don't know you or your mama." Mother Doreen pointed her finger at the man. "But if I ever do meet your mother, I'm certainly going to tell her about your actions here today, and I'm sure she won't be too proud about it."

"Lauren Casinoff," were the words he said. Lauren Casinoff were the words that shot from his mouth like a hot bullet, and they landed right in Mother Doreen's gut. The force was so hard that it shot her back into Wallace's arms. Her limp body felt lifeless. The bullet of a word had hit a major organ; two to be exact. It had hit her heart. It had hit her brain. The blow to her brain shook Mother Doreen from the present, all the way back to the past. It was far back into the past leading up to the day when the name Lauren Casinoff would alter her life, and now, all these years later, possibly come back to destroy it.

Chapter Six

Of all the men in the state of Kentucky, Doreen Nelly Mae Hamilton had to be smitten with William Tucker. No one in town saw that love connection coming. The two were total opposites. Doreen was raised by parents who regularly attended and volunteered in the church. Willie's parents ran a juke joint named Our Place, which Doreen's parents referred to as a sin hole. Doreen dressed clean-cut and pretty; nice, handmade dresses as a result of her mother's handiwork. Willie wore a style that the children of Generation X think they started—sagging. Why smooth, well-groomed, good girls always seemed to be a magnet for the boys who were rough around the edges, a.k.a. roughnecks, has yet to be figured out. Or was it the other way around? Was it the bad boys that attracted the good girls? Although the vote may still be out on that one, it was as clear as a bell that when it came to Doreen and Willie, the attraction was mutual. No one, not even Doreen's parents, could deny that—try as they might.

"The oldest of all three girls, what kind of example do you think you're setting for your sisters?" Doreen's mother rubbed her tiny baby bump that six months later would turn out to be yet another beautiful, bouncing baby girl for the Hamilton family.

Doreen just stood in the kitchen looking down at the ugly green designs on the linoleum kitchen floor. She could not figure out for the life of her why shades of green were such a popular décor color. She looked up and around the kitchen at the chipping mint-green paint on the walls.

"Child, are you paying me any type of never-mind?" Mrs. Hamilton asked her eldest daughter.

"Yes, Mama, I'm listening," Doreen lied, because she wasn't. Why did she need to? She'd heard that same old song and dance a thousand times already. She'd heard it for over six months now, ever since old Willie boy introduced himself to her one night while she was walking home from the Jaimesons' after babysitting their little one.

He'd been hanging out at one of his boy's houses after helping him and his young wife move into their new place. After a long day's work, Willie and the fellas were hanging out on the front porch eating fried chicken and drinking beer, the payment for their labor.

Doreen had been able to hear the lively bunch long before she ever saw them. Their language, that's what had gotten her attention. Their mouths were just as foul as week old collard greens left out in the sun in the summertime . . . with a hunk of salt pork right in the middle of the pot. Doreen had thought their breaths had probably smelled like it too. Stinking words such as the ones they were using could only come from a stinking source.

Disgusted and no longer willing to allow the men's words to infiltrate her ear ducts, Doreen began to hum song 104 from the church hymn book. The closer she got to the men, the louder she had to hum until eventually she was singing. Even though she'd sung in the church choir since she could remember, Doreen wasn't the best of singers. As a matter of fact, she'd never had a true desire to even sing in the choir. In her opinion, she'd chosen the worse of two evils when her parents made it clear to her that the Hamilton children would do something in the church, be it ushering or singing in the choir.

Doreen's younger sisters had chosen to usher, reasoning there weren't weekly rehearsals for ushers, so they didn't have to worry about giving up yet another one of their evenings to the Lord. They already gave up Tuesdays for evening devotional, Wednesdays for Bible Study, and then both Sunday mornings and evenings for the two services. Giving up Thursday evenings to rehearse songs that they could sing right from the church pew was out of the question.

It was no biggie for Doreen, though. Actually, she looked at it as an opportunity to get out of the house and away from her nagging siblings. All they wanted to do was to sit up under Doreen and be in her business. They didn't mean to be so annoying to Doreen. The girls were just so fascinated by their oldest sister, that they watched her every move. They wanted to walk like she walked, talk like she talked, and dress like she dressed. Their parents had indeed put their firstborn on a pedestal. She was the mold that all the Hamilton children would have to fit.

At first, Doreen didn't feel any pressure in having to be the perfect child. She liked it. It made her parents proud. She could see it in their eyes every time they looked at her. Not only that, but it made God proud too. Doreen could feel it in her spirit. God, her mother, and father were who Doreen would live to please. And as a result of the way she carried herself, she would receive favor from them all.

Her mother would take in extra laundry in order to make money for the more expensive material to sew Doreen's dresses. Her sisters never complained. They just waited around for their turn, because they knew it was only a matter of time before they'd get to wear Doreen's hand-me-downs.

Her father would always get his oldest daughter an extra quarter of a pound of licorice on Friday night after work and after cashing his paycheck. Of course, behind his back, she'd split the extra evenly among her siblings.

God? Well, He was just God, showing Doreen how much He loved her on a daily basis through His grace and mercy. In addition to that, God always seemed to answer every single last one of Doreen's prayers in the affirmative. If she prayed she'd get an A on her test, she did. If she prayed she'd not get picked on to do a church solo, she didn't get picked. Although Doreen could carry a tune back in the day, she knew dang well she didn't stand a chance in being on one of today's church praise and worship teams. Half of them might as well go ahead and sing rhythm and blues instead of gospel.

Singing from her heart though, God allowed Doreen's voice to blend in well enough so that there were no complaints from the choir director. Doreen's voice had been included in the many local choir competitions, of which her church had won a few. The winning church always received a nice-size monetary donation that would ultimately go to some sort of building fund or another after each member of the choir and their families were treated to dinner.

Much favor was Doreen shown by those she aimed to please most. In all honesty, she felt like Joseph from the Bible, only her siblings weren't jealous of her. They'd quickly learned that if their older sister got blessed, then they ultimately got blessed too. If basking in their sister's overflow was this rewarding, they could only imagine the favor and rewards that would come to them if they could be just like her.

The perfect sister to her younger siblings, the perfect daughter to her parents, and the perfect Christian to God, that is what Doreen strived to be. And she'd been well on her way until she tried to add yet another task on her "Perfect List," which was the perfect wife. Trying to be the perfect wife to William Tucker would end up being a perfect mistake.

Chapter Seven

Looking back on Doreen's tenure with Willie that evening when she was walking home humming to drown out the expletives of her new neighbors, some might say when Willie stepped down off that porch and approached her, she should have kept right on going. The truth of the matter is that she had.

"That sure is a pretty sangin' voice you've got there, Missy," Willie had complimented after Doreen's voice had lured him off his friend's porch and in her direction.

"Get thee behind me, Satan," Doreen sang loudly toward the silhouette coming up beside her.

"Oh, it's like that?" Willie chuckled as Doreen kept on walking as if he wasn't even there. Ordinarily, his ego would have been bruised, but for the first time since he could remember, his mind was fixed on something besides himself. It was fixed on that pretty young thing named Doreen Hamilton.

Upon his return to the porch after being completely ignored by Doreen, Willie would learn from one of the fellas that Doreen was the daughter of a preacher who ran his own church. Next he was told that he didn't have a chance in hell, literally, to get with her. Plenty guys had tried, but that Doreen had only given two other men the time of day in her life: her preacher man daddy and God.

Words meant to discourage Willie only ignited the desire in him to hook up with Doreen. So that following Sunday when he showed up at her daddy's church just as dapper as could be, Willie was only looking for one thing. Trust and believe that one thing wasn't Jesus.

To this day, Mother Doreen had no idea that the same fella that wooed her that Sunday morning in church was the same fella she'd shot down on her way home one dark evening. It was a good thing for Willie she hadn't paid him enough never-mind to recognize him as the drinking and cursing hoodlum she'd basically referred to as Satan. This allowed him to make what Doreen thought was his first impression in a different light; actually, in the light.

Knowing exactly what he was working with, a preacher's kid, Willie upped his game and put on his charm to the tenth power. It was that same charm that had enabled him to get in the skirts of many a gal. Truth be told, though, ever since he'd set his sights on Doreen, no other woman had occupied his thoughts. He never even gave another woman the time of day. He was too busy planning and plotting on how to get with Doreen. What started out as a challenge for Willie turned into love. All his boys even teased him about going soft. Willie never let the peer pressure get to him, as six months later, he stood in Doreen's daddy's church prepared to make her his wife.

Good thing for Willie that Doreen never let peer pressure get to her either; otherwise, Willie would have long been kicked to the curb. Instead, though, Doreen was standing in front of a full-length mirror in the church bathroom wearing an all-white gown—rightfully so considering she was a virgin—about to become Mrs. William Tucker.

"The oldest of all four girls, what kind of example do you think you're setting for your sisters?" Once again, Doreen's mother had posed the question. This time, she held her newborn daughter in one arm and touched up her eldest daughter's hair with her free hand.

"Oh, Mama, you've been saying that since I started seeing William six months ago," Doreen had replied to her mother. "Can't you just let me be on my wedding day?" Mrs. Hamilton cast her eyes downward as she held back tears. Doreen turned to face her mother, touching her shoulders. "Mama, those betta be tears of joy."

Not wanting to cast a black cloud on her daughter's wedding, Mrs. Hamilton perked up and both forced and allowed a small smile to slightly split her lips.

"That's more like it, Mama." Doreen pulled her mother in for a hug as close as she could without smashing her new baby sister, Bethany. Doreen pulled away, and then looked down at the baby. While rubbing the baby's cheeks with her index finger she said to her mother, "And, Mama, whether you want to believe it or not, I'm setting a mighty fine example for my little sisters. I mean, I'm not out here gallivanting around, sleeping with all kinds of menses. I saved myself for my husband, Mama. I'm getting married. What better example can I set for the girls?"

Mrs. Hamilton thought about it for a minute. "Yeah, I guess you're right." She then shook her head. "But William Tucker? Of all the menfolk out there you could'a married, you chose him." She closed her eyes, sighed, then opened them again. "But I reckon I don't know much about him—only what I've heard on the streets. But I know his daddy and his momma. I went to school with his daddy, and if he's anything like his daddy was back when he was his age . . ." Once again, Mrs. Hamilton shook her head while closing her eyes. After exhaling, she opened her eyes, stared at her daughter, and continued talking. "Oh, child, if William is anything close to being like his daddy . . ." she placed her hand on Doreen's cheek, "I'm going to pray for you."

Doreen smiled at her mother. "Oh, Ma, well, even if he ain't like his daddy, pray for me anyway, all right?" Doreen requested, still smiling. "All right?"

All her mother could do was nod while she held back tears. At that moment, her spirit confirmed in her that Willie would be nothing like his daddy. He would be ten times worse.

Chapter Eight

"Willie, who is that lady?" Doreen could barely contain her Christianity right about now.

This had been the second night this week where Doreen looked at the clock. It was after midnight, and yet, the spot next to her in the bed was empty. Having been married to Willie for not even a good six months, surely he wasn't tired of her already. Surely he wasn't the cheating, drinking, lying, gambling man that her mother had warned her he was. She'd pulled herself out of the bed to go hunt Willie down and see for herself.

Considering that he was sitting up in his parents' drinking establishment with a beer bottle in one hand and four empty ones in front of him on the table proved he was definitely a drinking man. The fact that he had playing cards in his other hand and a pile of money sitting in the middle of the table proved he was a gambling man. That heifer sitting on his lap proved that he was a cheating man. The words that came out of his mouth next confirmed that he was a lying man.

"What lady?" Willie answered his dumbfounded wife. "I don't see no lady." He threw out a card and focused on the game as if Doreen wasn't even standing there.

"Don't you dare try to play me like a fool—like I'm dumb and blind or something," Doreen spat. "I'm talking about that woman sitting right there on your lap."

Doreen pointed at the thick, long-legged, barely wearing any clothing woman that sat on Willie's lap like he was Santa and she was telling him what she wanted for Christmas. Whatever it was must have been a secret, because she'd been whispering in Willie's ear when Doreen first spotted them.

"Oh, her right here?" He took a swig of his beer, and then set it down on the table. "This ain't no lady. This is Agnes."

The other three men sitting at the table chuckled. Agnes gave Willie a playful punch and chuckled right along with the fellas.

Doreen looked Agnes up and down, rolling her eyes along the way. "I might have to agree with you on that one—that this is no lady. Because a lady wouldn't be settled on the lap of another woman's husband. Only a whore would be doing that."

Agnes jumped off Willie's lap and made a move toward Doreen, but Willie grabbed her arm. He never said a word to Agnes, just gave her a look. It was a look that only allowed Agnes to roll her eyes at Doreen sharply and walk away.

"What the heck is going on here, Willie?" Doreen asked. "Is this why when I wake up in the middle of night I'm alone in my bed? 'Cause you're down here at your parents' place with other women?" She looked down at the pile of money on the table. "And is this why the lights was off last month? Because you gambled the electric bill money away?"

"Now, woman, you betta go 'head with all that." Willie didn't give Doreen the look. He gave it to the cards in his hands instead, but she knew it was for her. She knew that look meant for her to walk away just as Agnes had.

"All right, I will go on, but only with my husband in tow," Doreen agreed.

"Look, I just got a couple more hands to play; then I'll see you at home."

"Fine," Doreen said, turning away. She didn't go far though, only far enough to grab a chair, pull it up, and plant herself next to Willie.

The men at the table looked at Willie as if to ask, "You ain't got yo' woman in check yet?"

"I meant for you to go ahead home without me," Willie explained to Doreen, throwing out a card. "I'll see you when I get done playing out this game."

Doreen let out a harrumph. "Do you think I'm gon' head back home while my husband hangs around so he can be in the likes of another woman's company?" Doreen rolled her eyes. "Puhleeze." She then looked at the man who was sitting at the table directly across from her and Willie. "It's on you," she told him, informing him that it was his turn to play his hand.

"If you're here babysitting me because you think me and ol' Agnes there got something going on, then you're losing sleep for nothing. She's just a friend of the family is all. Been waitressing here since my parents opened the place. She's like family. A little sister almost."

The men did all they could to keep from laughing, but a small chuckle escaped from one of their mouths. Willie smirked at him as if to say, "I'm the man." He turned his attention to Doreen, finally looking his wife in the eyes. "I'm sorry if Agnes made you feel uncomfortable. She don't mean no harm."

Doreen stared at Willie for a moment. "If you think you married some dumb little church girl who's going to let you do whatever you want, and then come back with some jive 'I'm sorry,' and everything is going to be okay, then you've got another think coming. You married a saint, but you didn't marry Jesus." Doreen stood. "Fellas, it's been real," she said to the other men at the card table. "William, your wife is ret-ta-go."

One man sank down in his seat, embarrassed for Willie for being checked by his wife in front of his boys. Another man let out a whistling air and tried to pretend he just hadn't witnessed Doreen take authority of the situation.

"Guess she told you," the other man mumbled under his breath while picking at his cards.

Willie's light brown skin turned as red as a beet. Through gritted teeth he said to Doreen, "Like I said, I'ma finish this game, so you head on home and I'll meet you there." He turned his attention back to the card game. "Hopefully with all these fools' money."

That fired the men up as they all focused back on their game. Doreen stood there feeling defeated, but not willing to give up. "If I go home by myself tonight, then that's how it's gon' be."

Willie paused before saying, "Then that's how it's gon' be." He'd only said that because his boys were there. The last thing he wanted to do was to lose a showdown with his wife in front of them. It would set an awful pattern for some of the other womenfolk. Willie was the smoothest player in town. If other men's wives got wind of how Doreen set him straight, they might get the same idea about pulling the same stunt with their own husbands. And heck, those husbands were who kept his parents' place in business. He couldn't allow all that to happen now, could he?

Although Willie stopped going to church regularly a little while after he and Doreen got married, he recalled a similar Bible story. Now he knew firsthand how King Ahasuerus felt when he had to kick Queen Vashti to the curb and get with Esther.

God knew how much Willie loved Doreen and how he'd rather lose a leg than lose her as his wife. He loved her as much as any man could truly love a woman. But he was loving his wife the same way he'd witnessed his daddy love his mama over the years. He'd witness his daddy sit up under all types of women in their spot, right while his mother wiped down all the tables. He'd dared her to speak on it, so she rarely did unless she'd had a few too many drinks. So this type of behavior and treatment was all Willie knew. It was like it was in his system—in his DNA. It was a curse, one that only prayer and deliverance could break off of him. Thank God he'd married a praying woman indeed. There was nothing like the power of a praying wife. But as Willie watched the back of Doreen exit through the doors, all he could do was pray that after all was said and done, he'd still have a wife.

Chapter Nine

"Baby, can you just come back home? I . . . I need you, girl. I love you. Please come back home." Those weren't the words Willie had rehearsed on his way over to Doreen's parents' house, but those were the only words that managed to roll off his tongue now that he stood on their doorstep. He'd planned on showing up at her parents' doorstep and laying down the law, demanding Doreen to come home. But what he was doing now sounded a lot more like begging and pleading.

It had been two nights since the couple's falling out at the juke joint, and Willie swore he couldn't stand another day being apart from Doreen. He'd held out the past two nights from even calling her, holding on to the idea that she'd realize she couldn't stand to be without him and make her way home. That hadn't been the case, however. Ever since coming home that night after their argument and finding her and her bags gone, Willie hadn't even been able to think straight. The funny thing was, all the times when Doreen had been waiting for him to come home, he'd been in no rush getting there, stopping off to do whatever it was that he wanted to do. Sometimes he wouldn't even stop in from work first just to say hello. Now that Doreen wasn't there waiting for him, lo and behold, there he'd been sitting in his favorite chair staring at the television box. It was a scene on television that had prompted him to get out of that chair, grab his britches and his pride, and go get his wife.

In the movie, the leading male had pretty much taken his wife for granted, with her ultimately leaving him for another man. Willie gritted his teeth at just the thought of it. Thinking maybe that movie was some kind of sign—that God was trying to tell him something—he wasted no time going to the only place where he knew Doreen would be.

"You need me? You love me?" Doreen repeated Willie's words through the screen door as she stood inside the house. "Humph; word around town is that you be saying those same exact words to Agnes." Doreen stood in the doorway of her parents' home with folded arms.

"Who been telling you those lies?" Willie asked. "Because that's exactly what they are—lies. I ain't been telling no other woman I love them, because you are the only woman I love." He touched Doreen's cheek that was steaming red with anger. "You're the only woman I've ever loved. That's why I just had to have you, girl. You are the only woman I've ever thought twice about making my wife. I never imagined in a million years I'd be the settling-down type."

"And from the looks of things, you're still not." Doreen's mother had heard enough. She'd been standing behind the half-open door, off to the side listening to Willie and Doreen's conversation. Now it was time she participated in the conversation and add her two cents.

"Good evening, Mrs. Hamilton," Willie greeted his mother-in-law.

"It was." Mrs. Hamilton cut her eyes at Willie, and then looked at her daughter who gave her a knowing look. She then turned back to Willie and gave a forced smile. "I'm sorry. I suppose that wasn't the Christian thing to say. Besides, it ain't none of my business nohow. Doreen here picked you, so she's the one who has got to deal with you. Since she married you in the house of the Lord and in God's name, that makes you my son-in-law. So, I'm thinking that means I have to deal with you too." She gave Willie the once-over. "So you gonna stand outside on my porch forever or are you gonna come in for supper, and then take your wife home?"

Willie tried not to smile, but one crept out anyway. Still, it wasn't as hard as he wanted to smile. "Uh, yes, ma'am. I will. I am." He put his hand on the screen door and took a step toward the entrance of the house. He halted his steps when he saw the not-so-welcoming look on Doreen's face. "I mean, yes, I will, that is, if Doreen will have me still."

All eyes turned to Doreen now in anticipation of her response. She looked at her mother as if she held the answer.

"I don't know what you are looking at me for," Mrs. Hamilton said. "Like I said, you picked him. God hates divorce, and I don't think He's too fond of separation either. Separation is like a crack for Satan to seep into and do his dirty work."

Knowing darn well that she loved Willie's dirty drawers and wanted nothing more than to skip dinner and get home with her man, Doreen still played it cool. She didn't want Willie to think he could get away with this type of behavior without any repercussion; with her just falling right back into his arms as if nothing had happened. So, after a brief pause, she sighed and relaxed her shoulders. This made Willie think she was game for the reconciliation, so he took another step into the house.

"I'll think about it," Doreen finally answered. On that note, she pushed Willie back outside and slammed the door in his face. Then she walked over to the window and watched him make a slow, dreadful trek back to his car, and then drive off home—without her. All Doreen could do was turn around and fall into her mother's arms. "Oh, Mama, I love him so much, but I don't know if I can do this. Marriage is forever. Can I really do this forever?"

"Look here, baby girl." Mrs. Hamilton separated herself from Doreen and grabbed her by the shoulders. "Willie is the same man today that he was when you married him some months ago. As much as you tried to act like you didn't, you knew exactly what kind of man you were marrying, so you have no right to complain about it now. Now all you can do is deal with him. Don't try to change him, because it ain't gonna work. Only God can change a person, and He can't even do it if that person won't receive it—if that person doesn't want to be changed."

Doreen felt hopeless. "Well, can I at least ask God to change him?"

"Sure, you can, but I have a better idea."

Doreen's eyes lit up. "What is it?"

"Ask God to change you and how you deal with ol' Willie, because trust me, dear, things are not about to get better any time soon. And I'm not trying to say all this just to scare you, but Doreen, baby, when you take up with the devil, you are bound to go through hell."

Chapter Ten

Doreen entered the church with thanksgiving. This was the day that the Lord had made, and she was so glad about that. She felt so blessed to see another day through God's grace and mercy that her spirit could do nothing less than rejoice. As the praise and worship team led the church in a few hymns, she sang like her life depended on it. She belted those praise songs out of her belly like she was giving birth. Her praise led to a worship so deep that even when the song was over Doreen didn't want to come out. She couldn't come out. She didn't come out—not until about ten minutes afterward when all the other praise and worship members had already left the stage and gone to their seats among the congregation. Even as she walked to her seat, tears streamed down her face as she mumbled in her prayer language to God.

The announcements had been read and her father had already started preaching by the time Doreen made it to her seat. She was none the wiser of what had been going on in the sanctuary, though. She had been in the Lord's presence. She had His attention. It was as if she'd reached out and touched His garment, and now that she had a good grip on Him, she didn't want to let Him go.

"That's right, Sis, give Him some praise," Doreen's little sister, Pauline, whispered in her ear as Doreen took a seat next to her. Pauline, or Paula as everyone called her, was the third daughter. She patted the top of Doreen's hand. "It's gon' be all right. You just keep praying, praising, and worshiping. God will get you through."

Doreen looked at her little sister and smiled. Pauline had always been wise beyond her years. That child loved the Lord and was after His heart so badly, she would have given David a run for his money. Preacher Girl was the pet name their father had for her. He said out of all his children, she was going to be the one to take over the church after him. And that was something big coming from Mr. Hamilton, because it wasn't too long ago that he felt women had no business behind the pulpit unless it was to do announcements or sing. Guess God showed him. God done went and born to him the very thing he felt shouldn't exist—a woman preacher.

God certainly does have a way of changing folks. Doreen was glad about that, because hopefully, God could keep working on changing her. Her mother had been right last year when she told Doreen that she was going to go through hell with Willie. The past year had indeed felt like hell.

That next day after Doreen had gone back to Willie from her parents' house, and for the next month or so after that, things had been great. Willie had even taken up joining Doreen for church three Sundays in a row. It wasn't too long after that, though, Willie turned back to his wicked ways. He was back hanging out at his parents' place all night, gambling, drinking, lying, and God knows what else. Doreen didn't know what else, but certainly God did. Doreen didn't want to know either. This was a time when she didn't mind being ignorant of Satan's devices, knowing some things just hurt too badly. The ironic thing about it was that sometimes not knowing hurt even worse. Doreen knew one thing though; she had a family that prayed, and with their prayers and those of her own, she could get the victory over any situation the devil threw her way.

After church, Doreen felt rejuvenated and brand new. God had restored so much in her, it was as if she had the strength of Samson now. She didn't even let the fact get to her that Willie had brought only half his paycheck home this week when he stumbled in drunk in the wee hours of the morning. He'd gamble off most of their bill money, but she would make it work. As a matter of fact, she would be prepared for things like this by finding a way to contribute her own money to the household.

"Pound cakes and dinners!" Doreen said out loud as she walked up to her house. "I'll sell pound cakes or chicken dinners. Heck, I might even sell 'em in that old juke joint," Doreen laughed. She then thanked the Holy Spirit for giving her such a good idea. Doreen was leaning more toward pound cakes. She made the best pound cakes that side of Kentucky. Everyone in the church had told her so. Every time the church was having a bake sale or some kind of event that required the members to bring food, the first thing everyone would ask was, "What did Sister Doreen bring?" Then they'd charge right over to her dish and get to devouring it.

Doreen could burn in the kitchen like nobody's business. She had to. With her mother helping her father so much with the church, she had to help out a lot at home. Cooking was her favorite thing. A gift from God is what most called it. Well, she would take her gift and use it to bless the finances of her home.

"Willie? Willie, guess what? The Holy Spirit just gave me a wonderful idea," Doreen exclaimed as she barged into the house. She couldn't wait to tell her husband about the entrepreneurial spirit that had just been dropped into her being. She was so excited to share her news with Willie that she didn't even stay for fellowship in the dining hall like she usually did. She had raced straight home instead.

Usually Willie was always sitting in the living room in his favorite chair watching television when Doreen got home from church, but to Doreen's surprise, not today. Only his shoes sat in front of the chair. Doreen walked over and picked them up and sighed. "That Willie. I've told him a million times about leaving his shoes laying around. What's he want me to do? Trip over them and break my . . ." Doreen's words trailed off as she spotted another pair of shoes, but unless Willie wore black open toe patent leather high-heel shoes, this pair was not his. They certainly weren't hers.

All of a sudden Doreen gasped, and Willie's shoes fell out of her hand and to the floor. Both her hands dropped to her belly, and she held it as if she was trying to keep her insides from spilling out. Her eyes became moist as she shook her head and mumbled, "No, Willie, not in my house—not in our house . . . in my bed."

She began to tremble as she picked up the pair of women's shoes. She began taking steps toward her closed bedroom door. The closer she got, she could hear some whispering and shuffling around inside. Doreen reached for the doorknob. Did she really want to know what was going on, on the other side of that door? Would whatever she saw lead her back to her parents' home, and for good this time?

Just standing there at the door with her hand on the knob she had yet to turn, Doreen waited for the answers to all of the questions that had been running through her head. None came—not soon enough anyway, because before she knew it, she had flung the door wide open.

"Doreen, baby! What you doing here?" Willie said as he stood over by the open window with no shirt on and his britches barely pulled up.

Doreen looked around the small room. Willie was alone. She walked over to the closet, opened the door, and did a search. No one was in there. She walked over to the bed, kneeled down, and looked under it. No one was there. She stood back up and shot Willie a glare.

Nervous as all get out, Willie asked, "Wha . . . what are you looking for, sweetness?" As he spoke, he inched in front of the open window. Just then, Doreen heard some tires peeling off. She ran over to the window, but Willie was there to block her.

"What you doing, honey? I'm so glad you're home. I'm so glad to see you." Willie swooped Doreen up and embraced her, spinning her around in the air as if he hadn't seen his wife in a month of Sundays.

"Put me down this instant, Willie Tucker," Doreen spat as she wiggled and squirmed out of his arms. She immediately stuck her head out of the window only in time to witness the dust the speeding car had left behind. Doreen wasn't no betting woman, but she was sure enough willing to bet the farm that whoever owned that getaway car also owned those high-heel shoes she held in her hand. "Who was she, Willie? Who did you have in my house?" Doreen was so angry, but she was hurt more than anything as she said the words, "In my bed? That's our bed, Willie."

"Woman, you crazy. Ain't no other woman been in this house," Willie said with a straight face.

"Oh yeah? Then who do these belong to?" Doreen held up the shoes to a dumbfounded Willie.

"Uh, well, uh, why, those belong to you," he stammered. "Yeah, I, uh, won them in a card game last night at the bar. I laid 'em out for you so I wouldn't forget to give them to you."

"Is that so?" Doreen asked, not believing a word that came out of his mouth.

"Yeah, that's the truth. I swear to God."

Doreen cringed and took a step backward, almost falling out of the window. She'd much rather fall out of the one-story window and land in the bush that sat outside their bedroom window than get struck by the lightning bolt that was about to come down and take out old Willie.

Sensing the disbelief in his wife, Willie added, "For real. Some guy made his wife take 'em off and put them right in the pot. I just happen to win them. I mean, I know they might be a little high for you, but I figured it just might be time for you to give a few new things a try."

Was Willie trying to tell his wife something with that last comment of his?

"Try new things, huh?" Doreen said. "Well, let me tell you this much, Willie; I don't want what another woman has already had."

He shrugged. "Fine; then. I'll just give 'em back to the fella whenever I see him again." Willie reached for the shoes, but Doreen pulled them away.

"That won't be necessary. You just go on about your business. Get yourself cleaned up while I fix you some lunch to hold you over until dinner," Doreen told him.

Willie swallowed hard. "But, uh, what about the shoes?"

"Oh, these shoes right here?" Doreen played dumb. She looked the shoes up and down. "They're not my style. But don't worry; I'll make it a point to find the owner of them myself and give them back to her personally."

"Uh, well, are you sure?" Willie looked as if he'd swallowed a rotten egg whole and was about to throw it back up.

"Positive." Doreen twitched up her nose.

"Well, fine then. I guess I'll go and take that shower." Willie turned around and practically ran into the door. He looked back over his shoulder at Doreen and smiled, then tripped out the bedroom door and made his way down the hall to the bathroom.

The strong, in control expression Doreen had on her face turned into a weak, sad one. Her head that she'd been holding up felt like it weighed 200 pounds as she let it drop.

"Why do I put up with his mess?" she asked herself out loud. She didn't have to ponder on the answer. She loved Willie. He was her husband. And like her mother and God's Word said, God didn't like divorce. Divorce would have most certainly been the easy way out, but Doreen feared a divorce might be more hurtful and painful for her to deal with than staying married.

The moistness in her eyes turned to tears and fell. She was hurting. She was hurting bad. "God help me," was all she could say as she turned and looked back outside the window. It was then she received a new revelation for the term "Ram in the bush."

Doreen looked down at the shoes again. "If the prince could find Cinderella with a single shoe, surely I can find the woman who has been sleeping with my husband with two."

Chapter Eleven

It was only early Wednesday evening and Our Place was jumping. One who didn't typically frequent such spots would have sworn it was a Saturday night. Well, Doreen was one of those people, but on this particular evening, something had led her here. This feeling took over her that literally had her jump right up from her seat and head over to Our Place to look into some things.

"So this is why Wednesday evening Bible Study has such a poor turnout sometimes," Doreen said to herself as she entered the joint. "Folks too busy up in here doing the devil's work." She scanned the room. Spotting Willie on the dance floor crooning to the music of the house band with some female, Doreen realized that her husband was one of them folks she was referring to.

The blood raced through her body as she watched Willie's hands start at the nape of the woman's neck, and then take an evening stroll down her back and land on the park bench—aka the woman's butt. He cupped her behind as if he were testing melons in the market.

Next, Doreen watched Willie whisper something in the woman's ear that made the redbone's skin flush with red. When he immediately whispered something in her other ear, whatever it was caused her to playfully slap him. But at the same time, it must have turned the woman on because she cupped Willie's bottom just the same as he was cupping hers and the two began crooning and rocking together. They were nose to nose. It looked as if Willie wanted to take his lips and lay one on her. He probably would have if he hadn't all of a sudden been hit with a Word from God.

Literally, Doreen had crept over to Willie and his dance partner, taken her Bible out of her purse, and whacked Willie a good one upside the head.

"Woman! What the he . . ." Willie couldn't even get his curse word completely out he was so stunned. Now his hands no longer rested on the woman's bottom, but massaged his throbbing head instead. "Doreen, what did you do that for?"

"Do you really have to ask?" Doreen stood there tapping an angry, agitated foot on the ground.

"Heck, son," Willie's father walked over and said, resting his hand on his son's shoulder, "why, your wife here was just trying to knock some sense into you is all." Willie's father couldn't help but start laughing. A few others standing around did the same as the house band ceased playing music since they were no longer the center of attention.

"Maybe if you had taught him how to treat a woman when he was coming up, I wouldn't have had to knock sense into him. It would have already been instilled." Beads of sweat formed on Doreen's forehead within seconds of her making that comment. She'd never been that bold in her life. Always the peacemaker, she was the one who tried to avoid tension and smooth out any that existed. But had she just said what she had to her father-in-law? By the look on his face—yes, she had.

"Excuse me?" Mr. Tucker said to his daughter-in-law. "What did you just say to me, little girl?"

Doreen swallowed hard, but didn't respond. Her own common sense, and to avoid even more tension, told her to take it back, but she couldn't. She meant it;

every word of it. The way her Willie was treating her was the exact same way he'd seen his father treat his own mother all these years. Doreen's mother had told her so. She'd warned her it was all her husband knew, and therefore, that's the way he'd treat her unless the good Lord Himself broke the curse.

Obviously, after thirty years of marriage, Mr. Tucker's behavior hadn't done any harm to Willie's parents' marriage. They were still together and appeared to be happy after all these years. Maybe her mother-in-law was cut out for that type of husband-and-wife relationship, but Doreen wasn't.

When it came to her own parents, over the years, Doreen had never seen her father treat her mother with anything but respect; and vice versa. So she didn't know how to deal with this type of behavior from her husband. And boy, oh boy, did she wish she had asked somebody before she'd gone and gotten on her father-in-law's bad side.

Doreen didn't know what kind of reaction she was going to get from Mr. Tucker as she stood there with sweaty palms . . . and a sweaty forehead.

"Son," Mr. Tucker said to Willie while he glared Doreen down, "I reckon you better get the wifey here in check." And that's all he said as he popped a cigar in his mouth and walked away while nodding to the band to continue playing. "Drinks on the house," he said over his shoulder, staring once again at Doreen as if to let her know that her words hadn't cut him deep at all. But they'd at least nicked him; that much she could tell.

Doreen let out a sigh of relief as Mr. Tucker walked away. She'd never heard that he was the kind of man to put his hands on a woman in a rough manner, but there's always a first time for everything. She silently thanked God she wasn't his first casualty. Instantly she felt as if there was no relief in sight as now Mrs. Tucker strolled her way.

When during Bible Study Doreen had gotten this funny feeling that something was going on with Willie, she had no idea it would erupt into all this. Now she wished she'd kept her behind planted right in that pew instead of sneaking out early and coming to the juke joint to investigate. Mr. Tucker may not have been the violent kind and resort to putting his hands on her, but the verdict was still out on Mrs. Tucker.

"You heard what my husband said," Mrs. Tucker said with a smile as she put her arm around Doreen. "Drinks are on the house, gal. Come on and throw one back with your mother-in-law."

Doreen tried not to show her nervousness. Mrs. Tucker was being too nice to Doreen after the way she'd just talked to her husband. "Well, uh, thank you, uh, ma'am, but I don't drink."

Mrs. Tucker leaned in and began talking to Doreen like she was telling her a top secret. "Do you see any of those good church folks of yours hanging around in this here juke joint?"

Doreen looked around. "Well, uh, no, ma'am. I don't think so."

"Then nobody will know. There's nobody in here to go run back and tell your pappy that his good little Christian daughter had a drink or two."

"But God will know," Doreen was almost afraid to say. Her mother-in-law was being way too nice. She had no idea what she had up her sleeve.

"Okay; then, I'll have a hard drink and you can just sip on some of that wine God's son, Jesus, whipped up." She chuckled, and to be courteous, Doreen chuckled. That's when Mrs. Tucker shuffled Doreen on over to a table in the back corner while Doreen looked at

Willie and pleaded for him to save her. But she had no such luck. She'd come to the juke joint looking for answers. Well, Mrs. Tucker was not only about to school her, but hand the answer key to her on a silver platter.

Chapter Twelve

"Doreen Nelly Mae Tucker! You left being fed at God's house to come have drinks with Satan?" Mrs. Hamilton was furious as she cupped her Bible in her hands against her chest. An armor bearer stood on each side of her, warding off the invisible evil spirits that they just knew were lurking in a place like that.

"Mama, what are you doing here?" Doreen had been laughing it up and joking with her mother-in-law just seconds ago. Now she pushed her drink from in front of her and stood like a serious soldier on the front line. She did everything but salute her mother.

"Shouldn't I be asking *you* that question?" Mrs. Hamilton replied, turning her nose up as she looked around. "Well, when you shot up out of the sanctuary like that right in the middle of Bible Study, I got this god-awful feeling in my spirit, so I came looking for you."

"Well, now that you've found her," Willie's mother stood, "can I offer you and your girls a drink?" she asked Mrs. Hamilton.

"I rebuke that offer in the name of Jesus!" Mrs. Hamilton stated, appalled. "I am the wife of a pastor; the first lady of the most successful and thriving church here in town. And as for these women standing next to me," she nodded to each of her armor bearers, "neither they nor myself are anybody's 'girls.' Grown women of God is who we are."

"Well, do you grown women want a drink or not?" Mrs. Tucker offered once again.

Doreen's mother cut her eyes at the complete disrespect Willie's mother was showing her. She turned her attention to her eldest daughter. "Doreen, get your stuff and let's go—right this instant."

Doreen went to move, but her mother-in-law put her arm out to stop her. "The same way yous all are grown women, so is this one here." Mrs. Tucker nodded toward Doreen. "And we were having us a nice little conversation before you all stormed up in her like yous the law or something." She put her arm around Doreen. "We were bonding. I was teaching her a thing about how to deal with real life, in the real world. Not some make-believe world Holy Rollers have created and think that's how life is supposed to be. Church is good for some folks. But the same way college ain't for everybody, neither is church. You church people try to give other folks a false sense of hope and outlook on life. And don't get me wrong—I ain't got nothing against church, church folk, or even God Himself. Heck, I love God. The same way He's blessed you to have a successful thriving church, He's blessed me to have a successful thriving business."

Mrs. Hamilton gave off a harrumph. "Then God's Word is true. I guess He isn't a respecter of persons."

"You can quote as much Bible as you want, but when church is over, honey, real life begins. And if I were you, I'd get to teaching those girls of yours about real life. That way, a wretch like me wouldn't have to." She looked over at her daughter-in-law. "Excuse me, baby. It's been real good talking to you, but there are customers I need to attend to."

Doreen smiled at her mother-in-law, who, she had to admit, she'd had a wonderful time chatting it up with the past half hour—give or take. In just that small amount of time, Mrs. Tucker had taught her a couple of tricks on how to deal with a Tucker man.

"And remember what I told you, now, you hear?" Mrs. Tucker winked, then walked away, but not before saying to Doreen's mother and her armor bearers, "Good evening, women of God. God bless you."

One of the armor bearers whipped out some praying oil and began splashing it where Mrs. Tucker had sat and where she'd stood.

"Come on, Doreen, let's go so we can talk in a better atmosphere," Mrs. Hamilton requested.

Doreen was scared out of her wits. Sure she was a grown woman, but Mama was still Mama. No matter how old Doreen and her sisters got, her parents would always have some type of control and authority over their children's lives. Maybe that right there was what the problem was Doreen surmised. Maybe what Mrs. Tucker had just said to her only moments ago was on point. Maybe she needed to cut the strings from her parents and what they expected of a preacher's daughter and be what Willie expects of a wife.

When Doreen tried to complain about Willie's gallivanting with other women, her mother-in-law acted like it wasn't nothing but a thing. That's when Doreen whipped those high heels out of her nice-size purse to show her mother-in-law proof. Her intentions had even been to go around that entire juke joint making every broad in sight try on those shoes until she found the gal they belong to.

"Then what? Then what you gon' do, church girl?" Mrs. Tucker had asked her sarcastically. "You gon' beat the girl up with 'em?"

Doreen sat looking dumbfounded because, actually, she had no idea what she'd planned on doing after she found the woman. "Uh-huh, I thought so. You being the perfect little Christian girl that you are wouldn't have done a dang on thing but been able to put a face with a pair of shoes—a face that was going to haunt you forever."

Doreen's eyes began to water.

"Don't you dare sit here and start crying." She pushed Doreen's drink closer to her. "Here, take a sip and get yourself together." After Doreen did just that, she continued. "First of all, that broad ain't married to you, ain't said 'I do' to you, and don't owe you no type of trust and loyalty. It's your husband you need to take those issues up with."

"I tried, but when I asked him about it, he played me like a fool."

"Of course, he did. That's what men do."

"They play women like fools?" Doreen questioned.

"They don't play all women like fools; only the fools who let 'em." Mrs. Tucker repositioned herself in her seat. "So if you got a man who likes to play, don't play the fool. Just play the game right back."

"I ain't going to hell for nobody." Doreen looked horrified. "So if you saying I should turn around and cheat on my Willie—"

"Oh, relax yourself—looking like you about to catch the Holy Ghost up in here or something," Mrs. Tucker said. "I'm just saying, if my son wants to try to play games, then you play right back until he loses."

"I don't understand." Doreen looked confused as she took a sip of her drink, keeping her eyes on her mother-in-law the entire time so as not to miss a beat.

"Them high-heel shoes you got there," she directed her eyes to the shoes, then back at Doreen, "put 'em on."

"Huh? What?"

"You heard me. Put those dern shoes on and strut around in 'em like you the finest thang walkin'."

"But I don't wear—"

"This ain't about you, gal; don't you get it?" Mrs. Tucker proceeded to help Doreen take off the flat loafers she'd worn into the joint and put the heels on her feet.

"Ouch! They're too tight," Doreen complained once the shoes were on.

"Good. See how easy it was for you to fill that woman's shoes? Obviously, you a size or two up on her, so it would be a lot more difficult for her to fill your shoes. Why, she'd fall right out of them." Mrs. Tucker leaned in and said to Doreen, as if her life depended on it, "Don't you ever, never, let no other woman fill your shoes. Now you keep those shoes on. Wear 'em home tonight. Even make sweet love to your husband in them shoes tonight. Let him know that no woman can, or will, ever fill the shoes of his wife. You got it, sweetheart?"

Strangely enough, Doreen felt encouraged as she replied, "Yes, ma'am," crossing her legs so that one of her feet dangled about, showing off the heels. She'd almost forgotten all about the shoes until her own mother, who she was now having a conversation with, said something.

"And what on God's green earth do you have on your feet?" Mrs. Hamilton said as she feigned faintness. Her armor bearers began to fan her. "Oh, in the name of Jesus, bless my child, Lord. Deliver her from the enemy that is trying to take over her life—the enemy that is trying to corrupt everything we've instilled in her, O God."

The house band was still playing, but they were playing slow tunes that enabled the patrons to be able to somewhat hear what was going on between Doreen and her mother. Embarrassed, Doreen said softly to her mother, "They're shoes."

"Huh? What did you say?" Mrs. Hamilton asked.

"They're shoes," Doreen repeated.

"I can't hear you."

"Ma, they're shoes!" Doreen yelled, and it just so happened to be when the band had finished up the song. So there was dead silence—all except Doreen yelling at the top of her lungs about her shoes. This caused all those who could to draw their attention to Doreen's shoes. Doreen then tried to say with confidence and a little more softly, "They're just shoes, Ma."

"You dang right they're shoes, but not any old shoes. Those are seventy-five dollar shoes, and they belong to my wife. Cost me a day's pay almost, so I was fit to be tied when she told me someone lifted them from her." Out of nowhere this gentleman appeared behind Mrs. Hamilton and her armor bearers. He squeezed through the women and walked up close to Doreen and got a real good look at the shoes before pointing at Doreen and yelling, "Thief! Somebody call the police now. I want this woman arrested."

Chapter Thirteen

"What in the world is going on over here now?" Mr. Tucker asked. It really wasn't until just tonight Doreen realized what a large man he was. Maybe he wasn't. Standing around six foot tall, he was actually pretty average. But his tone tonight and just his aura altogether had made him appear larger than life.

"What's going on is that one of your drunken customers is accusing my daughter of stealing," Doreen's mother said in her defense.

"*Accusing* my left toenail. She's *wearing* the evidence." The accusing man pointed to Doreen's feet. "I bought those for my wife, and she said someone lifted them—someone right here in this here juke joint. Who knew the thief would be such a fool as to wear 'em right back up in here?"

By now Mrs. Tucker had made her way over and figured out what was going on. Ol' Willie seemed to keep his distance though.

Doreen looked at her mother-in-law, her eyes yearning for Mrs. Tucker to help her out. Instead, Mrs. Tucker just gave her a look that said, "Ooops," sucked her lips in, and crept away.

"I'm telling you, we've been running this place for years and ain't never had no problems until you started bringing your wife around," Mr. Tucker called out to Willie, who was now making his way over to all the commotion.

"Willie, this here is your wife?" the man asked Willie while pointing to Doreen. "As much money as you take from me playing cards, you can't go invest in a pair of shoes for your woman? She got to run around stealing? What kind of man don't take care of his wife?"

Willie's body straightened out as his chest poked out. "Funny you should ask that last question, the one about what kind of man don't take care of his wife." Willie rubbed his chin, and his lips split into a mischievous grin. Both he and Doreen knew the underlying meaning to Willie's statement.

"And just what are you trying to say?" the man asked, now sticking his own chest out.

Doreen didn't like the fact that this man was challenging her husband one bit. And with the help of a couple glasses of wine, her level of boldness had increased even more. "What my husband is trying to say," Doreen spoke up in her husband's defense, "is that you're the kind of man that don't take care of his wife, because if you did, when I got home from church on Sunday, I wouldn't have found her shoes in my living room and her crawling out of my bedroom window, and then hightailing it off my property." Doreen went and stood by Willie proudly, snubbing her nose up at the man as if she'd just told him off. All the while she'd actually told on Willie, not to mention making herself look like the fool Mrs. Tucker had just warned her against being.

Willie shook his head, realizing the stuff was about to hit the fan now.

"Yous a liar," the man spat at Doreen. He then looked at Willie. "Not only is your woman a thief, but she lies. Word around town is that you don't have your broad in check. I guess the word is true."

Instinctively, Willie went to swing at the man, but his father caught his fist midair.

"Oh, so you want to hit me?" the man taunted now that Willie's father was holding him back and he didn't fear immediate bodily harm. "You mad at me 'cause you married a klepto."

"I'd rather be a klepto than a ho," Doreen spat at the man.

"Doreen!" Mrs. Hamilton gasped at hearing one of her saved, sanctified, Holy Ghost-filled children use such language.

"I'm sorry, Mama, but it's true. I caught his woman in my house with my husband," Doreen declared. "She left these shoes in my living room—too busy escaping out the bedroom window, and that's the truth."

"Like heck it is!" the man roared, not wanting to face reality. "My wife would *never* crawl around with the likes of Willie Tucker." He shot Willie, who was trying to wedge away from his father, a dirty look. "She's much too classy for that."

"Well, is she too classy for this?" And *bam*, there it was, the ram in the bush. Doreen held up a pair of purple with cranberry trim lace underwear that she pulled out of her purse. "I found these in the bush outside my bedroom window. Did your wife say somebody stole these too?" Doreen dangled the panties in front of the man's face. Everyone around blushed with embarrassment. Willie was humiliated for his business to be put on Front Street like that in front of his parents and mother-in-law, no less. Doreen was the only one wearing a smile of victory on her face. No, the panties in the bush weren't literally a ram, but at least now she couldn't be accused of being a thief.

The man snatched the panties out of Doreen's hands and began to fume as he stared down at them. "That no good, sorry excuse for a . . ." He let out a grunt, and then looked at Doreen. "Look, ma'am, I'm, uh, sorry, for, uh, you know, accusing you, and uh, well . . ." The man started to look heartbroken as he went from being angry to sad.

"It's all right." Doreen slowly removed the shoes from her feet and handed them to the man. "Tell your wife she's got good taste." Doreen looked at Willie, then back at the man. "But if I ever see her around my house or my Willie again, the next person who comes looking for those shoes are going to find them shoved up her a—" And on that note, Mrs. Hamilton flat-out fainted, with her armor bearers too late to break her fall.

"Cursing and drinking and carrying on. Honey, you should have heard her," Mrs. Hamilton said to her husband while looking Doreen up and down. "You should have *seen* her." She massaged her temples. "Wearing those hooker shoes, sipping wine, and did I mention cursing like a sailor?" She walked over to Doreen and laid hands on her head. "Satan, I rebuke you in the name of Jesus! Rise up out of my girl right now! Let her be!"

Mr. Hamilton walked over and pulled an overzealous Mrs. Hamilton away from his daughter. Doreen just stood in their doorway, now rubbing her own head. She'd never had a drink in her life, so that little bit of wine her mother-in-law had talked her into drinking was giving her a headache. Two of Doreen's sisters stood on the steps witnessing everything, while baby Bethany slept in her bassinet.

"Girls, why don't y'all take your mother into the kitchen and fix her some tea while I talk to your sister?" Mr. Hamilton ordered.

"Yes, Daddy," the sisters replied in unison. Shortly thereafter, they made it into the kitchen with their mother in tow, leaving Doreen alone in the living room with her father.

"Well, Daddy, I think I better get going home," Doreen said. "I just came to see if Mother was okay. She took a hard fall back there at the juke joint."

"Okay, I'ma let you go in a minute," he said, walking over to his daughter. "I know you need to get home and take care of that husband of yours. I mean, after all, you're a wife now. You're a grown woman."

"Yes, Daddy," Doreen agreed, although she didn't feel like a grown woman at the moment. She felt like she was back in high school, had done something out of the ordinary like cut school or something, and was now about to get into hot water over it.

"But before you go, I just want to let you know that I love you and I am proud of you."

That wasn't what Doreen was expecting. She looked at her father with surprise. He wasn't joking around or trying to use some type of trick psychology. He meant his words from the bottom of his heart. Doreen could see that. She could feel it. Doreen sniffed, and her eyes filled with tears. "I love you too, Daddy, but right now, there is no reason under the sun why you should be proud of me. Mama was right—I was a complete fool tonight. I was outside of myself and my ways."

"No, dear, that's not true. Tonight, you were exactly who you are. You were yourself."

Mr. Hamilton noticed the puzzled look on Doreen's face and continued speaking. "You were true to yourself and who you are. It was God's ways who you were out of. Tonight, daughter, is the person who you are when you step out of God's skin and allow your own flesh to cover you."

Doreen broke down in tears.

"It ain't pretty, is it? It doesn't feel good being all exposed like that, does it?"

Doreen shook her head as she cried with heaving shoulders. "I'm sorry, Daddy. I know folks are gonna be talking up in the church. I never meant to bring you or Mama any shame, I promise."

"I know, sweetie." He walked over and embraced his daughter. "And you don't owe either me or your mama an apology. All you owe one to is God. Just repent, baby, and you know that God will forgive you." He held Doreen a few more moments while she was able to get herself together. "And when you repent, mean it, and don't repeat your wrongdoing."

"Yes, Daddy, I'll repent," Doreen assured him, pulling away from him and wiping tears. "I'm just so blessed to have such a wonderful father and role model of a man," Doreen cried. "I'm even more blessed that I serve such a forgiving God; a God who can forgive me for my sins and actions."

"Hallelujah," Mr. Hamilton agreed as Doreen turned to exit the house. "But just keep in mind, daughter, that even though God forgives us for our actions and sins, there are still consequences."

Those words stopped Doreen in her tracks. "So what are you saying, Daddy? That I should expect the worst to happen between Willie and me now that I done put all our stuff out there?"

"No, dear, never expect the worst," he said to his daughter as he walked over to her and rubbed her cheek, causing her to smile. "You should never expect the worst in life . . . just be prepared for it."

Chapter Fourteen

"Sis, do you know starting this pound cake business is the best thing I could have ever done?" Doreen said as she stood in her kitchen boxing pound cake after pound cake. Sarina, her younger sister by three years, stood assisting her. The two had been at it since five o'clock that morning. Doreen's father had dropped Sarina off on his and her mother's way to a couple's retreat. This single order of a dozen pound cakes was the largest Doreen had had yet. Charging five dollars per cake and with Christmas right around the corner, she was saving to get Willie a watch. That way, maybe he'd look down at it, notice the time, and make it home at a decent hour.

"Is it now?" Sarina asked Doreen.

"Yeah, well, that and marrying Willie."

"Is that all?" Sarina tapped her foot.

Doreen chuckled, looked down at her slightly protruding tummy, and added, "Oh yeah, and get pregnant with ol' Willie Junior here."

"Child, you ain't nothing but about eight weeks pregnant. How you know it's a boy?"

"'Cause I've been sick as a dog. Only those belonging to the male species can make me this sick," Doreen joked as she placed a pound cake inside a box and sealed it in securely.

Sarina wasn't chuckling. "How do you do it, Sis? How do you stay married to an unbeliever?"

Doreen took immediate offense. "Who says my Willie is an unbeliever? Is it them people at the church? Because they got a lot of nerves. Just last week Willie told me how he saw Deacon and Mrs. Smitherson leaving the juke joint hand in hand like they'd had the time of their lives . . . or were about to anyway."

"And what's so wrong with that? I mean, sure, Deacon Smitherson and his wife probably had no business up in some drinking establishment, but at least they were in there together. At least they're not just so . . ." Sarina searched for words. ". . . different; different as night and day like you and Willie are."

Doreen poked out her lips. "I guess that would have been more like right if it was Deacon Smitherson and his wife Mrs. Smitherson, but it wasn't. It was Deacon Milton with Mrs. Smitherson."

"The devil is a liar!" Sarina spat. She'd been drizzling chocolate icing down a yellow pound cake when she yielded.

"You calling my Willie the devil or something? Because he's the one who told me."

"Oh, by no means would I ever call your Willie a lying devil. Why, he's the most honest man this side of Kentucky," Sarina said sarcastically with a playful flutter of her eyelashes.

"Uh-huh." Doreen dipped her finger into the icing and put some on her little sister's nose. "You keep it up and I'ma turn you over my knee and skin you clean."

"You can't even keep your husband in line. How you gon' try to keep me in line?" Sarina chuckled, but it was Doreen who didn't chuckle this time.

Doreen sighed, wiped her forehead with her sleeve, then went and sat down. Sarina noticed her older sister's sudden change in demeanor.

"I'm sorry, Sis. I didn't mean anything by it," Sarina apologized.

"Oh no, you're all right. Just getting a little tired and feeling somewhat ill from this baby is all," Doreen lied. And she wasn't a good liar as Sarina could see right through her and to the truth.

"You tired of people and all what they got to say about Willie, huh?" Sarina sat down next to Doreen at the kitchen table.

"I know I shouldn't let what folks say get to me, and I know it shouldn't mean much, but it does, Sarina. It does, and it hurts sometimes too. Never knew words could cut so deep. It's like from the beginning of Willie's and my relationship, folks been saying we ain't gon' make it. Now I feel like I have to prove them wrong, like I've been challenged, and no matter what, I have to hang in there. Every couple has their ups and downs. But all folks see when it comes to Willie and me is our downs. So they keep right on talking negative things."

"So what are you going to do about it then?"

"What can I do? Folks talked about Jesus, and He was a man without fault. So do you think they're going to give Willie a break?"

"Tell me this, Sis, why did you marry Willie?"

Doreen shot Sarina an indignant look. "What do you mean why did I marry him? Because I loved him, of course," Doreen flat-out said, then stood up and went back to tending to the cakes.

"So you never felt like maybe you got tricked into this whole relationship with him?"

"Tricked how? Girl, what in the world are you talking about?"

Sarina stood and walked over to Doreen and watched her finish icing the cake that she had started. "I'm talking about the way Willie came to church just long enough to court you and get you to say 'I do.' You never thought just once that was a trick of the enemy? And that you fell for it? Hook, line, and Willie?"

Doreen paused but spoke no words. It was clear by the way she looked at Sarina, then turned her attention back to the cake, that she'd had those same thoughts a time or two.

"Then why are you staying in this marriage?" Sarina asked with urgency. "Why do you want to live like this? You just don't seem like the same sister I grew up with back at Mama and Daddy's house. You don't seem to have that same joy and energy. I'm not the only one who notices it either. We think it's because you spend all your energy chasing Willie around town and—"

"We? Who is 'we'?" Doreen was very defensive and angry. "So you just like the rest of 'em? My own flesh and blood running around town talking about me too? Well, you and all them other folks can go to—" The buzzing of the timer signaling that the last cake was ready drowned out the curse word that had just flown from Doreen's tongue.

"Guess you been hanging around old Willie so long that you're starting to even talk like him," Sarina said as she turned off the timer, put on oven mitts, and removed the cake from the oven. She set it on the cooling rack, and then continued her conversation with Doreen. "Maybe that's why you don't see nothing wrong with the way he treats you. Maybe that's why you don't mind coming up in church singing all these praises to God like you're the perfect Christian while you know darn well ain't nothing going on in your home to be giving God praises for. It's phony, and it's fake, and everybody can see right through it."

Sarina grabbed her cheek but still couldn't stop the stinging left behind from the slap Doreen had just placed there.

"Oh, God, Sarina, I'm sorry. I'm *so* sorry," Doreen apologized as she moved toward her sister.

"Get away from me. Just get away from me," Sarina demanded as she went looking for her coat.

"Where—where are you going?" Doreen asked as Sarina put on her coat.

"Home." Sarina stomped over to the door.

"But you don't have a car. Wait and I'll take you." Doreen started scrambling for her keys.

"No, thanks. I'll walk. As a matter of fact, I'd rather walk than ride in the car with you."

"Sarina, baby, don't say that. Why are you saying all these awful things to me? What did I ever do to you but love you and take care of you, and all my sisters? This is my life. Why can't you just let me be me?"

"Because I am you! All right? Okay, big sister, do you get it now? I am you. And so is Pauline, and so is Bethany." Sarina named their other siblings. "You're the mold Mama and Daddy shaped for all us other girls to turn out to be. Trust me, they've made that clear over the years. And for so long I looked at you, admired you, and couldn't wait to be you. After all, you were so blessed, so highly favored. The anointing oil on you just trickled down right to us other girls. But then you got with Willie, and it's like slowly but surely the spigot is being turned off, and the flow is starting to stop.

"I used to see you as this strong woman of God who I couldn't wait to live my life like. And now . . ." Sarina swallowed back tears.

"And now what?" Doreen pressed. "Keep on talking. You've been big enough in your britches to say everything that's been on your mind thus far. Keep talking."

Sarina inhaled, stood straight, and said, "And now I'd rather be dead if this is the kind of life I have to look forward to living." Sarina shook her head. "You've ruined it. And with me being next to the eldest, now I'm going to have to battle the family curse you've started." Sarina shook her head as she opened the door. "It was never just about you, Reen. Couldn't you see that? It was never just about you." With tears flowing down her face, Sarina stormed out the door to start her three-and-a-half mile walk home.

The revelation that had just hit Doreen felt like lightning striking through her body. Her sister's words had penetrated her soul. She didn't even have much time to take in the words before the doorbell rang. "Oh, God, Sarina." Doreen rushed to open the door hoping Sarina had returned.

"Oh, Ms. Flanagen," Doreen said when she saw her customer outside her door.

"I hope you got all my cakes ready, gal, 'cause I'm running short on time." Ms. Flanagen was a big woman; big enough that one might think all twelve of those cakes were just for her. But she ran a little carryout where she planned on selling the cakes by the slice and by the whole. She'd make the most money selling by the slice. Upping the cost from the five dollars she paid for the cakes to the eight dollars she planned on selling them for, she'd still make a nice profit selling them whole as well.

Doreen helped Ms. Flanagen load the cakes in her car. After receiving payment, she went back in the house and tucked her money away in her top drawer where she'd been keeping the profits from her pound-cake business over the last five months. She hadn't spent one red cent. She had no idea how much a good watch for Willie was going to run her, but she wanted to make sure she had enough to buy the very best or close to it. But now, after once again allowing Sarina's words to play back in her mind, she was rethinking what she'd do with all that money as she thought out loud, "I wonder how much a whole new life would cost me."

Doreen was serious in thought. She pictured taking all her money and buying a bus ticket right out of Kentucky—away from her family, the church, just everybody, including Willie—especially Willie. But then, as her stomach began to churn, she remembered one person that she couldn't leave behind. She placed her hands on her pregnant womb, and then a horrible thought ran through her head as she gasped. "Oh, God, little one," she said to the unborn baby inside her stomach, "have I cursed you too?"

Chapter Fifteen

"I'm gonna kill him!" Doreen screamed as her tires screeched into a parking spot outside of Our Place. Even though it was cold outside, snow was on the ground, and the ice underneath it was thick. That meant no never-mind to Doreen. She hopped out of that car with no coat, shoes that were ordinarily confined to wearing around the house, and a scarf tied around her hair. She was so hot on the inside that it might as well have been July.

"Well, excuse me," Doreen heard a woman say as she was fixing to barge into the bar.

"Pardon me. I'm sor—" Once Doreen looked up at the woman she'd nearly trampled over, she almost wished she had—trampled her flat on the ground. An apology was definitely not in order at this point.

"Oh, it's you," Agnes said in a singsong tone. "The good wife. I almost didn't recognize you looking like . . ." She paused to give Doreen the once-over. "Looking like Aunt Jemima." She laughed. "Then again, I guess that's a step up for you." She laughed even harder as she took a cigarette out of the pack in her hand and went to light it.

With the cold winter wind blowing, Agnes was already going to have a hard time getting that thing lit. It didn't help that once she got close to lighting the cigarette, Doreen blew the fire out.

"What you go and do that for?" Agnes asked. "I came out here just to hit my drag in peace—to get a break from all that inside there." She nodded to the door. "Here you come to mess up that. What's your deal anyway? Why you mad at me? I ain't never did nothing to you." Agnes cupped her hands around the cigarette and managed to successfully light it this time. "Nothing you can prove anyway." She let out a gust of smoke into Doreen's face.

"I promise you on the Holy Bible, tonight ain't the night," Doreen warned Agnes. "I'll beat you like you stole something and repent to the good Lord later. So if you know what's good for you, you'll keep that cigarette in your mouth, and my Willie out of it. You dig?"

Agnes's mouth dropped open as a smile appeared on her face. "My, my, my, the Mrs. done went to see the wizard and got herself some courage. Ain't that about nothing? Either that or Willie's ways are rubbing off on ya." She took a hit from her cigarette and exhaled as she stared off into the night.

Doreen didn't want to bite the bait Agnes was throwing out there. She wanted to go inside and tend to the business that had brought her out at almost midnight. But Agnes's last comment had intrigued Doreen. "What do you mean by that? My Willie is just as kind as anybody I know."

"Guess you ain't done nothing to piss him off good yet then. Then again, I'm sure you probably haven't. After all, what reason he got to get ticked off at you about? You let the man do whatever he wants whenever he wants. Why would he want to mess up a good thing like that?" Agnes looked Doreen up and down, taking note of her appearance. "Then again, looks like all that might be about to change. Only a woman who is about to cut the fool will come out of the house looking like *that*." Agnes laughed as she took another hit from her cigarette.

Doreen shook her head in pity of Agnes. "I'm not even going to entertain you, girl. You don't know my husband. You don't know him at all." Doreen went and swung the door open.

"No, ma'am, I think you the one who don't know your husband at all," Agnes said, almost under her breath.

"What did you say?" Doreen had a major attitude at this point and was ready to rumble with Agnes if need be. Like she'd said before, she'd get with Agnes in a New York minute and repent about it later.

"Oh, nothing," Agnes said, swooshing her hand in Doreen's direction.

"Thought so," Doreen said, heading back into the juke joint.

"Oh, by the way, I hear congratulations are in order." She looked down at Doreen's stomach. "I hear you got a bun in the oven."

Doreen paused but didn't bother to say thank you. She knew Agnes wasn't sincere.

"It's nice of Willie to let you have his child. Spite his actions, he must really love him some wifey." A look of hurt and sadness seemed to shadow over Agnes at that point as she dropped her cigarette to the ground and put it out with her shoe. "If it was anybody else, he'd probably force them to go visit some back-alley doctor with a dirty knife and a hanger and get it taken care of, if you know what I mean."

By the look in Agnes's eyes, Doreen knew exactly what she meant. Doreen had heard the rumor that Agnes was pregnant with Willie's child. She turned a deaf ear and just waited to see for herself. She was a Christian—she didn't run her life based on gossip and rumors. As a matter of fact, she wanted no part of it. That wasn't of God. Doreen was glad she hadn't reacted to the rumors when Agnes never appeared pregnant—when her belly never grew. Guess now she knew why.

"Anyway," Agnes said, brushing past Doreen, "thanks for keeping me company while I took me a smoke break. It can get lonely for a girl like me." Agnes stopped and looked Doreen in the eyes. "But I promise you, I'll be finding other ways to keep myself company, so you won't have to worry about me anymore. You know what I mean?"

Doreen nodded. She nodded because she couldn't speak. All that Agnes had just told her without actually telling her had her feeling some kind of crazy. But as she pulled herself together and marched into the juke joint, she was about to find out what crazy truly was. And unfortunately, so was Willie.

"Where is it? Where's my money," Doreen demanded to know of Willie. She'd stormed into the juke joint and marched right on over to the table where Willie was playing cards.

"Hey, Willie, is that your wife, or did you place an order for some panny cakes?" a gentleman at the table joked as everyone else at the table roared out in laugher.

Doreen ignored the men and repeated, "Where's my money? All that money I been saving up in my drawer. All those cakes I been baking for months and now the money is gone!" Just a half hour ago Doreen had gotten up off her knees from praying. She went to remove her housecoat to get ready for bed. It had been a late night for her. Someone had called on her at the last minute to bake two cakes for a funeral that was the next morning. Once the cakes were picked up, Doreen had placed her pay in her housecoat pocket. Thank goodness she always checked her pockets before going to bed, or she might have forgotten all about the ten dollars.

She excitedly went to add it to her stash. When she opened her drawer, dug around in it only to find that her entire bankroll was gone, she was fit to be tied. With it being just her and Willie in the house, it didn't take her long to figure out who might have taken her money. And now here she was to confront Willie about it.

Willie stared up at Doreen. He couldn't believe she'd actually come out of the house looking like that. He too burst out laughing.

"Oh, you think this is funny? You think this is funny?" Doreen spat. "I'll give you something to laugh at." Like a woman gone mad, Doreen started picking up the beer bottles from off the table and throwing them on the ground at Willie's feet. Each time a bottle crashed she asked, "Where's my money?"

"Now hold up, gal." Here came Mr. Tucker with his larger-than-life self. "You ain't gon' just come up in here destroying property."

"It's just beer bottles, Dad," Willie shrugged.

Mr. Tucker looked at the ground. "Oh, I guess you're right, son." He looked at Doreen. "Carry on, daughter." And as he walked away he yelled, "Agnes, clean up!" Now if Doreen got to throwing chairs and turning over tables, it would be another story.

Doreen was getting angrier by the minute. She'd already been ready to blow her top once she'd pulled up in the parking lot. Her conversation with Agnes added gasoline to the fire. That had only made things worse. At first, every bottle Doreen threw to the ground represented every dollar that had been taken out of her drawer. Then the crashing of the bottles started to represent all the times Willie had probably slept with Agnes, how he had impregnated her, and then probably given her money for an abortion. All of Agnes's words were embedded in her head. She could hear them playing over and over, and she just wanted the crashing sound of the bottles to drown them out.

When Doreen got to the last bottle she yelled out, "Where's my money?" Next, she shocked herself with curse words she never thought she'd fix her lips to say.

There was dead silence at this point, and everyone was waiting on Willie to spill the answer.

"What money?" was all he said; then Doreen walked over to the table next to them and proceeded to pick up a bottle to start throwing. "Okay, okay, okay. I'm just messing around with you, girl. You want to know where your money is? Well, here it is." Willie pulled out a huge wad of cash from his pocket and placed it in Doreen's hand.

Doreen looked down at the knot of money. It was much thicker than the one that had been taken from her drawer. She had a puzzled look on her face.

"That's all your money with interest," Willie smiled. He then turned to one of the men at the table and ordered, "Come on, Rufus, get to dealing so I can get to taking the rest of y'all's money." He yelled over his shoulder toward the bar. "Another round of drinks at this table. And since these fellas barely got a pot to piss in, drinks are on me."

Willie and his boys proceeded to playing cards as if Doreen wasn't even standing there. She continued to look down at the huge wad of cash. At this point, she didn't know what her next step should be. She'd anticipated going up to the joint and finding that Willie had gambled away all her money, like he'd done with his last paycheck, forcing them to miss paying a month's mortgage and her dodging phone calls from bill collectors. It looked as though there wasn't too much more of a fuss she could make. She'd gotten what she'd come there for.

Agnes showed up with a broom and dustpan and began cleaning up the mess Doreen had made. Doreen briefly locked eyes with Agnes, and then Agnes turned away. Doreen thought about speaking on Willie's situation with Agnes; asking her husband if what Agnes had insinuated outside was true. But what good would any of that do? The deed was done. And in all honesty, that was one truth Doreen didn't know if she could withstand.

Perhaps both her sister and Agnes were right. Maybe she wasn't as strong and powerful in the Lord as she thought she was. Otherwise, why did she sit back and allow Willie to disrespect her and their marriage like that? She had no answers besides the ones she'd been feeding off of: the fact that she truly loved Willie, was afraid of the pain and stigma attached to divorce, and that she had to prove everyone wrong who said she and Willie wouldn't make it.

She might have had her money back, but she had no other answers. So with nothing but a wad of money, with interest, Doreen headed back out the door. Dazed and confused with her mind still wrestling with unanswered questions, she missed that patch of black ice that landed her flat on her back. The last thing she saw was a twinkling star in the night sky. The last thing she said was, "God, help me."

Chapter Sixteen

"So how many more weeks you just gon' lay around in this bed?" Willie asked Doreen.

Doreen didn't so much as shrug at Willie's question as she lay in her bed staring off yonder.

With even less compassion in his tone than when he'd made the previous comment, Willie said, "You act like you're the one that died."

Through dry, cracked lips, Doreen spoke softy and slowly. "A part of me did die, Willie, and a part of you too. Now if you're able to function normal through life as you were before I lost the baby, then good for you. But forgive me for having not as easy of a time getting back to normal."

"I didn't have no choice. If I stayed around this house all day instead of worked, we'd never eat because I wouldn't be able to make no money." Willie cleared his throat. "Speaking of work, I wanted to wait and tell you this when you got to feeling like your old self again, but it looks like that's a long time coming." Willie looked down, then continued. "Work is going to be carrying us away from here. West Virginia, I think—something like that. You know how the railroad business is."

Doreen knew how it was. Her mother had warned her about that too. She'd told her that Willie's job could pick up and send him anywhere across the map to work on railroads. Her being his wife and all, she'd have to go with him. About a month ago, Doreen probably would have felt sad about having to leave Kentucky, where all her family was and her church, but nothing could make her any sadder than she already was. Hearing they'd have to pick up and move to West Virginia was nothing compared to hearing that her unborn baby would never be born. Her fall outside the juke joint last month had been fatal for the baby.

It was no secret that Doreen blamed herself. Had she not been out that night cutting a fool over Willie's behind she never would have been out there on that ice to fall in the first place. Inside she was so angry, not just at herself, but at everybody. She was angry at Willie, blaming his shenanigans for driving her to be out in that nasty weather. She blamed his parents for not doing something about all that snow and ice that was building up outside their establishment. She had a mind to sue them, but she knew that would only drive even more of a wedge between her and Willie.

In spite of Willie's actions, Doreen loved the mess out of that man. Love was what was keeping her from leaving him every time he gambled their money away, came home with dings in the car from driving drunk, every time he lied to her in her face like she was plum dumb, and every time he had another woman upon his knee. Oh, it was true love all right. Even if love hadn't a thing to do with it, Doreen still probably would have never left Willie. She knew the history of the Hamilton women. None of them, not a nary one of them, had ever gotten a divorce—no matter what their maiden name ultimately got changed to. Doreen came from a long line of first ladies, deaconess, and women who just loved the Lord and His ways. They knew how to pray their way through circumstances and situations. Yea, just like Doreen had done a time or two, a few of the Hamilton women had packed up and went to stay with their parents for a spell, but they always went back to their husbands.

Sarina had already accused Doreen of cursing the women that would come after her by letting Willie walk all over her. She wasn't about to cast another one upon them by walking away from her husband. Funny thing was, she couldn't figure out the worst of the two evils.

"Okay," Doreen said to Willie. "I'll get to packing just as soon as the good Lord gives me strength. I've been praying for strength. Prayer works, so I should get that strength any day now."

"Well, I hope God answers your prayer soon, because we head out in two weeks."

"That's fine. Maybe it's best we get out of Kentucky anyway—start fresh somewhere else. Leave all these memories behind." Her eyes began to tear up. This surprised Doreen, because honestly, she thought she was all cried out.

Willie thought she had been too. "Oh, God, are you gon' start that crying stuff again?" Willie, who had been sitting on the bed next to Doreen stood up in a huff. "I understand what could have been, that we could have been the parents of a nice, bouncing baby girl or boy. And we still can. You heard the doctor. He said your female parts work just fine to produce us another baby . . ." Willie looked off proudly. ". . . that son I've always wanted to carry on the family name." He then looked at Doreen. "But what you lost wasn't even a real baby yet. It was just this little jellyfish-like thing. I could see you acting like this over a real live baby, but—"

"Stop it! Stop it right now, William Tucker." Doreen shot up in the bed, as the burning heat through her body evaporated all the tears. "I don't care what it looked like—that was a baby. Once it's conceived, it's real. It's a person, not some thing—or as you put it—a jellyfish. You should repent right now," Doreen demanded as tears streamed down her face once again.

Willie could see how shaken up Doreen was. He didn't realize how insensitive he was being until that moment. He hadn't meant to be. Sure, he'd wanted his wife to bear a baby to carry on his name, but in his mind, Doreen had been only a little bit pregnant. It confused him to see her acting so depressed over a baby that had never made it outside her womb—that she'd never bonded and made a connection with. For the life of him, he just couldn't understand it. He silently wondered if other people felt the same way as he did. All that mattered now, though, was that his wife didn't feel that way.

"I'm sorry, baby. I didn't mean it like that." Willie was truly apologetic.

Doreen sniffled, and then let her body fall flat in the bed again.

"And don't you even worry about packing. I'll do it all. I'll get some of the fellas and they wives to come help. You're right; I think my job moving us away from here is a blessing in disguise. We do need a fresh start. We can pretend like we newlyweds all over again—like we just got married and picking up to start our new life together somewhere else. Don't that sound good?" Doreen didn't reply. She was still trying to cool off from Willie's previous comment about the baby. "No one will know us, and we won't know nobody. Only God. And speaking of God, heck, I just might get to West Virginia, find me a church I like, and get baptized or something."

"Really, Willie?" Doreen shot up in the bed once again with the most excitement she'd felt in a long time.

"Well, yeah, you know, like I said, if I find me a church I like." He shrugged. "Anything is possible." He slowly sat down on the bed with his back toward Doreen. Good thing his back was to her too. That way she wasn't able to see the look of regret on his face.

"Oh, Willie!" Doreen threw her arms around Willie. "You've just made me the happiest woman in Kentucky right now. Soon to be the happiest woman in West Virginia." Doreen couldn't describe the emotions that were going through her right now, but she made an attempt to verbalize them to her husband. "If losing that baby meant you getting born in Christ, then maybe it ain't so bad." She held Willie in her arms as she continued. "God has a mysterious way of bringing His children to Him so that they may have eternal life. Maybe He used the death of our baby as one of His ways."

"Yeah, maybe," Willie agreed.

Doreen moved her body so that it was now sitting next to Willie. "I'll get to packing. You don't need to call over none of your friends. I'll do it all. And I don't need the help of none of their wives either." Doreen grabbed Willie by the cheeks and looked him in the eyes. "I don't ever want another woman doing what I can do myself. You hear me, Willie?"

Oh, Willie heard her all right—loud and clear.

Doreen hopped out of the bed. "Go on out to the supermarket and get us some boxes that they've thrown out by the Dumpster. While you do that, I'ma cook you up a nice breakfast. Okay?"

"Sure," Willie replied. He stood and went to do as Doreen had suggested.

"Willie, guess what?" Doreen smiled as Willie stopped, turned, and looked at her with questioning eyes, urging her to speak.

"God answered my prayers just that quick." She snapped her fingers. "I got my strength back." She held back tears. "And I got my man back. All of him. Right, Willie?"

Willie nodded, and then walked away. Doreen watched the back of him until he was no longer in sight. Once again, good thing Willie's back was to her too. That way, she couldn't see the look of regret on his face. He was regretting that he wasn't able to tell his wife the *real* reason that was taking him to West Virginia.

Chapter Seventeen

The first three months in West Virginia weren't bad at all for Doreen. She and Willie had gotten along swell. Well, actually, she and Willie had always gotten along. Them getting along never was a problem in their marriage. It was her trying to get along with all his wicked ways that had caused her stress. But never once had Doreen really displayed just how stressed out the things Willie did had made her. Just when hate would try to rise up in her, she'd suppress it with the love of the Lord. Love covers a multitude indeed. But for how long was the question.

"The blue tie or the black one?" Willie held up a tie in each hand and waited for his wife to make the decision for him as to which one to wear.

"Now, Willie, we've been over this a thousand times already, and I keep telling you the blue one," Doreen replied. "How many more times are you going to ask me? 'Cause I'm telling you now, my answer ain't gon' change none. But if it pleases you, wear the black one then." Doreen gave Willie the once-over. "After all, anything would look good on you, baby." Doreen blushed. Talking that way to Willie always made her a little coy. She wasn't used to expressing herself like that. In her head, though, she'd always tell herself how lucky she was to have a man as fine as Willie.

Willie was sharp, so she didn't blame all those other gals for trying to get a piece of him. She blamed Willie for cuttin' 'em off a slice. But that was neither here nor there. It had been three months, and all Willie had been doing was working all week and going to church with Doreen on Sunday. As a matter of fact, that's where the two were headed now.

On the way to their new place in West Virginia, they'd driven past a couple of churches, but West Va. Jesus Is Lord Church of Christ was the one Doreen settled on. Willie had suggested a thousand times that they at least give the other churches a try and visit around. But from the moment Doreen saw it, she knew it was home. Something about that church had just spoken to her. It was as if the Lord Himself had led her there.

"You don't just go attending the first church you see," Willie had tried to reason with her. "How will you ever know if the others aren't better if you don't try 'em out?"

"Willie, now you know I ain't never church hopped my entire life, and there ain't no reason to start now," Doreen had countered. "Besides, it was like I was drawn to West Va. Jesus is Lord Church of Christ. For some reason, I'm just supposed to be there." Although Willie wasn't convinced and still tried to talk Doreen into visiting other churches, her mind was set on making it her home church.

Even from just the outside of the church Doreen could feel the pull—the anointing on the building as they drove by it. Her eyes even watered. It was like the Lord was in there waiting on her, and she felt overwhelmed about getting to Him. It pleased her soul to have that feeling every Sunday. She always had a level of expectation when it came to church. Doreen had never been one to attend church out of routine or habit, because she was raised in the church or because it was what was expected of a preacher's daughter. Sunday morning services were like a date with the Lord that she prepared for all week long. The fact that deep down inside Willie seemed to actually like this church too made it all the better.

"Do you mean that?" Willie asked Doreen. "I would look good in anything?"

Doreen blushed as she finished making up the bed. "Of course," she blushed again. "Am I one to lie?"

"Oooooh, woman, don't you start nothing you ain't willing to finish," Willie grinned.

Doreen looked down at her watch on her wrist, and then back up at Willie. "Who says I ain't got time to finish?"

And on that note, a few minutes later, Doreen would find herself having to make the bed up all over again. Willie had made her feel so good with his attentive lovemaking that she wore a smile all the way to church. Willie was good; oooooh, Willie was indeed good when he was good. But when Willie was bad, oooooh, Willie was bad.

Doreen and Willie had arrived at church just as the praise and worship team took the stage. They'd missed opening prayer and the reading of the scripture, but praise and worship was Willie's favorite part anyway. Doreen would sometimes just stand there and admire how into the songs Willie would be. He'd be staring up at praise and worship like he was looking at Jesus Himself. Then she'd have to catch herself and remember that her eyes were supposed to be on Jesus. So she'd close her eyes, allow the words of the songs being sung to penetrate her heart and go into her own personal praise and worship with the Lord.

"Praise and worship was something else today, wasn't it?" Willie said as he and Doreen drove home.

"That church is something else, period. I love it!" Doreen exclaimed. "And you know, I've been thinking," she turned her body toward Willie, "maybe it's time we join the church. I'm just itching to join the praise and worship team, but you know you have to be a member to join any of the ministries."

"Praise and worship?" Willie swallowed hard. "I don't mind you joining the church, but I don't really think joining praise and worship is such a good idea. Theirs is different than the one at your mom and pop's church," Willie reasoned. "I mean, they good up at this church—really good."

Doreen took offense. "So what you trying to say? That praise and worship back home was bad? So what's that say about me, your wife? You trying to say I can't sing?"

"Calm down. Calm down." Willie rested his hand on Doreen's. He peeked over at her with a smile on his face, and then studied the road again. "Now you know I've told you that you've got the sweetest voice I've ever heard. As a matter of fact, heck, you'd be able to show their choir a thing or two. But they ain't that good because they practice for only an hour once a week like you all did back at home. They practice twice a week for two hours. And you done started up with that pound-cake business again too. How you gon' take care of home and your husband doing all that?"

Doreen thought for a moment. "Hmmm, I guess you are right about that. I mean, that's a lot of practice. That's a lot of time away from the house."

"And a lot of time away from me," Willie winked.

And there was no way Doreen was going to leave Willie unattended that much. Surely he'd find some drink-

ing hole to start hanging out at with that much time on
his hands. Things were good right now; too good for
her to go messing it up. "Maybe joining the praise and
worship team might not be such a good idea, but I still
think we should consider joining the church. We need
a church here in West VA. that we can call home. So
will you at least think about that?"

"Sure," Willie nodded. "I'll think about it."

And while Willie was thinking about that, Doreen
should have been thinking about just how in the world
Willie knew the rehearsal schedule of West VA. Jesus
Is Lord Church of Christ Praise and Worship. But not
to worry. She'd find out soon enough. And it wasn't going to be good.

Chapter Eighteen

"Amazing grace, how sweet the sound . . ." Doreen sang as she piled seven pound cakes into her car. Three had to go to one place, while the other four had to go to another. She was running a little bit behind schedule, but that little bit would make a big difference considering she had two different places she needed to be. Where was that Willie when she needed him? Had he come straight home from work this evening, he could have dropped off one order while she did the other. But he'd been having to work overtime a couple times a week here lately, so Doreen assumed that's probably what had happened this evening. And if that was the case, she had no complaints about that. Overtime meant extra pay. Extra money was always a good thing.

". . . who saved a wretch like me." Doreen coughed after a failed attempt to hit that last note. "Oooh, maybe Willie is right," she laughed. "Maybe I ain't fit for praise and worship anymore. I got to get these pipes tuned up," Doreen said before hitting the road.

Doreen made it to her first destination with absolutely no time to spare in getting to the next the one. She collected her money and was on her way to the second stop. Having earned an extra three-dollar tip, she was singing a more upbeat tune now. She was rocking her head and smiling. As she zoomed by a couple buildings only to have to screech her wheels at a stoplight, her smile soon faded. It wasn't because she'd gotten caught by a stoplight with one more delivery that needed to be made. It was because of what she thought she might have seen while speeding past those buildings.

"Was that . . ." she said out loud, but then shook the thought away. Had she *really* just seen what she thought she'd seen? "No. No. No. No," she told herself as she shook her head and forced a smile back on her face. "Oh, devil, I see what you're up to now. You're just mad things are going so good and that God is showing up and showing out in Willie's and my marriage. I will not allow you to influence my mind or make me think I'm seeing things that are not there." Doreen shook her head even harder.

As the light turned green, in spite of the little pep talk Doreen had given herself, everything in her wanted to turn that car around or at least look through the rearview mirror and double-check. But she didn't. She had a delivery to make. She didn't have time to risk or waste feeling like a fool when what she thought she'd seen she really hadn't.

Pulling off from the stoplight, Doreen picked back up on the song where she'd left off. She wasn't singing it as upbeat anymore, though. She might as well have gone back to singing "Amazing Grace."

Arriving at her second drop-off, Doreen made the exchange of cakes for money and was on her way back home. She drove in silence this time. There was no singing, not even the humming of a note. She had a lot on her mind and decided to verbalize it to the Lord. "God, I know you ain't gon' let me go running around this town made to be no fool." She swallowed hard. "I . . . I just can't do it, God. Not this time. Not anymore. I'll break, I swear I'll break." Doreen's words trembled out of her mouth. "But God, you know exactly how much I can handle, so I trust you'd never put on me more than I can bear. So if there is something that needs to be revealed to me about my Willie, then God, I ask you to do it now so I can get it over with. In Jesus' name."

Doreen finished her prayer just as she drove past those same set of buildings she'd passed before. Driving a little slower this time, she looked over as she drove by. She scanned the parking lot. She let out a deep sigh and kept driving. She kept driving, but not for long. The next thing she knew, she'd made a U-turn and drove back to the buildings. The second building was a local motel. That's the parking lot she pulled up into; right next to Willie's car. "God, you are so faithful." Doreen threw the car in park, turned it off, and jumped out of the vehicle. "My Willie may not be, but Lord in heaven, you sure are faithful."

Now that Doreen was out of her car, she didn't know what to do. There were several motel rooms before her. She didn't know exactly which one, but she knew Willie had to be in one of them. Why else would his car be parked there?

"Lord, you brought me here, now show me what to do." Doreen paced back and forth before three doors. "Show me what to do," she yelled. Catching herself, she realized she had to do something besides stand out there looking like some deranged fool. She paused and looked around. Spotting the motel office, she made her way in there.

"Good evening, can I help you?" the clerk behind the desk asked Doreen.

"Uh, yes, well, uh, I hope so," she stammered, looking down at the clerk's badge to see the word "Manager" printed on it. "You see, it's my husband's and my anniversary. We got a room here under his name. He left to go to the store, and I done locked myself out of the room when I went to get some ice. I could wait for him to get back, but I was really hoping to decorate it up nice while he was gone. You know—to surprise him."

The manager looked at Doreen suspiciously. "Oh yeah?"

"Yes, sir."

"And Missy, just what is your husband's name?"

"It's Willie. It's William Tucker. I'm Mrs. Tucker."

Still looking at Doreen suspiciously, the manager proceeded to examine his check-in log. He looked down at the log, and then looked up at her. He was looking at her like she was up to no good, and for good reason too. She was stammering and a sheet of sweat had formed across her forehead. She looked nervous about something. That didn't sit too well with the manager. "What did you say your husband's name was again?"

"It's William—William Tucker."

"Oh yeah, here it is, right here. William Tucker. Room 111." He looked at Doreen almost apologetically, then thought for a minute. "And you say you're his wife, huh?"

Doreen nodded, wiping the sweat from her forehead with the back of her hand.

"Then you got some ID on ya you can show me?" he asked.

"Yeah, uh, sure. But I, uh, left my purse in the car." Doreen hadn't thought to grab it.

The manager stood there looking at Doreen as if waiting for her to say something else. She never did. She just looked at the clerk.

"I'll wait," the manager finally said, not picking up on the fact that there was no logical reason why Doreen's purse should have been in her car. If anything, it should have been locked inside the motel room. And even then, hadn't she just told him that her husband took the car to the store? Thank goodness this guy's picnic basket was light a sandwich or two.

"Excuse me?" Doreen had no idea what he was talking about.

"I'll wait while you go to your car and get it."

"Oh yeah, right." Doreen smiled, and then headed out of the office.

"Uh, ma'am," the manager called out, causing Doreen to pause and look back at him. "I thought you said your husband went to the store. Wouldn't he have driven?" Guess he hadn't missed that little slipup after all.

Doreen hadn't thought about that herself. With only a few seconds to reply before she looked even more suspicious she said, "Yeah, but, uh, we drove separate cars. We met up here. Kind of like role-play; two teenagers sneaking around. You get it?" Doreen hoped he did—get it and believe it.

Still eyeballing her like she'd stole something he said, "You just go on and bring me that ID back, ya hear?"

"Yes, sir, right away." Doreen scurried out of the motel office. "Oh, God, I'm so sorry. I repent right now in Jesus' name for telling that man a bold-faced lie. I'm sorry." Doreen opened her car door and pulled her purse out. She went back into the motel office while digging around in her purse.

The clerk watched her with a hawk eye as she scrambled through it. After a moment or so and Doreen coming up with nothing, he began tapping his finger on the counter impatiently.

"Just a minute, I know it's in here," Doreen said as she continued to fumble around. Stuff began to fall out of her purse onto the counter. Some items even rolled off the counter onto the floor. The manager sucked his teeth. "I'm sorry, sir. I'm trying to find it." After still coming up with nothing and both the clerk and Doreen getting agitated, she finally just dumped the entire contents of her purse on the counter and began picking through it. "Voilà! Here it is." She held up her ID as if she were carrying the torch in an opening ceremony for the Olympics. She handed the ID to the manager with a smile.

He eyeballed it while Doreen wiped another wave of sweat off of her forehead. "Hmm. Mrs. Doreen Tucker." He looked at the ID, then looked at Doreen. He looked back down at the ID again. "That's you, all right," he sighed with defeat. Then without further delay, he turned around and grabbed the motel key for room 111. "Here you are, Mrs. Tucker." He handed Doreen the key. "Sorry about the delay. It's just that we can't go around letting any ol' body into motel rooms. You could have been a murderer for all I know."

Doreen accepted the key, having no idea that the manager's last statement would contain such irony.

Chapter Nineteen

After nervously scooping up and shoveling all the contents from the counter and floor back into her purse, Doreen thanked the motel manager and headed for room 111. She walked out of that motel office a nervous wreck. Now that she had lied her way into entry into Willie's room, she had no idea what to do next.

"Go into the dang room," she told herself. She passed room 101. "Lord, you are an all-knowing God." She passed room 102. "You already know what's behind that motel room door I'm about to go to." She passed room 103. "Do I want to know is the question?" She passed room 104. "Do I need to know?" She paused in front of room 105. Did she need to know?

She couldn't help but really think about that answer. She knew Willie was a cheat. The circumstantial evidence had always been there. No, she'd never really caught him in the act except for the couple times women had made themselves comfortable in his lap or in his arms on the dance floor. That wasn't nothing to go out and get a divorce about. Now going out and getting another woman pregnant, that would be grounds for divorce. But for all Doreen knew, Agnes was just jealous and full of lies. Agnes probably made that stuff up because she wanted Doreen to get mad and leave Willie so she could have him all to herself.

As quiet as it's kept, Doreen never questioned Willie about it or dug around to find out whether it was the truth or not because deep down inside, she didn't want the answer. Before leaving Kentucky she had, though, had a talk with Mrs. Tucker about what Agnes had insinuated.

"Okay, so let's say it is all true," Mrs. Tucker had said to Doreen. *"What you going to do about it? I mean, for real, what you gon' do?"* She threw her arms up in the air.

Doreen really didn't know what to say. She shrugged while saying, "I don't know—I guess pray about it and see what God—"

"Look, honey child, I been there and prayed that, so take it from me; nothing is what you're going to do. I mean, yeah, you gon' be mad. You gon' fuss and argue and might even try to come up into the juke joint and cut the fool again." She chuckled, *"Although your father-in-law swears to God he's gon' ban you from the place if you do. And he ain't too sweet on God, so whenever he brings His name up,"* she nodded upward, *"there just might be some truth to it. Anyway, gal, like I was saying, you ain't gon' do nothing but be mad for a spell, maybe hold out on the lovemaking for a week or two, but then you and Willie gon' be as good as new."*

"No." Doreen shook her head, but weakly, as if there was some truth to what her mother-in-law was saying.

"You say that now, but I done seen it happen a million times. A woman comes up in the joint and finds some other woman dangling all over her man or vice versa. She cuts the fool, threatens to leave him, tells him how he ain't gon' just treat her no any kind of way; then the very next week, he comes back into the joint now with that same woman who threatened to leave him dangling on his arm."

Mrs. Tucker chuckled. "I don't know why women do that to themselves. We compromise everything that we are and who God meant for us to be, and for what? Some man?" She looked far off as if she was looking into her past. As if she was wondering if she might have done some things differently, how her own life might have turned out to be. She then looked at Doreen seriously and rested her hand upon her shoulder. "Baby girl, don't be like me, spending the first few years of your marriage all stressed out trying to sneak and creep around to see what your husband is up to. Don't do it unless you know for certain what you find is going to change some things. If you just looking for answers in order to have something to fuss and complain about, then why bother? If you looking for answers because you gon' walk away from the bull crap, know your worth and live your life; now that's another story."

Doreen allowed her mother-in-law's words to sink in. "Mrs. Tucker—and I hope you don't mind me saying this—but you sound like you're speaking from experience." Doreen waited for a response, which came a few seconds later.

"Could be, could be not. But look at me. I'm still with Mr. Tucker, who, let me just say this, is a mirror of your Willie. I just loved that man so much I was willing to fight for him. I was willing to show myself, the world, and most sadly, my son, that a woman's worth ain't more than a welcome mat at a saloon— 'cause I just kept letting him walk all over me. My actions basically cosigned to my son that how his father was living was right." She looked down at Doreen's now-vacant womb. "You ever wonder if that's why your God took away your baby? So the same thing wouldn't be repeated."

Doreen instantly grabbed her stomach as if a gush of wind had blown and was about to carry her insides away. She became teary eyed at just the thought that the reason why God had allowed her to lose her baby was because He knew she would be too weak to stand up for herself. She would be too weak, like her mother-in-law, to teach her child any different.

With her hands on her belly, still standing outside motel room 105, Doreen said, "God, give me strength. Give me strength to walk in the God-given authority I have inherited from the throne." Doreen continued her trek past room 106. Her pace picked up as she passed room 107, then 108. She was at a full jog as she passed 109 and 110. Then finally, she stood outside room 111. Almost out of breath. She stood there for a moment before taking the key the clerk had given her, stuck it in the lock, and quickly opened the door.

Any question Doreen had about her Willie had just been answered. Like Mrs. Tucker had inquired of her, now what was she going to do about it?

Chapter Twenty

Speechless, shocked, disgusted, hurt, pissed; no, none of those words could truly describe the emotions circling through Doreen's head as she watched her husband thrusting, moaning, and groaning on top of a woman who was expressing the same sentiments in return. Everything was like HD. Although Doreen was quite a few feet away from the scene, it appeared to be so up close and personal. It was so in her face. It was as though her eyes were camera lenses and had zoomed in, capturing a close-up shot. The upper body of Willie was drenched in sweat as his lower half was covered with a motel sheet. The sweat droplets were magnified as they rolled down his back. The movements his lower body displayed were so gentle and choreographed. So tender.

Her mind couldn't help but wander back to their own lovemaking sessions. For the life of her, Doreen couldn't recall him ever being that gentle and tender with her.

"Oh, baby."

The moan from the female up under Willie immediately brought Doreen's thoughts back to the present. She stood there, longer than she could explain why, watching her husband make love to another woman. They hadn't a clue she was even in the room. Perhaps they would have heard her enter had they not been so loud in expressing their pleasure with each other.

"*What you gon' do?*"

Doreen looked over her shoulder for the voice that had just relayed that question to her. It was the voice of Mrs. Tucker. Doreen had heard it so clearly in her head, as if her mother-in-law was standing right there. Doreen pictured that she was. With a glass of liquor in one hand, Doreen envisioned her posing the question once again. "*Well, gal, what you gon' do? You got your answers.*" The Mrs. Tucker that was only visible in Doreen's mind right now looked over at Willie and the woman making love. She chuckled. "*Heck, and now it ain't just hearsay. You see it with your own two eyes. So what you gon' do? Cut the fool and end up looking like a fool when next week you still living with Willie and the week after that he'll have some other woman up in here? And the cycle will repeat itself over and over again, just like it did with me and his daddy.*" Mrs. Tucker laughed again. "*You young girls crack me up always looking for answers—like that's going to change anything. Ha.*" She took a sip of her drink and continued with a wicked laugh that echoed throughout Doreen's head.

Doreen stood in the motel doorway covering her ears with her hands. She began shaking her head as tears formed in her eyes. She was protecting her ears from the truth Mrs. Tucker's voice was speaking inside her head. Why had she bothered? Why should she even bother doing anything about it now? After all is said and done, she's going to end up being the one looking stupid. Passing women up in grocery stores that have been with her man. Having to endure those snide looks on their faces, reminding Doreen that they'd been with her husband and could be with him again if they wanted. If in her heart she knew she wasn't going to leave Willie for his unfaithful actions and sins, then she might as well leave that motel room right now and save herself the drama.

Slowly Doreen began backing out of the motel room.

"You don't care about me and your other sisters, do you?"

Doreen stopped in her tracks. It was as if she'd physically bumped into Sarina. And now, instead of Doreen visualizing her mother-in-law standing behind her, it was her little sister. She could hear the words from her sister inside her head scolding her.

"You just gon' keep taking it and taking it and taking it, huh?" Sarina's eyes spilled with tears. *"Is this how you are going to pay back Mama and Daddy for all the years of them bringing you up to be a good Christian girl? Is this the example you want to set for me and the girls? How many generations of us Hamilton women are going to have to endure this same thing because you set a pattern? How many generations will be cursed?"* Sarina looked over at Willie and the woman he was cheating with. *"You just gon' walk away and do nothing but pretend to be the perfect little wife and the perfect little Christian."* Sarina shook her head. *"What you gon' do, Reen?"*

"Nothing. She ain't gon' do a dang on thing." Now the vision of Mrs. Tucker was back. She took another sip of her drink and laughed.

"Baby, baby," the woman underneath Willie moaned again, almost in a panic.

"I'm sorry. Was I being too rough?" Willie asked, slowing down his pace.

At that moment, in Doreen's ears she could hear Willie and his mistress talking. In her head she could hear her mother-in-law and her sister. There were too many voices. She couldn't take it. Too many voices.

"Baby," the mistress said.

"Is that better? Does that feel good to you?" Willie murmured.

"She ain't gon' do nothing," Mrs. Tucker said.

"Do something, Reen," Sarina urged.

"Noooooooooo," Doreen yelled out. "Noooooooooo!!!!"

"Doreen!" That was Willie, shocked as all get-out to look over his shoulder and see his wife screaming, crying, and covering her ears in the doorway. "My God, what are you doing here?" Doreen didn't reply; then moments later, she heard Willie asking, "My God, what are you doing?" Still Doreen didn't reply. She didn't know how much time passed after that, but the next question Willie posed to her was, "My God, Doreen, what have you done?"

As far as Doreen knew, she'd been standing in the doorway the entire time. She hadn't moved a muscle. But when she looked down at the sheet she held clinched in her fist, she knew that wasn't the case. She looked up at Willie for answers as to how the sheet had gotten into her hands, but he just stood there looking horrified at his wife. Next, Doreen turned her attention to the place where she had more than likely gotten the sheet—at the bed.

Upon seeing blood—blood everywhere—she had no choice but to pose the same question to herself that Willie just had: "My God, what have I done?"

Chapter Twenty-one

Doreen felt like she was a very, very long way from home. It felt more like Germany or something, rather than West Virginia. It may not have been Germany, but it was still foreign, nonetheless. She had never stepped foot in jail a day in her life; not to visit anybody or nothing. And now, she would call this place home.

Although she was a grown woman now, she wanted her mommy. She wanted her daddy. But there was no way in hell or on earth she would summon them to come see her; not in a jail cell, that was for sure.

"You gon' eat that or what?" a voice boomed into Doreen's ear.

She looked down at the beige clump of mess that had been scooped up into the bowl that sat on her tray. She gagged, holding back puke. It wasn't just the cold, old oatmeal that made her sick to her stomach. It was her nerves—the fear that was lurking inside her belly like a bully's prey at three o'clock after school.

Doreen shook her head and scooted the bowl toward the woman who'd just inquired about her food.

"Thanks. But just so you know, the chow they give us here don't get much better than this. So unless you plan on turning into skin and bones, you better get used to it." The woman took Doreen's bowl and dumped its contents into hers. She then scooted the bowl back toward Doreen and began eating. "So what you in for and how long?" the woman asked with a mouthful of mushy oatmeal.

Once again, Doreen wanted to gag. Now it was because the girl next to her, with half her teeth missing and the other half just as rotten as could be, was talking with a mouthful of food. The yucky concoction of oatmeal and saliva settled in the cracks of the woman's mouth.

Doreen quickly turned away and put her hand over her mouth. She managed to keep from throwing up, but absolutely could not look back at the woman who had no table manners whatsoever. "I don't know."

"You don't know what?" The woman scooped food into her mouth, chewed, and talked all at the same time.

The churning of Doreen's stomach could be heard. Although she couldn't see the mess in the woman's mouth, she could hear the stickiness of it as she spoke. She couldn't talk for fear it wouldn't just be words that came up.

"Well, I don't know what. Is it you don't know what you're in here for, or you don't know how long you're in here for?"

"Both," Doreen managed to say.

"Oh, I see. You ain't a transfer or nothing. You came in with the new girls in the middle of the night. You ain't been arraigned yet. They'll tell you the charges then. They should be rounding y'all up soon to transport y'all to the courthouse. The judge will set bail, and then maybe you can get out of here." The woman then asked with a mouthful of food, "You married?"

"Isn't it obvious that I'm married?" is what Doreen wanted to reply. *Can't she see as clear as day the wedding ring on my fing* . . . Doreen's thoughts trailed off and her heart almost stopped when she saw that each of her fingers were bare. She began to panic. "Oh my God, my ring. My ring is missing. Someone stole my wedding ring."

"Slow your row," the woman told her. "Ain't nobody stole nothing. They made you check all your stuff in when you checked in. You'll get it back just as soon as you check out. That is, if your stuff don't mysteriously 'get lost.' My girl Josie swears up and down she seen one of the guards wearing her diamond studs." The woman nodded her head up and down as if what she'd just said was Bible.

Back then there was no Tyler Perry or Madea movies, but if there had been, this woman would have been a perfect match for Mr. Brown. She looked like him both in the face and physically. She even talked like him. Everything she said she spoke with such seriousness, as if the last days were here.

"Anyway," the woman continued, "you better pray you ain't been getting on your old man's nerves. That way, he won't hesitate to come bail you out of this place." She looked around, and then at Doreen. "But if you been nagging and worrying him something awful, he'll look at your being here like a gift from God."

Finally, Doreen spoke. "How could a man see his wife being in jail as a blessing from God?"

"It's like a minivacation of him getting to be away from her. He ain't got to hear her mouth talking about 'Where you going' and 'Where you been.' You'll be the one locked up, while he'll be out there feeling mo' free than he ever has in his entire life." The woman dipped her head up and down to drive her reasoning home.

Burying her head in her hands, Doreen tried to think back. Had she been worrying and nagging Willie? Had she? She strained her brain to recall just the past twenty-four hours, let alone the last days or so. Her mind was blank. It was like her memory slate had been wiped clean. It felt as if she were outside herself and would return when she got good and ready.

"If you been good to yo' man, though, do everything for him, then he'll rob a bank to get you out of this place." She laughed. "'Cause he know if he don't, he might to die. A man used to having a woman around to do everything for him ain't no good when she's not around. He can barely pull up his own britches. He like to starve to death 'cause he can't even boil water to make a hot dog." She let out one more hearty laugh, and then it faded. "That's what happened to my pops, you know. When my moms died of a stroke, he went to his own grave not too much after her. He was so used to having her there for him, doing for him, that he didn't know how to live without her. He couldn't live without her, so he didn't. He died off shortly after. He had no will to live."

"I'm sorry to hear that," Doreen told her.

"Oh, no need to be sorry. Well, you can be sorry 'bout my mama dying. She was an angel. But the old man, he was Satan himself. Us kids was glad to see him go. He made coming up in our house a living nightmare. Always fussing and hitting on Mama and us kids. He the one who gave Mama her stroke in the first place. I know he did. All that hell he raised—her poor, kind heart couldn't take it no more." The woman looked down as her bottom lip began to tremble.

"You . . . you all right?" Doreen asked her.

The woman let the spoon fall from her hand into the bowl of oatmeal. "Yeah, it's just that I feel kind of bad. I feel bad about something I prayed for after Mama had the stroke." The woman took a break, contemplating whether she'd share the details with Doreen. Then she decided to do just that. "After Mama had her stroke and was lying there on that hospital bed, I closed my eyes and prayed to God." The woman mocked the scene in the hospital room that day by closing her eyes and folding her hands. "Dear God, I love my mama. But don't let her live, not here on earth. God, take her with you. She's the perfect angel. I don't know how heaven has survived without her thus far. But I know one thing; if you don't take her and leave her here with my father, she ain't gon' survive long anyway. So please, God, just take her." Once the woman realized a tear had escaped her eye, she quickly wiped it away, picked up her spoon, and continued piling heaps of cold oatmeal into her mouth.

"So you prayed for your own mama to die?" Doreen was a little shocked.

"I just wanted her to be happy," the woman reasoned. "She deserved to be happy, you know? If you had a choice to see your mother die and go on to eternal life or stay here on earth and suffer, which would you choose? A selfish person is gonna choose the second one. A selfless person will choose the first one. Yeah, I loved my mama and wanted her here to be able to love and caress me. But that was so selfish. I couldn't make it about me. For once in my life I had to make it about somebody else. I had to make it about her." The woman looked upward as if looking straight into the gates of heaven. "I know she's up there happier now than she ever would have been here on earth with my daddy."

The woman smiled a huge smile. This time, Doreen didn't even get disgusted by her mouth. She was too moved by the story she'd just told.

The woman turned and looked at Doreen. "You know, I ain't never, never told a living soul about that prayer." She shook her head. "I don't even know why I told you." The woman was about to shovel another bite of oatmeal in her mouth before she stopped and looked at Doreen. "Yeah, I do. I know why I'm telling you all this stuff. Because you remind me just like her. You remind me just like my mama—your spirit and all, that is." The woman gave Doreen such a warm smile, that for a moment, Doreen didn't even care that she was in jail. She didn't even care about how she'd gotten there. She just wanted to comfort this woman.

Doreen placed her hand atop the woman's hand. The woman looked down at her hand, and then smiled up at Doreen. Just then, a couple of beasty-looking broads walked up behind the woman. One bent down and whispered in the woman's ear. The woman immediately looked at Doreen with horror in her eyes. She slipped her hand from up under Doreen's, picked up her bowl of oatmeal, and dumped the exact portion she'd taken from Doreen back in her bowl. Next, the woman stood up and went to walk away.

"Wait a minute," Doreen called to the woman. "Where are you going? You don't have to go." Doreen felt bad that the woman had picked up and was leaving. For a minute there, the woman had made her forget all about herself. For a minute there, she felt like she was tending to one of her own sisters' worries.

Folks at her mother and father's church always told Doreen that she had these natural motherly tendencies, even at such a young age. Obviously, this woman had seen the same thing in her, but now, just like that, the woman was treating Doreen like she had cooties or something. "At least tell me your name," Doreen practically pleaded.

The woman adamantly shook her head. "Uh-uh. Don't no baby killer need to know my name." The woman hurried off behind the other two women.

Doreen turned her attention back to her tray horrified. "Baby killer?" she mumbled. "Had that woman just called me a baby killer? But why? Why on earth would she say something so—" And it was at that very moment that everything came back to Doreen like a gushing tidal wave. She remembered. She remembered everything that had happened in that motel room, especially why she now found herself in jail.

Chapter Twenty-two

Breakfast was over, and now Doreen was back in a jail cell. Originally, she'd been in a cell with multiple other women, but now she was alone. After that woman had called her a baby killer, whispers and chattering made their way around the room like a high school cafeteria with a whole bunch of babbling girls. Doreen could only wish she could turn back the hands of time and find herself in a high school lunchroom instead of jail. She wanted to be anywhere but there as voices started getting louder and sounding like a swarm of bees. An uneasy feeling had come over Doreen. It was if the bees were going to strike and attack her at any moment.

She had simply sat at the cafeteria table, closed her eyes, and prayed for God's protection.

"Prayer works on the outside world, but it ain't gon' help you none in here," Doreen heard a voice say as someone passed behind her. She felt a thump as the owner of the voice brushed by her. She was too afraid to even look up from her breakfast tray to see who had, without many words at all, threatened her. No, no threatening words had been outright spoken as to any harm being done to Doreen, but she'd felt the threatening presence back in the cafeteria. She now still felt it in her jail cell. Evil was around her. Evil spirits lurked in that entire place. Doreen could feel it, but what scared her most was the evil that dwelled in her.

It had to have been nothing but pure evil that caused Doreen to do what she'd done to land herself in that place. The vision of the actions of exactly what she'd done eventually being triggered by two little words: *baby killer*.

"Why didn't I just leave?" she asked herself as she sat on the floor of the cell. She could have sat on the bed, but there really wasn't a big difference between the floor and that two-inch piece of mattress.

She closed her eyes and tried not to think about what had happened several hours ago at that motel room. She couldn't help it, though. The entire incident consumed her mind.

"Doreen!" That was Willie, shocked as all get-out to look over his shoulder and see his wife screaming, crying, and covering her ears in the doorway of room 111. She'd been watching him make love to another woman in the bed of a cheap motel. Willie had no idea how long his wife had been standing there watching. Doreen hadn't the slightest clue as to how long she'd been standing there either. "My God, what are you doing here?"

What had gotten to Doreen was Willie's tone. He'd asked her that question like she was his teenage daughter on punishment and had shown up at the school dance in spite of being forbidden to do so. What got her even more heated was when he said, "Go on home, Doreen. You've got no business here."

He hadn't even sounded sorry or regretful for the position she'd just caught him in. He continued to turn the knife already in her heart even more when he said, "Get to gettin', woman, and I'll talk to you when I get home." He said all of these things without even attempting to remove himself from on top of the Jezebel beneath him.

There was no "Please, baby, please—it's not what it looks like." There was no "I'm sorry—it will never happen again." There was no empathy whatsoever, and this cut to Doreen's bones as tears began to fill her eyes, blurring her vision. Although she couldn't see as clearly anymore, the silhouettes of her husband and his lover in that bed were still there. That vision taunted Doreen that very moment to no ends, but what happened next would haunt her forever.

"Sister Doreen, it's, it's . . ." The woman was stuttering and seemed scared for her life. "It's not what it all seems. I swear to God." The woman managed to push a still stunned Willie off of her. He was now positioned in bed next to the woman. Doreen wiped her eyes, and for the first time was able to clearly see the woman's face. Because the woman had clinched the sheet between each fist and pulled it up to her neck in shame, Doreen couldn't see her nakedness, but she sure could see her face, and a familiar face it was.

The rage was building up inside of Doreen more and more each second. She couldn't believe the woman she'd just caught her husband with was a member of the church choir. Ironically, it had hurt less when Doreen thought Willie might have been cheating on her with some juke-joint floozy of a tramp. But with one of her sisters in Christ? This was the ultimate betrayal. How in the world could a woman of God do such a thing, and to another woman of God, at that? Surely that soprano-singing soloist was going to go to hell for this, and Doreen was going to send her there personally.

"My God, what are you doing?"

Doreen heard Willie ask her that question, but answering him was far from her mind as she pounced on the woman who lay in the motel bed next to her husband. Doreen had dived on top of the woman. All of Doreen's weight landing on her stomach nearly knocked the wind out of the poor girl. Blow after blow Doreen landed on the woman and not once did the woman even attempt to hit Doreen back. She was too busy clinching and crying out, "No! Stop it!" The woman's pleas fell on deaf ears, though. Her perpetrator was in a zone. Doreen swung wildly. Never having fought a single day in her life, not even with one of her sisters, there was no precision to Doreen's aimless swings. That didn't keep her from landing every single blow, though.

As Doreen pummeled the woman, the woman was reaching out to Willie. Doreen could even feel Willie trying to pull her off of the woman, but it was as if he was trying to do the impossible. A wave of strength had come over Doreen that she didn't even know was in her.

The more that woman tried to get to her husband and the more her husband tried to protect that woman, the madder and stronger Doreen got.

"Baby!" she heard the woman cry out, still reaching for Willie.

This woman was just brazen to be referring to Willie as her baby right in front of his wife, Doreen thought as she swung and punched everywhere, hitting the woman on almost every inch of her upper body. Inch by inch, Willie was finally able to make some lead way and slide Doreen off of the woman, but Doreen still kept kicking, pounding, and throwing blows the entire time.

"My baby!" the woman cried out again, reaching for Willie.

"Doreen, stop it! Stop it right now. You have no idea what you're doing. Stop it! I'm sorry! I'm sorry!

*I didn't mean to hurt you like this. I've never meant to
hurt you. I'm sorry."*

*There he'd said it, and Willie's apology was like the
antidote the raging beast inside of Doreen needed to
calm down. Suddenly Doreen had stopped swinging and was no longer like deadweight to Willie as
he pulled her off the woman—off the bed. In Willie's
pulling Doreen off the bed, the sheet came off with
her, and the woman lay there baring it all in the bed.
That's when Doreen saw it. That's when Willie saw it.*

"My God, Doreen, what have you done?"

*Now Doreen was the one who was in shock; who
looked like a deer not only caught in headlights, but
inches away from the Mack truck to which the headlights were attached.*

*"What have you done?" Willie repeated again, and
again with no reply from his wife. "Doreen? Doreen?"*

"Doreen? Doreen Tucker?" When Doreen felt the
guard snatching her up off the floor, she realized she was
no longer having a flashback, but that someone besides
Willie was calling her name.

Doreen looked up at the female guard. "Come on
with me," the guard ordered, pulling Doreen up to her
feet. "It's time for you to have your day in court."

Chapter Twenty-three

About an hour after the guard had snatched her up, Doreen found herself in a holding room, waiting on her case to be called in court. Surprisingly enough, she wasn't worried, nervous, afraid, or anything; not about the case itself anyway. What she was worried about, though, was whether Willie had contacted her parents. Would they be sitting in that courtroom watching for their daughter who'd been raised on the church pew— who knew better—to come through the door hand- cuffed and wearing jailhouse clothes?

She'd tried to make a phone call to Willie when she'd been given the opportunity around the time they first processed her into the jail. There was no answer. They'd given her another attempt a little while after that. Still, there was no answer.

"You sure you don't want to try someone else?" the guard had asked Doreen. "Ain't you got nobody else here in West Virginia you can call?"

Doreen simply shook her head and was escorted back to her cell. That was the last time they offered for her to make a phone call. Willie hadn't even answered the phone, so Doreen's nerves were on edge, afraid that Willie wouldn't be out there.

She threw her head back against the wall and ex- haled. Her flesh wanted to tell her, "Willie just better be out there. This is all his fault anyway. Not nary none of this would have ever happened had he just kept his pants up." But Doreen had never been one to blame someone else for her actions. Her spirit man, who had already told her that she couldn't blame anybody else for the way she acted, was working overtime to beat down the flesh inside her. Too bad that spirit man had not prevailed in room 111. It was one point for her flesh and zero points for her spirit man.

"Tucker, you're up on deck," a guard said to Doreen, signaling for her to stand up. Just as Doreen stood, the inmate who had gone out to the courtroom before her was being escorted back into the holding room. She hadn't come willing, though.

"Twenty-five-thousand-dollar bond? Is that judge done lost his mind?" the woman yelled as the guards tried to keep her limbs under control. The woman was kicking, screaming, and cussing so bad that they eventually had to remove her from the room. All that ruckus had delayed Doreen from going into the courtroom. The judge had ordered a brief recess to go get himself together and bring order back to the court.

"You can sit back down until court is called back to order," the guard had instructed Doreen.

Doreen didn't want to sit back down. She wanted to get out there and get this mess over with. Realizing the guard had told her to sit down more so than ask her, Doreen allowed her body to go into a sitting position.

"I can only imagine what that judge is going to hit you with," the guard said while shaking her head and smiling at Doreen. "That chick," she nodded to the door the raging woman had been dragged out of, "all she did was rob an old couple at gunpoint." The guard shook her head even harder. "But what you did . . . ummph, ummph, ummph."

Okay, now Doreen was worried, nervous, and afraid about her case. Because she wanted so badly for the visions of the incident to stop replaying in her head, she never consciously thought about it. But thanks to the guard, Doreen felt as if she was standing in that motel room all over again.

"My baby!" she could hear Willie's mistress crying out.

Again, Doreen had thought what nerve of that woman to be calling out to Willie as her baby. That had caused Doreen to subject her with a few more good licks. Doreen wasn't aiming; she was just swinging and landing. As a matter of fact, her eyes had been closed the entire time she swung. Because if the woman decided to hit her back, she didn't want to see it coming.

The more the woman cried out about Willie being her baby, the more Doreen swung, and the harder. Even as Willie finally managed to start pulling Doreen off of her, Doreen continued kicking and swinging, landing some powerful blows. Doreen didn't know she had it in her. She didn't know she had the devil in her to cause bodily harm to someone else.

"Baby!" the woman had cried out louder than ever. But by now Doreen had ripped the sheet off of the woman who lay buck naked in that bed. She was cradling her belly and began whimpering, "My baby. My baby."

That's when Doreen got the shock of her life. She watched this woman lay in a fetal position in a bed surrounded by red. The sheet she was lying on hadn't originally been red, but the blood pouring out from her womb had been like food color to the icing on some of the pound cakes Doreen had made.

"My God, Doreen, what have you done?" Willie had asked her. She had no idea what she'd done. As a matter of fact, she had no idea she'd done it. Still, at this very moment, as the guard again instructed her to stand, she had no idea of just exactly what she'd done. What had been the result of her horrendous actions?

As the guard escorted her into the courtroom, she was about to find out.

Chapter Twenty-four

Doreen's eyes were filled with tears by the time she made her way into the courtroom. As the vision of that woman caressing her very visibly and very pregnant belly settled in her head, it got comfortable in her heart as well. The anguish the woman displayed now seemed to fill Doreen's own heart. Doreen remembered holding her belly and echoing the woman's cries the night she fell down outside of the juke joint. She remembered what it was like to wake up in that hospital only to be holding an empty womb.

Doreen gasped. Was that woman now in the same predicament herself? Was she now, like Doreen had been months ago, holding an empty womb? Had her baby come and gone from this earth without ever having been there in the first place? Is that why that woman had referred to Doreen as a baby killer? Yes, that's it. That had to be it. That had to be what had triggered the memory of her horrible actions.

"Oh my God," Doreen gasped.

"God can't help you now," the guard chuckled, leading Doreen into the courtroom.

With her eyes cast downward initially, Doreen finally raised her head and the first thing she saw was Willie. He stood as if a queen was entering the room and he was required to stand by law in her presence. Doreen saw where he slightly went to extend his hand to her, as if he wanted to reach out to her, but then he held back, knowing that wouldn't be permitted. This act forced even more tears down Doreen's face. Whatever it was she had done, Willie still cared about her. Whatever she had done wasn't so bad in his eyes that he'd turn his back on her. Whatever she had done wasn't so bad that he would forsake her in her time of need.

The guard placed Doreen, who was smiling with her eyes for a quick second, next to a man in a suit facing in the direction of the judge. Her back was now to Willie. As she stood facing the judge, Willie's presence and how he might or might not now feel about her faded into the background. Now she had to see if the real person who mattered still cared. If the real person who mattered would not turn His back on her and forsake her. Not the judge, but God. Would God show her grace and mercy as He had done all the days of her life and get her out of this situation? Even if He didn't get her out of it, would He get her through it?

God, if you do help me, Doreen prayed, *I promise to never let you down again. I promise to pray more, read the Bible more, and even start back singing for you again, Lord. Please, God, just don't let me spend the rest of my life in jail. Please! I'll do whatever you want me to do and go wherever you want me to go. You can give me any assignment anywhere on earth, and I'll do it, Lord. Just please help me.*

"I'm sorry I didn't have a chance to speak with you before now," the suit standing next to Doreen said to her. "It's just that this case got thrown in my lap only an hour ago." The man nervously fumbled through one of many files.

The young man didn't look a day older than Doreen herself. He was drenched in sweat, and his hands were shaking as if it were his life at stake.

"Are you . . . are you all right?" Doreen asked him.

"Uh, yeah, uh, sure." He wiped so much sweat from his forehead with his forearm that it left a huge stain on his suit. He wiped his hand down his cheek, scooping up more sweat. "By the way, I'm Mike England. I'll be representing you in your case." He held out the hand he'd just wiped his face with.

Doreen looked at it strangely. He followed her eyes to his wet hand.

"Oh, I'm sorry." He wiped his other hand down his pant leg, then extended it to her to shake, which she did. He turned his attention back to his paperwork. "You have no criminal history. Is this your first offense?"

"Yes, sir, it is," Doreen replied.

"Wonderful, just wonderful. Then we have something in common." Doreen raised an eyebrow at his comment; then he said, "Because this is my first case." A look of horror covered Doreen's face. "Oh, don't worry. Like I told your husband when he hired me, I graduated the top of my class. Although my focus was on civil matters and not criminal," he shrugged and let out a laugh, "how much different could they be?"

Doreen shook her head. Had God indeed forsaken her? Whatever she was being charged with didn't matter. This guy next to her couldn't defend her in a jaywalking trial.

The bailiff announced Doreen's case, and the judge began to proceed.

"Mrs. Tucker, you are being charged with attempted murder. It is alleged that you knowingly attacked an eight-and-a-half-month pregnant victim. You brutally beat her with the intention of killing her. You used deceit to gain access to the motel room in which the crime was committed in order to execute your attack. It was a well planned and thought out act that, as a result, left the victim hospitalized in serious condition. And even worse, as a result of your criminal actions, Mrs. Tucker, the unborn life in which the victim carried was lost." The judge leaned in and looked into Doreen's eyes with nothing but pure hate. "In other words, you are responsible for the death of that baby, Mrs. Tucker." He leaned back comfortably in his chair. "How does the defendant plead?"

And just like that, in a few sentences, Doreen learned exactly why she was in jail and what she was being charged with.

"Mrs. Tucker, I asked, how do you plead."

Doreen looked at her attorney for help. She didn't know what she was supposed to say or do. Yes, she'd attacked the woman, but it hadn't been all maliciously calculated like the court was trying to make it sound. And she had no idea the woman was even with child. Was it possible she could plead guilty to some of it and not the rest?

"What do I do? What do I say?" she whispered to her attorney.

"Not guilty, of course," he told her.

"But I did do some—"

"Mrs. Tucker, not guilty," her attorney said, cutting her off in a raised tone and raised eyebrows . . . dripping with sweat.

By now, both he and Doreen appeared to be the perfect couple. She was dripping in sweat, he was dripping in sweat, and standing in front of a judge was a first for both of them. So even though Doreen managed to get the words, under her counsel's guidance, "Not guilty," out of her mouth, she felt nothing but guilt. She felt doomed.

Jesus had definitely not been the attorney and the judge in the courtroom in her case. As a matter of fact, how Doreen saw it, He hadn't shown up in the courtroom at all.

Chapter Twenty-five

"Willie, oh God, Willie?" Doreen cried just as soon as the guard walked her out to the visiting room where Willie was waiting on her. "A hundred thousand dollars? That judge set my bail at a hundred thousand dollars." Doreen hadn't even sat down yet when she started going on about the high bail the judge had set. "Can you believe that? I'm never going to get out of here. Oh, God, Willie." Doreen buried her face in her hands and bawled.

At first Willie just stared at his wife. He didn't really know what to say. As he watched Doreen weep he searched for some comforting words. "Come on now, Reenie, you know I could never stand to see you cry. Don't do that now. Everything is going to turn out just fine. I done hired that law firm to take care of you. Everything is going to be all right. You'll see."

Wiping her eyes and calming down, Doreen looked up at her husband. His words, although try if he might to make them tender and sincere, weren't. Willie was just going through the motions, and Doreen knew it. He was just saying what he thought a husband should say. The look in his eyes didn't match his demeanor. He sat in the chair like the strong, supportive husband, but his eyes were full of hurt. They were full of pain. It wasn't worry and heartache that he should have felt for his wife. No, he was feeling something else for somebody else. Doreen could discern it.

"Little girl, you've got the gift of discernment," her father would always say to her. "God done blessed you to just get a feeling about people, places, and things. To just be able to tell things by strong feelings."

That indeed was true. Doreen could sometimes just tell things weren't right. That's why she'd popped up out of Bible Study that day and went to the juke joint. That's how she was able to catch that floozy in Willie's lap. She had a feeling. That same feeling that sent her to the juke joint was the same feeling she ignored in her gut when she knew she should have walked away from that motel room.

"That gift of discernment is special," her father had continued to say. "Make sure you tune into it real good. It can help keep you out of trouble. It can help keep you away from the wrong people, places, and things."

If only Doreen had followed her father's advice. Speaking of her father, Doreen asked Willie, "My daddy and my mama—did you call them? Do they know?"

"Naw, I, uh, figured I'd let you be the one to do that. I mean, I didn't even know if you wanted them to know. I guess I was figuring you'd just do like some of the folks do back at home when they get out of line and Pops has to call the man on them. They usually just spend a night or a weekend in jail and that is that." Willie put his head down. "But it ain't looking like that is gonna be the case."

Once again, Doreen observed how Willie appeared to be more broken in spirit than she was.

"So do you want me to call your folks?" Willie lifted his head.

"For God's sake, no!" Doreen was quick to say. "No, don't do that. There is no way they can find out about this. It would destroy them and possibly ruin their ministry." Doreen thought for a moment. ". . . and my

little sisters . . ." her eyes filled with tears. "My little sisters can never ever know their big sister done gone and
got herself thrown in jail."

Willie pulled a handkerchief from his pocket and slid
it to Doreen. He didn't even look up at her when he did.

Feeling a coldness coming from Willie, Doreen
picked up the handkerchief while looking at him in a
peculiar way. She wiped her tears away. "I tried to call
you while I've been in here. I never got an answer."

Willie repositioned himself in his chair. "Yeah, well,
I, uh, probably was out."

"Oh," was all Doreen said—at first. "Where were you?"
she asked on second thought.

Once again, Willie repositioned himself in his chair.
"At the hospital." His words were hardly audible, but
Doreen had heard them. Still she wanted to make sure
she'd heard Willie say what she thought he had.

"Where?"

This time he straightened himself up in the chair and
spoke louder and more clearly. "I said I was at the hospital." Now he was looking at Doreen. His eyes were almost daring her to ask why he'd been up at the hospital.

Never one who was big on dares, Doreen couldn't let
this one slide. "At the hospital for what?" she chuckled
nervously.

"I needed to be there with her—to see what was going on with her and the baby."

"Oh, I see." The fact that Willie had been sitting up
at the hospital with his mistress stung a little bit, but
Doreen played it off. "How is she doing?"

"Not good. She's all messed up in the mind." Willie
shook his head as if he was trying to shake away the
tears that were forming in his eyes. "It was a boy. He was
almost eight pounds. He was light as a feather too." That

last comment had brought a slight smile to Willie's face as if he was reminiscing on something nice.

Doreen did a double take. Was this the same Willie sitting in front of her getting all emotional over the loss of another woman's baby? The same Willie who had acted like he couldn't have cared less when the two of them had lost their own baby just months ago? Although Doreen had been thinking it, eventually she spoke it to Willie and waited on him to respond.

"This was different. This was a full-grown baby pretty much," Willie reasoned. "He could have lived and functioned outside of this world if you hadn't of . . ." Willie's words trailed off. He sniffed and wiped a tear that hadn't made it as far as the corner of his left eye.

All Doreen could do was sit back in her chair feeling like the monster everybody probably thought she was. She felt like a monster because at this moment, she honestly couldn't have cared less about that woman and her baby. All she cared about was why her husband cared so much. With the right questions, she was hell-bent on finding out.

Chapter Twenty-six

Before she spoke, Doreen sat and dissected the few words Willie had spoken to her thus far. She worded her questions carefully in her head before she spoke them. In the past, Willie had been able to lie at the drop of a dime and make it sound believable. It was as if he had mastered the art of lying. Well, today, Doreen was going to see to it that Willie met his match.

"You said the baby was as light as a feather," Doreen started. Her next question normally would have been, "How do you know?" but that was too general. That left open far too many options for Willie to dig up a lie about. She needed to close up the margins, so instead, she asked, "Did you hold him?" There, all that required was a yes or no answer. There wasn't too much room for him to twitch and squirm on this one.

What tripped Doreen out was that Willie didn't even try to weasel his way around answering the question. He flat-out said, "Yes." Then he had the nerve to add more. "The doctors said it was okay. I mean, the boy was gone and all, but he was still warm. Still fresh." Willie paused for a minute, and then that smile that had appeared on his lips before was back. "He had the biggest hands I'd ever seen on such a little fella. He would have been a ballplayer for sure." Willie had the proudest look and the proudest tone in his voice ever.

"So the mother was okay with letting you hold the boy, huh?" Doreen stated, then once again calculated her words before she spoke them. "How did the daddy feel about that? I mean, not too many men are gonna be in a good way about another man holding their child." Doreen knew she should have stopped there, but the woman in her just pressed right on. "Especially under the circumstances. Most people would already be disgusted at the fact that you was running up inside another woman while she was with child." Doreen expressed her own disgust with the look on her face. "I mean, really, Willie, of all the women here in West Virginia, you pick the unwed pregnant soprano girl from the choir. You couldn't have messed with somebody else?"

Maybe not at the moment did it make sense to Doreen, but the more she kept talking, the more sense she started to make of things. "I mean, is that why you dragged me all the way here to West Virginia, so that you could shack up with a pregnant woman? Is it, Willie?" Finally Doreen had taken a breath long enough to let Willie answer. Once again, Willie didn't even try to square-dance around the situation or make up a lie.

Willie simply said, "Yes, Doreen. That's exactly why we needed to move here to West Virginia." He lifted his eyes from the ground and directed them to Doreen. "I knew it would be next to impossible to be there for my child with me living all the way in Kentucky." He'd said it. He'd just come right out and said it without Doreen even having to have poked and prodded him.

"Your . . . your child," she muttered with trembling lips.

"Her cousin lives in Kentucky. She'd come up for a two-week visit. You was all into sitting up in church dang near every day of the week. When you was home, all you focused on was baking them pound cakes. So I just hung out with her. She headed on back to West

Virginia. We kinda sorta kept in touch. She came back to visit a couple more times—once on my dime."

Okay, Doreen had not asked for all this, and she surely wasn't prepared to hear it. But Willie continued anyway, and she listened.

"The next thing I know she calls me and tells me she's pregnant. I tried to talk her into . . ." Willie's words evaporated.

Doreen decided to finish his sentence for him, ". . . going to see the same doctor Agnes went to see?"

Willie's eyes shot up at Doreen. He couldn't believe she knew about that. There was no need in trying to lie about it now. "Yeah, that's what I tried to get her to do. She wouldn't hear of it, though. She insisted on keeping the baby and made it known how she intended for her child to have his daddy in his life too. She was gon' move to Kentucky, Doreen. We had to move here. It was easier that way."

Doreen honestly couldn't believe what she was hearing. She was dumbfounded. "Now I see why you put up so much of a fight about us attending that church. You knew that was the church she attended."

Willie didn't deny it.

"And the way you'd look up in the choir stands like you was filled with the joy of the Lord. Heck, all you was thinking about was being close to her and her baby."

"My baby. He was my baby too. That baby you beat to death was mine too, Doreen. I know it hurts your soul to hear that, and I've never wanted to hurt you, but that baby she was carrying was mine. And I moved here from Kentucky to help take care of it the best I could."

Doreen wanted to pretend like she was a little girl and throw her hands over her ears and block out Willie's words. But instead, she just sat there and took it.

She took it like she'd taken all Willie's mess for years until she had finally exploded inside that motel room.

"I can't do this, God," Doreen cried out. "It's too much. It's too much for me to be knowing."

"I'm sorry, Doreen, but I had to tell you the truth. They was gon' tell it in court, so I knew you had to hear it from me first. I'm sorry." For the first time Willie reached over and touched Doreen. He cupped one of her hands into his. "But I just want you to know I'm not gon' leave you. I'm gonna be here for you no matter what. I don't hold it against you what you did to my baby. I know I brought it all on myself by living a lie. But I promise you, when you get out of here, I'm going to be waiting for you. And I promise you one other thing. I'm going to be a better man." By now, tears were streaming down Willie's face and his nose was running. "I'm going to be a better husband to you, baby. I know it shouldn't have taken all this, but at least I learned something from it. At least I learned from my mistakes. I'm hurting, baby. I feel like I done lost the two most important things in my life." Willie gripped Doreen's hands. "I can't bring that baby back, but I still have you. And when you get out of here, you can give me another son. We can start fresh—even move again where nobody knows us for real this time."

Willie had never been so emotional in his life, at least not that Doreen had ever witnessed. Although she managed to keep it together and hide her true pain, which she'd sort of mastered thanks to Willie and her many attempts to try to be the perfect wife and the perfect forgiving Christian, Doreen was hurting inside. She was hurting because of the lie Willie had lived. She was hurting because she was watching her husband suffer more from the loss of the baby he'd made with a mistress, rather than the one he'd made with his own wife. She was hurting because she'd done the unthinkable. She'd taken away a child's life. She was hurting because she didn't have to imagine, but she knew how that woman must be feeling as a result of her loss.

"Okay, Willie," fell from between Doreen's lips. "I forgive you, and I pray you can forgive me for causing the death of now two of your babies." Doreen broke down just hearing herself say those words. She pulled herself together so that she could finish saying what she had to say. "I want to get past this. We will get past this. I know the God I serve will bring us through this, and we can start over and live the life we were meant to live together as husband and wife. Okay?"

"Okay, baby. Okay," Willie nodded.

"All right, it's time for Mrs. Tucker to return to her cage," the guard said in a slick attempt to refer to Doreen as an animal. "I mean her cell." She scooped Doreen up.

"I'm going to go talk to your attorney and see what he can tell me; see how much time you could be looking at," Willie called out to Doreen. "But just remember what I said; no matter how much time it is, I'm going to be waiting when you get out. Do you hear me?"

"I hear you," Doreen cried as the guard pulled her off. "And I'm so sorry, Willie. I'm gonna pray for that baby's soul. And I'm going to lift the mother's name up too." That's when Doreen realized she had no idea what the woman's name was. She knew she sang in the church choir and had spoken to her a time or two, but was never officially introduced by name. "What's her name?" Doreen asked right as the guard got her to the exit.

"Huh?" Willie called out.

"The woman's name—the baby's mother. What's her name?"

As Doreen was pulled from the room and out the door she heard Willie call out, "Lauren. Her name is Lauren Casinoff."

Chapter Twenty-seven

"Lauren Casinoff," the words fell from Mother Doreen's lips as she stood at that altar on what should have been her perfect wedding day to Pastor Frey. But so far, it had turned out to be a complete mess. No, maybe *disaster* was a more fitting word. For some reason, not even that word described the full magnitude of what Mother Doreen would now describe her wedding day as.

"Aha; the name rings a bell, does it?" the man that had interrupted the wedding ceremony said. He bobbed his head up and down with a knowing grin on his face. "I thought saying her name would."

This man started out as a stranger, but now Mother Doreen knew him to be the son of Lauren Casinoff. But a stranger, to a degree, he was. Exactly who was he? Meaning, why was he there? What did he want from Mother Doreen?

"Honey, what's going on? Who is this young man?" Pastor Frey asked Doreen, who had not taken her eyes off the young man once.

Mother Doreen remained frozen, still gazing at the young man.

"Go ahead, Doreen, answer the man," the stranger said. "Tell him what's going on. Tell him who I am."

Mother Doreen snapped out of her daze. "Uh, oh, yeah. Uh, he's, uh . . ." Mother Doreen couldn't even focus enough to speak a complete sentence. With just hearing the name Lauren Casinoff, her mind had traveled way back into the past, and then all the way to when she'd heard that name for the first time.

Not even in the courtroom during Mother Doreen's arraignment had they said Lauren's name. They simply just kept referring to her as the victim or the alleged victim, like she wasn't real or didn't even exist. Like the only thing that had existed or allegedly existed was the incident itself. Ironically enough, for years, she didn't exist—not in Mother Doreen's thoughts anyway. Mother Doreen had served her time in jail, repenting daily at first. Coming to realize that God had indeed forgiven her, she was released from jail and moved on with her life.

As promised, Willie had been there waiting for her once she got out of jail. As promised, they moved to another town in Ohio. They started their lives over together. They never looked back, never speaking about the incident that had cost Mother Doreen a year of her life behind bars and had cost Willie his son.

Not only did Mother Doreen and Willie never speak of it to each other, but the two never spoke of it to anyone else either. Willie never told his parents, and Mother Doreen never told hers. For that year she was in jail, her family had always thought she was caught up and consumed with chasing Willie around. They'd even shared that mysterious year of Mother Doreen missing in action with her baby sister, Bethany, over the years, citing Willie for being the cause. Mother Doreen never allowed them to think otherwise.

It wasn't until about a year ago that Mother Doreen finally decided to share the dirty part of her life she had swept under the rug for years. First she told her pastor of New Day, Margie. Next she'd told Pastor Frey. He'd been so persistent in courting her in an attempt to make her his wife, she knew there was no way she could marry him without telling him.

Mother Doreen thought once Pastor Frey learned that she was a murderer, he'd withdraw his desires for her. That didn't happen though. He loved the woman Mother Doreen was today, and he showed her so by proposing with a diamond ring the very next day after she'd shared her past.

Although Mother Doreen hadn't told them herself, some of the New Day members even knew about Mother Doreen's past. Margie's former secretary had a problem with eavesdropping in on Margie's prayers and conversations with the saints. The secretary would then spill what she'd heard like a toddler just learning to walk carrying a cup of Cherry Kool-Aid around a white-carpeted house. Some of Mother Doreen's Kool-Aid, so to speak, dripped into other folks' ears. Gossiping and rumors started, but Mother Doreen never really put a stamp on what was true and what wasn't. She just let folks talk. She allowed people to think what they wanted to think. But now what's-his-name was here, obviously to give his version.

"My apologies for not introducing myself to the groom," the gentleman said, sticking his arm past Mother Doreen to Pastor Frey. "My name is Terrance Casinoff, and I drove all the way from my hometown in West Virginia just to be here today." He smiled a cunning, devious smile.

Pastor Frey hesitantly shook Terrance's hand. "I'm—"

"Pastor Wallace Frey," Terrance said. "You're all set to head back to Kentucky after the wedding and take over the reigns of Living Word, Living Waters, isn't that correct? Congratulations." Terrance began to shake Pastor Frey's hand harder.

Pastor Frey kindly pulled his hand away and looked at Terrance suspiciously. It was written all over his face that he was wondering how the man knew that bit of information about him.

"Oh, you're wondering how I know that," Terrance said, responding to the expression on Pastor Frey's face. "Well, you know I've been keeping up with the bride here," he pointed to Mother Doreen, "for quite some time. As a matter of fact, my latest Google search pulled up a local article about Kentucky's hometown preacher man to wed the woman of his dreams. It went on about some type of comeback from a scandal you'd been a part of and how you'd redeemed yourself to the church. There were quotes from church members supporting you and your works and how they couldn't wait to welcome you back with open arms as the head of their ministry." Terrance opened his arms wide.

"Uh, yeah, I know exactly what article you're talking about," Pastor Frey acknowledged.

"It just moved my heart." Terrance sarcastically put his hand on his heart and shook his head. "Heck, by the time I finished reading it, even I was cheering for the underdog. That's why I couldn't let you do it. I couldn't let you ruin your life . . ." he glared at Mother Doreen, "or should I say, I couldn't let her ruin your life. She's ruined one life too many as it stands." He looked back at Pastor Frey. "Man to man and just me looking out for a fellow black man, you're better off dead than marrying this woman."

Pastor Frey instantly flexed toward the gentleman. That's when everyone at the altar either jumped to hold him back or jumped in between him and Terrance.

"Oh, feisty old man, are you?" Terrance chuckled. "Maybe you two are a match made in heaven after all. You both like to jump on people." He shot Mother Do-

reen a glare before turning his attention back to Pastor
Frey. "So, tell me, Pastor Wallace Frey, do you like to
jump on pregnant women, beat 'em half to death, killing the baby inside their wombs too? Or is that something you leave up to the old lady here?"

Once again, Pastor Frey flexed and everyone put
their guards back up to keep him from getting at Terrance. They almost didn't move quick enough this
time, as Pastor Frey's hand had almost got the collar of
Terrance's suit coat in a grip.

Terrance dusted off his suit coat and held his hands
up. "Hey, don't shoot the messenger." He let his arms
drop. "I'm just here with your best interest in mind.
I'm here to stop you from possibly making one of the
biggest mistakes in your life. I'm here to share with you
something I bet you never would have guessed about
this woman." He pointed an accusing finger at Mother
Doreen. "She's a killer. She even served time in jail for
it."

There were gasps about the sanctuary. "I told you
so," and "I knew those rumors were true" could be
heard sprinkled throughout the sanctuary. A hand-
ful of folks even had the audacity to get up and leave,
taking their gifts they'd left on the gift table out in the
foyer with them.

"I'll have you know that Mr. Frey here is well aware
of Mother Doreen's past," Margie interrupted. "So, Mr.
Casinoff, you've pretty much wasted your time and
ours. So if you don't mind, please remove yourself from
the sanctuary. We have a wedding we need to finish up
here."

Terrance looked at Pastor Frey. "So this is the type
of leader you are? This is the type of first lady you are
knowingly going to present to your church? I wonder
what the parishioners are going to think when the local

journalist prints that story in the paper." He looked at Mother Doreen, Margie, and then Pastor Frey. "Pardon me. Looks like I'm going to have to leave before the nuptials are exchanged. I need to get to Kentucky before it's too late." Terrance bowed as if he'd just performed on Broadway and was making a grand exit.

"No!" Mother Doreen shouted, stopping Terrance in his tracks. "Don't go. There's nothing to tell that journalist. There's no need to make the saints of Living Word think they are going to have someone like me as their first lady."

Pastor Frey said nervously, "Doreen, what are you saying?"

Mother Doreen looked at Pastor Frey with tear-filled eyes and said to him, "I'm sorry, Wallie, but I can't marry you. The wedding is off."

Chapter Twenty-eight

"The coast is clear," Deborah said, entering the dressing room.

Mother Doreen had been sitting in there the last hour or so waiting for the coast to clear of all guests who had come to see a wedding that never took place.

"Some folks ate and lots of people took food to-go in those foam containers. Unique wouldn't let anybody cut the cake though. She said she was going to freeze it for a couple days just in case you changed your mind."

There was silence for a brief moment; and then Mother Doreen spoke. "How's Pastor Frey?"

"Other than the times he came back here and you refused to see him, he's been at that altar praying." Deborah sat down next to Mother Doreen. "You know I love you, and I have the utmost respect for you. You're like a mother to me. You're like a mother to everyone at New Day. And I'm sure you're going to be like a mother to everyone at Living Word too."

Mother Doreen began shaking her head. "That's not going to happen, Sister Deborah. I can't take this mess to Kentucky and destroy everything Pastor Frey has worked to build with that congregation. They have to trust his judgment. He's already been involved in the scandal when he was covering for his once senior pastor's affair with my sister."

"And the church got over that," Bethany interrupted, "so they'll get over this too. Trust me; I know what you're going through." Bethany entered the room, closing the door behind her. She walked over and sat beside her sister. "You know how hard it was for Uriah, me, and the kids to start going back to Living Word again. It was crazy. People were talking, whispering, gossiping, pointing fingers, and turning up noses. But God wasn't. Some folks were even bold enough to walk up to Uriah and ask him how on earth he could still be with a woman who cheated on him with his pastor and got pregnant by him. Church folks, the ones who are supposed to be practicing forgiveness, will sometimes be the first people to write you off. But God didn't write me off." Bethany went over to Doreen and put her hand on her shoulder. "And God is not going to write you off either. He knows your heart. You're like the perfect Chri—"

"No! Don't you say it!" Mother Doreen stood up in a gust of anger. "I'm not now, nor have I ever been the perfect Christian. And if that's what I've been portraying to people for all these years, then I repent right now in the name of Jesus." Mother Doreen was in such a huff, it silenced both Deborah and Bethany. They both had shocked looks on their faces. "Jesus was the only perfect somebody who ever walked this earth, and don't you forget it."

Her big sister had spoken. Just like when she was younger, Bethany had planned on taking Mother Doreen's word as bond, allowing her older sibling to have the final word. But this time she just couldn't. Too much was at stake, namely her sister's happiness.

Bethany stood up and stomped her foot like a spoiled four year old throwing a tantrum. "Now you listen to me, Doreen, and you listen to me right now. You're as close to perfection as I've ever witnessed. No, you're not God, but God is in you. And the God in you is the only God some folks are ever going to be blessed enough to see. So you better own it. You better own the fact that God chose you to work through all these years; that God gave you a testimony powerful enough to change other people's lives. Just think about all the people at New Day whose lives you've touched."

"Like mine." Deborah stood up to cosign for Bethany.

"God has a calling on your life," Bethany continued. "You know that, and everybody else knows that. And He's requiring that you take that calling to Kentucky— to Living Word." Bethany walked over to Doreen and placed her hand on her sister's belly. "God don't care nothing about a person's age. He's birthing a new thing in you. God don't care how old a woman is in order for Him to impregnate her with something. Ask Sarah from the Bible."

Bethany began to rub her hands on Mother Doreen's stomach as she began to speak in unknown tongues. Deborah extended her hands toward Mother Doreen and began to pray.

"God is birthing something inside of you, Sis," Bethany said. "God is requiring more of you. You once said, 'Lord, wherever you want me to go, I'll go.' Did you mean that, Doreen? Did you really mean it? When you said yes to God's will and yes to God's way so many years ago, was it a complete yes? Was it a yes to everything or a yes to some things?"

"It was a complete yes," Mother Doreen replied with closed eyes. Even with closed eyes, the tears managed to seep through and down her face.

"Then why is it you are going to allow that Terrance fellow to come up in here like a doctor putting on his rubber gloves and perform an abortion on you?" Upon Bethany saying those words, the entire calm atmosphere changed. Mother Doreen opened her eyes immediately and even Deborah was at loss for words to pray. Noticing words were no longer coming out of Deborah's mouth, Bethany turned to her and said, "Keep praying, Saint. Please keep praying. The Word says where two or more are gathered . . . I need you to touch and agree with me, Sister Deborah. We need to send this demon off to flight that's trying to abort what God is birthing in Doreen. Pray!" Bethany demanded.

Deborah went right back into praying. She was praying harder than ever.

"That's right," Bethany said. "We're coming up against you, Satan. I know you don't want to kill, steal, and destroy my sister. No, you ain't thinking about Doreen. It's the gifts inside of her that you want to kill, steal, and destroy. See, that's where folks get it twisted; thinking you're after them, Satan. But it's what's inside of them that you're really after. It's what's inside Doreen that you're after. But you can't have it, Satan. This thing inside of my sister will be birthed. I declare it so in the name of Jesus."

"Hallelujah!" Mother Doreen cried out as tears continued to flow from her eyes. "Hallelujah!"

"That's right, give Him the highest praise," Bethany ordered her sister as Mother Doreen continued to cry out praises to God. "You can make it through the labor pains, Doreen. I know it's hard. I know it's painful, but if you don't get this thing out, it's just gon' die up inside of you. You are not death, but are life. Do you hear me?"

"Yes, I hear you," Mother Doreen cried. "I hear you." She turned and embraced Bethany. "Oh, God, thank you for your Word. Thank you so much for bringing forth that word, Sis. I love you, Beth. I really do."

"I love you too, Reen. And that's why I want to see you happy. I know what makes you happy is doing God's work. If God didn't have you on some type of assignment, then you'd be all up in the rest of our business driving us crazy."

All the women in the room laughed.

"You know I love you, Mother Doreen," Deborah laughed, "but Bethany's right."

"Oooh, y'all ain't right," Mother Doreen said as she pulled her arms from around Bethany and wiped her face with her hands.

"Oooh, and if Unique was in here to see the mess you've made of her makeup job . . ." The women shared another laugh until a knock on the door interrupted them. "Speaking of the devil . . ." Deborah tiptoed over to the door, assuming it was Unique. She cracked the door open, and the smile that had been on her face as a remnant of the laughter faded. She turned to face Mother Doreen. "Someone wants to see you. But I'm not sure if you're ready to see him yet."

Mother Doreen took a deep breath and looked at Bethany. "I guess I'm going to have to face Wallace sooner or later. Do you think he'll forgive me for my little stunt and still want to marry me?"

Before Bethany could answer, Deborah spoke. "I'm not sure what Pastor Frey is going to do, but he's not the one who wants to see you." Deborah opened the door wide enough for Mother Doreen to see Terrance standing in the doorway.

Chapter Twenty-nine

"There you are!" Unique came up behind Terrance. "I saw you still roaming around. Didn't our pastor ask you to leave?"

"The sanctuary—but not the church," Terrance answered. "Besides, I'm not finished with what I came here for."

"Oh, you're finished because *I* say you're finished," Unique spat, kicking off her shoes. "Now I've tried to stay saved—Lord knows I have—but there is only so much a girl from the hood can take."

Terrance looked at Unique with his nose turned up. He sniffed the air. "I thought I smelled a rat . . . a hood rat. My senses were correct."

"Oh no, he didn't!" Unique started taking her earrings off next.

"Oh, Lord. Not again," Deborah said under her breath, and then rushed over to get Unique under control. "Come on, Unique. There are not going to be any more fights today."

"Let me go," Unique demanded, "'cause I'll fight a man. I promise you I'll fight a man."

"Stop it right now!" Deborah ordered as she dragged Unique out of the room. Once they were no longer visible, Deborah could still be heard saying, "Acting like a bunch of heathens in the house of Lord. I'ma pray for every last one of you. Honestly I am."

"Pardon me, Mr. Terrance," Bethany said as she walked in between Mother Doreen and the gentleman. "I apologize for Sister Unique's actions. That's no way for a saint to act and certainly not in God's own house. Perhaps I can say more diplomatically what my sister in Christ there was trying to say." Bethany held a smile. "I don't think my sister wants to see you, speak to you, or have anything to do with you." She looked back at Mother Doreen. "Isn't that right, Reen?"

"Reen—oh, what an endearing term between two sisters," Terrance said before Mother Doreen could reply to Bethany's question. "You got any other siblings?" he asked Bethany.

"Uh, yes, well, no; I mean, I had other siblings, but they've gone home to the calling of the Lord," Bethany answered.

"Oh, I'm sorry to hear that."

"Thank you." There was a brief moment of silence, and then Bethany was about to speak again, but Terrance spoke instead.

"I guess you could say I'm an only child. I could have had a sibling—a brother—but he never had a chance in the world." He looked over Bethany's shoulder at Mother Doreen. "Nope, never had a chance in the world thanks to your sister here."

"Okay, look . . ." Bethany put her hands up. "Pastor might have asked you to leave the sanctuary, but now I'm asking you to leave the church." She walked over to the door and held it open, signaling for Terrance that he should leave.

"No," Terrance said. What surprised both Bethany and Terrance was that Mother Doreen had said the same thing in unison.

"Wha—what?" Bethany asked with uncertainty. "Come again, Sis."

"I said, no—let him stay. I'll talk to him."

"Doreen, I really don't think that's a good—"

"He needs to finish up what he came here for," Mother Doreen said, walking toward Terrance. "I know what it's like to be on assignment and don't finish up the job. It haunts you and always sits in the back of your mind until you go back and do something about it. Well, let's not give Mr. Casinoff any reason to have to come back for any unfinished business. Let him say all he's got to say right here and right now." Mother Doreen looked at Terrance. "All right, Mr. Casinoff?"

A little caught off guard by Mother Doreen's support of his not leaving, Terrance replied, "Yes, fine."

Bethany looked from Terrance to Mother Doreen, then said, "Okay, Reen, if you insist." She went to close the door with her still inside of the room.

"Uh, Bethany, Sis, if you don't mind, I'm sure Mr. Casinoff here wants to talk to me alone."

"It's Terrance. You can call me Terrance," he offered. There was something about Mother Doreen showing him formal respect that tugged at his conscious.

"Fine," Mother Doreen agreed. "I'm sure Terrance wants to talk to me alone."

Bethany walked over to Mother Doreen hastily. "There is no way I'm leaving you in here with this man alone. No telling what a man who will come and interrupt the wedding of complete strangers is capable of—"

"Beth, please." Mother Doreen put her hands up. "I'm covered in the blood. I feel protected. I just think there are a few things Mr. Casi . . . Terrance needs to get off his chest, and then he'll be well on his way." Mother Doreen looked over at him. "Isn't that right, Terrance?"

He swallowed without saying anything. Mother Doreen's kindness seemed to be eating him alive.

Once again, Bethany looked at Terrance, and then back at Mother Doreen. "All right, if you say so," she agreed with much reservation as she walked toward the door. "But if you need me, just shout, because I'm going to be right outside this door . . ." she glared at Terrance as she walked past him to exit, ". . . praying." On that last note, Bethany left the room, closing the door behind her, leaving Mother Doreen at the hands of the enemy.

Chapter Thirty

Initially, after Bethany had closed the door behind her, there was silence. Mother Doreen soon broke that silence.

"Well, Terrance," she threw her hands up, and then let them fall to her side. "Let's do this. Finish up what you started; I mean, whatever there is left to finish. Heck, you've already interrupted the wedding. You succeeded in stopping the wedding from taking place. Being that that was your goal in coming here in the first place, what else could there possibly be left for you to do? What else is there, Terrance? You came here to have a brotha's back, as you called it—to keep Pastor Frey from making a mistake by marrying an ex-felon. Well, you succeeded at that. So what else is there? Please, let's do this so we can both go on with our lives. No, mine might not be the life I thought I was going to live once I walked out of this place today, but I'm not going to fret on that. Sometimes life doesn't turn out the way we want it to. But you know what? We simply gotta make due. So come on, Terrance. Let's do this."

It was as if Mother Doreen was putting up her dukes and challenging Terrance to a fight just like Unique had done moments ago. Only instead of like it was for Unique, with Mother Doreen, the brawl wasn't going to be physical. No, Mother Doreen knew better than to try to fight the enemy with flesh. Her pastor had taught her a long time ago that the flesh can't win battles, not really. It's the spirit that is victorious over all enemies. So Mother Doreen put on the full armor of God and was in position to fight.

Terrance didn't appear to be intimidated one bit though. The same way Unique professed that she would fight a man, Terrance would definitely fight an old woman . . . with words, of course.

"I thought I'd be satisfied, but just seeing the wedding being called off wasn't enough," Terrance said. "The same way only serving one year in jail hadn't been enough of a punishment for you for what you did to my mother."

"So is that why you're still here? To punish me some more? Well, you've succeeded. For years I lived with the weight of having not told anyone about my past. Do you know that it wasn't until a year ago that I actually finally shared it with someone?"

"Well lucky you. I had to hear about what you did every day of my life since I could remember." Anger filled Terrance's tone. "I was reminded of my mother's loss every day my grandma would take me to visit my mother. Probably the same way your former husband was reminded of his loss every time he came to visit you in that jailhouse." Terrance stepped closer. "Speaking, of which, you were in the joint for about a year. Didn't you wonder what that husband of yours was up to all that time? I mean, it had to be lonely for ol' Willie boy out there."

Mother Doreen's eyebrows sunk in at the way Terrance spoke of Willie with such familiarity.

"Oh, yeah, the same way I did my research on you and everybody else I felt the need to know some things about, I did my research on Willie too." He snickered. "That Willie was some player, that's for sure. At least that's what I heard. I mean, I heard so many things about Willie that I would have never guessed he was a married man." He shook his head. "I guess that's what they mean by the good old days, because I'm sure today you can't find a black woman on earth who would turn a blind eye to all of Willie's doings. But then again, womenfolk ain't built like they were back then. Because you have to admit, it takes a certain kind of woman to allow her husband to sleep with other women, drink, hang out in the streets, gamble all their money away, and then lie about it all." He laughed.

Mother Doreen stood there not finding one thing funny. "I agree, Mr. Casinoff . . ." she'd gone back to being informal. "I was a different kind of woman back then, but I'm a new creature in the Lord. I'm not that woman anymore. She's dead."

Terrance looked Mother Doreen up and down. "Then I guess I'm like that little white boy in that movie, *Sixth Sense*." He leaned in and whispered, "I see dead people," then pulled back and burst out laughing. "'Cause from what I can see, Doreen Tucker is alive and well; living her life like it's golden." He frowned. "Well, she was about to anyway."

Now Mother Doreen was the one who snickered. "You can stand here all day and insult me any kind of way you want to. You can bring up my past all you'd like, but I ain't going back to live in it. But if it makes you feel any better, I'll stand here and take it. If you want to stand here and say to me what your momma never got a chance to, I'll allow that. Because I can only imagine the pain your mother must have felt and probably still feels to this day."

"Oh, my momma isn't in pain anymore. Her pain is long gone. See, Lauren Casinoff is dead now. For real. Not the old her, not the new her, just her, period. She's gone." Terrance looked as though it was taking every bit of strength he had to hold the hurt inside resulting from thoughts about the loss of his mother.

"I'm sorry . . . I'm sorry to hear that." Mother Doreen slowly extended her hands. "I can see that you're hurting. And if you don't mind, I'd like to pray for you." Her hands lingered in the air while Terrance stared down at them, almost contemplating on whether to allow Mother Doreen her request. "Please, son, let go and let God. Don't let the past haunt you. Allow forgiveness to enter your heart. I'm telling you, keeping all this bottled up inside will drive you crazy."

Terrance's eyes darted from Mother Doreen's hands to her eyes. "What do you know about something driving a person crazy? Trust and believe, you don't know crazy." Terrance, still shooting daggered eyes at Mother Doreen, began closing up the space between them. "But here in a minute you are going to know just what crazy is." Terrance reached into his pocket before saying, "Because I'm about to show you exactly what crazy looks like."

Chapter Thirty-one

Mother Doreen stared down at what Terrance had pulled out of his pocket. She stood there breathless with no words to say. She looked into the eyes of the woman in the picture Terrance held in his trembling hand. She'd remembered the first and only time she ever really truly looked into those eyes. It wasn't when she was on top of her beating her and her unborn child. It hadn't been when she'd been in the choir stands singing praises to the Lord. It was that day in the courtroom when Mother Doreen had been sentenced after pleading guilty—per the advice of her attorney. Plea deal. Just as Mother Doreen's thoughts had traveled back to the past earlier when she was in the sanctuary, that's exactly what her thoughts did again.

Soon, the eyes on the Kodak paper turned into real live eyes that Mother Doreen stared into as she was escorted out of the courtroom after having been sentenced to prison. "I'm sorry," Doreen managed to let come from between her lips as the guards escorted her out of the courtroom.

"Too late to be sorry now," the guard snorted.

Later, as Doreen was driven to the prison, she thought the entire time of whether she'd done the right thing by taking the plea. One year tops if she plead guilty to felonious assault.

"You could spend that much time in jail waiting for a trial date," her attorney had told her while they discussed her options prior to her agreeing to take the plea.

"But, but it was an accident," Doreen had told him. "It just happened. I didn't wake up that morning planning to do that. Even when it was happening, I had no idea that she was pregnant."

"Well, that's not what the court is going to say. What the court is going to say is that you were jealous. You were jealous that another woman was pregnant by your husband. Not only that, but you were angry because you yourself had miscarried your husband's child. Now here's this other woman giving him what you couldn't."

"But that's a lie!" Doreen blurted out.

"Oh, really now?" The attorney began flipping through the file he had before him. "So the information I have here is incorrect? You didn't miscarry in the first trimester of your pregnancy? Ms. Casinoff wasn't pregnant by your husband, and your husband knew the child was very much his? As a matter of fact, hadn't they even planned the pregnancy? Your husband, while telling you his job relocated him, had actually put in a transfer request to his boss to relocate him to West Virginia, right?" While the attorney made all his statements in question form, Doreen shook her head. "He wanted to be closer to Ms. Casinoff. Raise their child together and eventually leave you to be with his mistress and child, isn't that true?"

"No! No!" Doreen stood up and yelled. "That's not true."

"What? What part isn't true?" he scanned his files. "Please tell me, because your husband has been interviewed, Mrs. Tucker. Most of this information came straight from the horse's mouth." He slammed the folder shut and looked Doreen squarely in the eyes and began to speak in a whisper. "Come on, girl, you and I both know you did this."

"Not on purpose," Doreen interrupted.

"Yeah, but you did it. I mean, you're lucky they are not trying to charge you for murder for that baby. There's really no precedence for that right now, but I'm sure that judge would love to set one and make a name for himself using you. Me, personally, I'm sure prosecution would much rather take the easy route with a plea. So if I were you, I'd take the plea before everybody decides to try to make a name for themselves while dragging your name through the mud."

Doreen sat and thought about it.

"You're a preacher's kid, right?" the attorney asked her.

"Yes, sir. My father has a ministry back in Kentucky. He—they—him and my mother—they don't know anything about this."

"Well, if this thing goes to trial, they are certainly going to find out about this. Do you really want everybody's named dragged in the mud along with yours? I mean, what would become of your daddy's church if his members found out that his daughter had beat a poor woman half to death and killed her—"

"Okay, okay!" Doreen cut him off. She didn't want to hear one more time how'd she'd killed a baby—how she was a baby killer. She might have been in jail for what she'd done to the grown woman, but mentally, everybody was charging her for killing a baby. It might as well have been on the books.

"Okay, what?" the attorney wanted to be specific.

"Okay, I'll take the plea. I'll take it," Doreen broke down.

The attorney exhaled. Doreen buried her head down on the table and cried.

"Now, now," her attorney tried to comfort her by patting her arm. "You're doing the right thing." His thoughts mirrored Doreen's when he said, "Because look at it this way. Even though you'd be in that courtroom being charged for a crime against an adult, all that the jurors are going to have planted in their heads is that dead little baby who didn't have a chance in the world of surviving after the beating it took."

Doreen cringed. The way he'd just described it sounded so vile, so vicious, so evil. He made it sound like she'd taken this poor little innocent baby and pummeled it to death with her fists. If that's the way they would portray her act in the courtroom, then there was no doubt the jurors and judge would lock her up and throw away the key. Doreen had made up her mind; she was going to take that plea. And she had.

Now, after taking the plea and being sentenced, she was in a van on her way to begin serving out her sentence. Her heart ached. She'd have to go a year without being next to Willie. She'd have to go a year making her family feel she'd abandoned them to be up under Willie. It was a lie, but she'd rather hurt them a little with a lie than hurt them a lot with the truth. She'd write letters to her family to keep in touch with them, letting them know she was okay. She'd tell them she was going on a sabbatical for a few of the months she would be locked away. She'd figure out a way to get a call through here and there without them knowing it was from a jail. She had to do something to keep them at bay so that they wouldn't try to come looking for her. Lord knows she didn't want them to find her there.

By the time Doreen made it to the prison, she had convinced herself 100 percent that accepting that plea and making that courtroom think her actions had been carried out according to some devious plan was the right thing to do. It beat her going through a long drawn out trial and having lies and theories made up about her that, nine times out of ten, people would believe. No, she couldn't do that to herself, and she couldn't do that to her family.

She decided she would serve her time like a woman, accepting the punishment God had for her. Because although what she ultimately did that day at that motel might not have been intentional, she did it nonetheless. She committed a crime against man and God. There was a price to pay, but after only a week of coming to terms with her decision, Doreen would find out just how costly that price tag was.

Chapter Thirty-two

The days of Doreen's time served in prison thus far had felt like a lifetime. In real time, it had only been two months—two months of absolute hell. She wouldn't wish her predicament on her worst enemy. She didn't feel like herself. She wasn't her own person anymore.

Once upon a time she'd felt like she belonged to God—that that's whose she was. But now she felt like she belonged to the State of West Virginia. Some mornings when she woke up she didn't even know who she was, let alone whose she was. On this particular morning, waking up in her prison cell, she didn't even know where she was.

In a panic, she looked around her empty cell. She shared it with no one. She'd opened her eyes only to be staring up at the bottom of the top bunk above her. Quickly sitting up, she examined her surroundings, and then it dawned on her—she was incarcerated.

Her heavy breathing slowed as she tightened her lips and fought back tears. At least three times a week, this was how Doreen's day started. That was how many times she'd close her eyes at night and dreamed of an ordinary life. It was just her and Willie. They were back in Kentucky—had no reason to ever travel to West Virginia. Doreen was still baking pound cakes. As a matter of fact, in a few of her dreams she owned a cake shop, a very successful cake shop at that.

Her sisters helped her run things. When Willie got finished with a long day's work, he'd come straight to the cake shop and help her close it down. No juke joint. No gambling, drinking, cussing, or lying. No other women. Just Doreen and Willie. They were happy.

"Stop dreaming and get ya behind out of that bed if you plan on eating this morning."

The male guard's booming voice snapped Doreen out of her daze. Even if she hadn't recalled where she was just moments ago, that guard sure would have reminded her.

Doreen pulled her legs over the side of her bed and rubbed her eyes.

"Yep, that's right," the guard snorted obnoxiously. "You're not dreaming. Still in paradise. Now get your skank butt up and get to moving. You're a preacher's kid, right?" he asked Doreen.

She nodded.

"Then God done showed you favor. You got a job. Starts today. Means you'll get to earn money for luxuries. You know, things like Little Debbie Snack cakes, stamps, paper, envelopes." He snorted again, and Doreen wondered if he had something against speaking in complete sentences. "Got bathroom duty. You know how many broads would kill to have that job? Beats laundry, that's for sure. Least that's what I hear, anyway. Dunno, personally. Can't say I'd care too much for cleaning up after a bunch of nasty womenfolk. I got a wife and three teenage daughters. Bloody pads floating around in the commode. And you know how the food is in this place. Toilet full of sh—"

"If you don't mind," Doreen interrupted before he could release his expletive, "I'd like to use the bathroom and change clothes." Doreen nodded over to the toilet that sat out in the open in her cell.

"Oh . . . oh, no problem. No problem at all. Go right ahead," the guard told her.

Doreen stood up and walked over toward the toilet. Clearly that's what most people did the first thing in the morning. She went to pull her prison-issued bottoms down when she noticed the guard was still standing there, watching her.

"Uh, excuse me," Doreen stammered nervously. "Do you mind?"

The guard looked Doreen up and down, then rolled his tongue across his top row of teeth. "As a matter of fact, I do. See, my job is to keep an eye on you; a special watch. If I took my eye off of you for even a minute, anything could happen. You wouldn't want me to lose my job on the count of not doing it well, would you?" He had lust in his eyes as he eyeballed Doreen.

"Please, sir. I, I just want to—"

"Do you think I give a rat's behind about what you want? Now do what you need to do or stay in here and starve to death."

Doreen wanted to scream inside. She wanted to cry out for help, but who was there to come to her rescue? Certainly not Willie. He'd been to visit Doreen a few times, but not as much as he should. At least not as much as Doreen thought he should. And when she wanted to talk to him—when she really needed to talk to him—he never picked up the phone. She just hoped he was saving up all that money from all the overtime he was claiming he was doing.

"So what's it gonna be?" the guard snapped.

Doreen slowly gripped the waist of her pants and slid them down an inch or two—slowly. Just as slowly as Doreen moved her hands, the guard moved his . . . toward his private area. By the time Doreen's pants were mid-hip, the guard was fully clutching his manhood.

"Go on now, girl," he moaned, rubbing himself. "You hungry, right? How about I give you a taste of a li'l something else other than that slop they got prepared for you?"

Doreen couldn't believe her ears. Not only couldn't she believe the words that were coming out of the guard's mouth, but she couldn't believe the sound of his zipper being undone either.

"Please," Doreen pleaded, her insides trembling while she tried to keep her exterior calm, cool, and collected.

"Oh, you don't have to beg me, pretty chocolate," the guard cooed. "Now come on over here and do me right." By now the guard was exposing himself to Doreen as his hand moved back and forth along his flesh.

Doreen swallowed hard. She closed her eyes and said a prayer to God. Well, she didn't really pray. Prayer was supposed to be a conversation. She was doing all the talking asking God to get her out of that situation. To direct her path. She didn't know whether she should just do what the guard wanted her to do. She feared perhaps by not doing it, the guard would make her time in prison even more hellish than it already was. Whatever she was going to do, she needed to do it fast, as she really needed to go to the bathroom.

Doreen stood there talking to God and twitching her legs, trying to hold in her body fluids.

"I see you squirming," the guard snorted. "Got you all wet down there, huh? You know you want it. And I don't mind a little chocolate myself." His snort was mixed with a laugh.

With her hands still on the waist of her pants, Doreen went to move her pants another couple of inches or so, but this time it was upward instead of down.

Disappointment flooded the guard's face. "Wha—what you doing?" he said, no snorting, just a hint of anger is all. "Ain't you gon' do me?"

Doreen said nothing. She just stood there, securing her pants above her waist. She was hopeful her actions spoke louder than words and answered the guard's question.

"You black slut," he spat, tucking himself back inside his pants. "Ashy, black nigger witches ain't no good at going down nohow. But I thought I'd teach you a thing or two." He threw insults that Doreen was not moved by. "Think I care if you eat or not? Can stand to lose a few pounds. All y'all do is sit around eating chitterlings and pig feets, gaining weight. Bunch of nasty black pigs." He continued his insults using incomplete sentences. Still, Doreen never said a mumbling word. "Think you won this, don't ya? Well, you might not want to eat, but you still gotta take a morning piss."

The man standing before Doreen was as vulgar as she'd ever met. He was simply not going to let her be. She glared at him, his eyes burning through her like the devil himself. But she would not give in to him. She would not.

As the lust had begun to fill his eyes again, he looked Doreen over from head to toe. His eyes traveled from her head, appearing to peel the clothes off of her as they made their way down to her toes. That's when the look of lust suddenly turned into disgust. That's when the next sound Doreen heard was him zipping his pants back up. He turned up his nose and grunted as he walked away.

Doreen let out a sigh of relief. She looked down at her toes, the liquid now surrounding her feet. She felt disgusted too. But she had to do what she had to do.

All of a sudden she stood there and let out a chuckle. "I heard that garlic keeps the vampires away. But who knew a little bit of pee could keep Satan away?"

Chapter Thirty-three

Doreen's stomach growled as she attempted to listen to the female guard's instructions. Hopefully that devil of a male guard from earlier that morning was right; that this job cleaning the bathrooms would afford her the luxury of snacks. Because if they sent that piece of work to escort her to breakfast every morning, she'd be missing the most important meal of the day for the next ten months.

"Those chemicals are kept track of," the guard warned Doreen, "so don't think of doing any funny business. You got that?"

"Yes, ma'am," Doreen replied as she held on to the mop handle.

The guard looked down at her watch. "And I'm timing you too. You best be finished up in here in forty-five. Don't try to milk the job. That's the best way to lose it."

"Yes, ma'am," Doreen said again as the female left her to tend to her new job. It was just mopping the floor and wiping down sinks and toilets. The guard had given Doreen instructions on how to clean as if she was working for a maid service.

Doreen slopped the mop out of the industrial-size bucket on wheels. "I'd take baking pound cakes any day over this." She proceeded to mop up the bathroom with perfection. For a minute there she was acting like she really needed this job. She acted as if just because

Willie wasn't readily assessable to her physically, that he wasn't looking out for her by putting money on her books. He was, and Doreen appreciated that. It's just that she'd used it up already, not really realizing how quickly the money could be used up in jail. And she thought she overspent in Woolworth's . . .

She hadn't mopped a quarter of that floor when a voice sounded off in Doreen's head reminding her that she did, in fact, need that job. That job was what was going to keep her mind from being idle for a good part of the day. That job was what was going to keep her from fixating on time—the ticking of the clock and the pages of the calendar. This would make the days go by quicker; one by one.

What this job didn't do, though, was keep her mind off of Willie. She worried from minute to minute which day would be the day Willie decided he didn't want to wait around on her anymore. Which phone call would be the last one he'd take from her. Which visit would be her last visit from him. She'd done a horrible thing and wouldn't blame him if he decided to leave her. She stripped him of a legacy, a child—a son. Yes, she wished the circumstances under which that baby had been conceived had been different. She wished it had been conceived with her. But the child had no power over its predicament. The child didn't deserve its predicament.

Doreen felt as if she was the only one who deserved her predicament, which is why she would not complain. Which is why she would not place blame. It would be easy to say that Willie and Lauren had no business making a baby together—sneaking around together. Some scorned women would even say that Lauren had it coming; that Doreen had every right to go off on her. That's not how Doreen felt, though. What other people did was their business. What other people did and how they acted should not affect the way she acted. As a child of God she knew better; yet, she grieved Him anyway with her actions. This was her punishment. Be if from God or just the state of West Virginia, it was her retribution, and she would take it like a woman.

Now halfway finished with the floor, Doreen allowed her thoughts to travel to good places. They fast-forwarded to thoughts of her getting out of jail and Willie right there waiting for her with open arms. Him taking her into those arms and whispering in her ear how much he loves her and how he's forgiven her. Even fast-forwarding after that, she envisioned herself in Willie's arms, making love to her husband, then learning later that he would be a father after all. She would fill the void, his feeling of loss, by giving him what she had taken from him in the heat of passion—a crime of passion. She would carry his seed.

As the good thoughts consumed Doreen, she picked up the pace on her task at hand, finishing up the entire floor in prison-record time. It wasn't necessarily a record she'd been striving to break, but she had nonetheless.

A loud whistle caught Doreen's attention. She'd just kneeled down on her hands and knees to begin cleaning her first toilet.

"It's sparkling clean in here," the voice said after whistling.

Doreen looked up to see a group of women. She noticed two of them off the bat as the women from the cafeteria when she first got locked up. They were the two who had whispered something in the woman's ear she'd been dining with. After further observation, Doreen even noticed the woman she had been sitting with. The woman who had scurried off after the women had whispered in her ear—but not before hurling the insult of "baby killer" at Doreen.

"Thank you." Doreen accepted the compliment as if she had just invited some sisters from the church into her home and they'd complimented on her cleanliness.

A couple of the women in the group of five looked at one another and chuckled. One got serious and said, "You're welcome." She looked around the floor, then said to Doreen, "But you missed a spot."

Doreen followed to where the woman's eyes had just roamed. "Where?" Every spot she looked at was clean.

"Right here." The woman with her hair swept back into a ponytail and a lightly made-up face hocked up a wad of spit and spat it within inches of Doreen.

Doreen looked at the woman, her jeans fitting a little snug and her prison-issued shirt tied at her belly button, almost like a halter. To look so ladylike, she sure wasn't acting ladylike.

Taking the rag she had been cleaning the toilet with, Doreen went to wipe up the fluid next to her.

"Uh-uh." The woman was quick in bending over and snatching the rag out of Doreen's hand and throwing it on the ground. "That ain't how you get it cleaned up." She bent down, squatting in Doreen's face. "If you want something cleaned up real good you gots to lick it up. And I bet that little tongue of yours is just magic." She winked while the other women chuckled.

A feeling began to rise up in the pit of Doreen's belly. Something wasn't feeling right. She took a deep breath and simply went for the rag that had been taken out of her hand. Another one of the women was quick to walk over and kick it away.

"You heard what my girl Lecia said," the kicker told Doreen. "She wants you to lick it up."

"Yeah," Lecia said, eyeballing Doreen. "Then after that, I got something else I'm gon' need you to lick."

"Oooh, can I watch?" one of the other girls mumbled while another chuckled.

Doreen just sat there now, staring down at the ground. *Yea thou I walk through the valley of the shadow of death,* Doreen prayed in her head. Because right now, under the shadow the women hovering over her were casting off, it felt like death was on its way.

"Did you hear me?" Lecia spat. "Why you just sitting there? You heard me; lick it up . . . now. And if I have to tell you again, it ain't gon' be nice."

Doreen swallowed hard, keeping the vomit down that wanted to rise up at just the thought of licking up that woman's spit off the floor. *But do I deserve this, God?* Doreen asked in her head. *Is this part of my punishment too?*

She couldn't imagine God would want her to do something so degrading—so disgusting. But as she looked up at the women, she had to remind herself that this wasn't God giving her the order. She knew that God did not give her the spirit of fear, but she was scared. She was afraid that if she didn't do what these women wanted her to do, there would be hell to pay. She had ten months with them and an eternal lifetime with the Lord was how Doreen saw it as she kneeled over and positioned herself to do as she was told.

"I can't believe that stupid broad actually licked up your spit," one of the women said to Lecia as Doreen now hung over the toilet gagging and spitting out the mixture of the woman's body fluids and the remnants of the cleaning solution.

"Heck, me either," Lecia said, laughing. "She's easy. Witch ain't got no backbone. But then again, I suppose someone who beats a baby to death is no match for a grown woman like myself."

"Please," Doreen said in between gagging and spitting in the toilet, "it's not what everybody thinks. It's not like that."

"Waaa, waaa, waaa. Somebody pull out the string instruments and give this sad song some background music," Lecia said sarcastically. She got down on the floor with Doreen, grabbing her by the throat. "Yeah, I roll with some hard-core broads up in here. They done done a little murdering, robbing, assault—you know—that type of thing. But what ain't none of 'em ever done was harm a helpless child. But you did, and you're going to pay for that." Lecia released Doreen and watched as Doreen went on a coughing spell.

By the time Doreen finished coughing, choking, and getting her breathing back in order, she looked up to see that Lecia now had the mop in her hand. Doreen looked deep into Lecia's eyes that told a story. They told a horrific story about what Lecia's plans with that mop were going to be. And before Doreen could even register it all, she felt hands and knees pinning down every limb of her body. She felt someone's weight sitting on her stomach while hands clawed at stripping her naked from the waist down.

After that, she felt nothing. It was as if God had spared her; removing her from her fleshly vessel, allowing her spirit to rise above it while the women did the unthinkable.

Chapter Thirty-four

"I can't give you no babies, Willie," Doreen stated as she lay in the hospital bed, handcuffed to the bedpost. "After what those women did to me, the doctor says I'm never going to be able to have babies." Doreen burst into tears as she lay there in agony crying. Her body hurt. Her heart hurt. Everything hurt.

No, there was no way this could all be part of God's punishment. Or was it? Doreen, whether intentional or not, had taken the life of a baby. Now she had been robbed of the ability for a new life to exist within her. Had God resorted back to the ways of an eye for an eye? But Jesus had preached to not think in that manner. Surely God wouldn't act in that manner. No, God would not take away her ability to have a baby because she had taken the life of a baby. God would never go back on His Word. It would never return void.

"It's . . . it's okay, baby. It's okay." Willie rubbed Doreen's head. "Don't you worry about a thing, Reen. Everything is going to be all right."

"But it's not. The one thing I took from you, your son, now I can't give it back." She pulled her body up as far as it would go. Then she looked upward, lashing an angry tongue at the Lord. "Why, God? Why?" Then she rested back and had to remind herself that when all this drama first went down, she'd basically told God to "bring it on." She'd served herself up to Him on a silver platter letting God know daily how whatever punishment He deemed fit to give her, she would accept it. It looked as though Doreen was having a hard time keeping up her end of the bargain.

Almost robotically, Willie dazed off and repeated, "It's . . . it's okay, baby. It's okay." He continued to rub Doreen's head. "Don't you worry about a thing, Reen; everything is going to be all right."

Willie didn't mean that. Doreen could tell by his voice. He was just saying that in order not to make matters seem any worse. But they couldn't get any worse as far as Doreen was concerned. Wasn't nothing else God could do to her now in order to get a reaction out of her. She'd been raped by those women in the bathroom, with objects and with their flesh. As a result, she'd been raped of the ability to ever have children.

Since the miscarriage, Doreen had dreamed of getting pregnant again and giving Willie a son. She became even more desperate after taking the life of his son that only had a couple more weeks in the womb before joining them on earth. She loved Willie. He was every other heartbeat in her body. He was her first. In spite what those women did to her, he was the only person she'd had sex with—made love to. He was her one and only. She couldn't imagine life without him. Rather than get released from jail and go home to nothing—nobody—she'd rather stay behind bars.

But would Willie even be there waiting for her now? Now that she couldn't give him what could make things whole again, would he still be there? For Doreen, it already felt like Willie's contact with her was forced. Even now, as he attempted to comfort her, he didn't look her in the eyes. He just stared off in a daze. What was he afraid he'd see in her eyes if he looked into them? Would he see his wife? The one who he took vows to love until death do them part? Or would he see a killer? The woman responsible for the death of his baby?

"I don't blame you if you want to leave." Doreen sniffed as she calmed down.

"Aw, no, baby. My boss said I could have the rest of the day off to be with you," Willie replied.

"That's not what I meant, Willie. I mean, I don't blame you if you want to leave me . . . forever . . . divorce."

"Now you just talking straight-up nonsense, woman." Willie stood up and shooed his hand, turning his back to Doreen with folded arms. "I ain't gon' leave you. Why would I go and do a thing like that?"

"I just told you why. I can't give you no babies."

"Then it will just be me and you," he turned back toward her and said. "Whoever said God meant for us to have babies together in the first place?" He shrugged.

"Don't you try to downplay it, Willie. I know how much you want a child. And you know how much I wanted to give you one. And you would have one if it wasn't for . . ." Doreen's words trailed off. She wasn't sure what circumstance she should bring up. The one of her losing their baby because she came out on an icy winter night to cut the fool and ended up falling and miscarrying. Or the one with her cutting the fool in the motel room. Either way it went, both losses were because of her.

It was then, though, when she thought about a third loss; the one with Agnes. But she didn't have anything to do with that one. Doreen almost felt like a monster for finding solace in not having anything to do with Agnes deciding to abort the baby she conceived with a married man.

That's when it hit Doreen. Maybe God wasn't punishing her. Maybe He was punishing Willie. Maybe it was Willie God didn't see fit to raise any children. Maybe this was God's way of breaking a curse, one that Doreen had no idea how far back in Willie's bloodline it ran. Again, she felt like a monster finding solace in that thought as well.

"Having babies and all," Willie said, "it just ain't that important anymore, you know? What's important is you making it through your prison sentence and coming out of this place in sound mind and body." Willie went back and sat down next to Doreen.

Her heart leaped bounds hearing his words. Maybe it took such a time as this to bring about a change in Willie that would lead them to true marital bliss. And for that, Doreen was willing to give up one year of her life in order to have a lifetime with Willie. Tears fell from her eyes she was so moved.

Upon noticing the tears, Willie kicked right back into gear. "It's . . . it's okay, baby. It's okay." Again, he rubbed Doreen's head. "Don't you worry about a thing, Lauren; everything is going to be all right."

Doreen's eyes froze open as she looked at Willie. He'd just called her Lauren. She waited to see if he would correct himself. He never did. He just kept rubbing her head, telling her that it was okay and that everything would be all right. She could tell that must have been what he'd done, what he'd said to Lauren when she found out the fate of their child. She figured when he'd been so hard to reach, that's where he'd been—with her—comforting her. He'd been by her side doing and saying the exact same things he was now doing and saying to Doreen.

Doreen relaxed her body, letting her head fall even deeper into the pillow on which she lay. Tears spilled from the corner of her eyes. She wasn't so sure of things anymore like she'd been a moment ago. She was sure Willie would be there physically when she got out. She felt the deep sincerity in his words when he'd promised her that he would be. But what Doreen wasn't sure about was whether everything would be okay—if everything would be all right. Would he be there for her emotionally as well? Would Willie's heart and mind be with Doreen, or would his heart and mind be somewhere else, like with Lauren?

Chapter Thirty-five

"Well, does this look like crazy to you?" Terrance shot, snapping Mother Doreen back to her present thoughts. Looking at the photo of Lauren, looking into that woman's eyes, it had taken her back, way back, to a place she hadn't been in years.

"Your mother was a beautiful woman," Mother Doreen said, looking away from the picture and at Terrance. "I could see why my Willie would . . ." Mother Doreen stopped her words right there in their tracks. She couldn't even believe she was about to tell that boy she could see why Willie would want to be with his mother. That would have been a lie. She couldn't see it. She didn't understand why Willie, after taking vows with her, could cheat on her with any woman.

Knowing what Mother Doreen had been fixing to say, Terrance said, "Well, I can't see why my momma would want to fool with his sorry tail. And you either, for that matter."

"Now you hold on right there, young man. I will not let you speak ill of the dead, especially not about Willie." She looked up. "God rest my Willie's soul." She drew an invisible cross across her heart with her index finger.

"How on God's green earth can you stand here to this day and defend that man? After what he did? Not just to you, but to everybody? That man destroyed every woman along his path in one way or another. Trust me, I know. Like I said, I done did my research," Terrance stated. "His lying and cheating ways changed everybody's life . . . forever. But no, just like all those years ago, instead of being mad at him, you blamed the women. You blamed my mother. You beat her down like a dog in the streets while you should have had your foot up his a—"

"Mr. Terrance. Please. Not in God's house."

"Then let's take it outside, because I don't want to have to hold back no more because of God. Besides, you wasn't thinking about no God back at that motel was ya?"

"As a matter of fact, I wasn't. I let my anger consume me."

"And that's understandable. I mean, I think any woman who walks into a motel room and finds her husband on top of another woman is gonna be angry. But it was your husband you should have been angry at. He's the one who took vows with you, not my momma. She didn't owe you nothing."

Staying as calm as she could, Mother Doreen explained. "I was angry at Willie. I was angry at your mother too. I think you are incorrect about something. I think we all owe each other respect, and to be decent and kind to one another."

"Yeah, what you did was real decent and kind," Terrance huffed sarcastically.

"Look, son, I understand you're angry. But you're going to have to let it go. It was all in the past. Everyone has moved on."

"She hasn't!" Terrance yelled, gripping the picture of his mother. "She never did." In a more relaxed tone he said, "She tried. For a minute there, she thought things were going to be better. When she got pregnant with me, she felt redeemed and restored." He looked upward, and if she wasn't mistaken, Mother Doreen thought she saw a fleeting smile on Terrance's face. "Those were her exact words; redeemed and restored . . . whole again." He looked at Mother Doreen, now with disdain on his face. "You know how I know?" He reached inside his suit jacket and pulled something out of his waist. "'Cause of this right here." He held up a hardcover worn book that appeared to be a journal.

Terrance held the journal against him as if he was holding his mother. "Thank God she decided to even keep a journal. If she hadn't, I don't think I would have ever known why Momma is like she is. I would have never known why for years she's been lying up in some place for crazy folks." He looked down at the picture again. "No, she might not look like crazy, but she is."

"She's alive?" Mother Doreen sounded confused. "But I thought you said she was dead."

"She might as well be," Terrance glared. "She's got no soul. Nothing inside of her. Just a shell of what once was. She's not even in her right mind."

Terrance walked up on Mother Doreen. "And you drove her to that state; you and that husband of yours. You walking around here all saved, sanctified, and Holy Ghost-filled while my momma can't even get out of bed without assistance. She won't pick up a fork and feed herself. She won't even talk to me." Terrance's voice broke, and he quickly pulled himself together, but turned away from Mother Doreen so she wouldn't see him becoming weak. "I have never, ever heard my own mother's voice." He sniffed, pulled it together, and turned back around to face Doreen. "I'm sure when I was just a baby she probably cooed at me, told me how much she loved me. But I don't remember that. I can't recall the sound of her voice then. And that's okay, because it's not then I'm worried about. I want to hear it now. I want to hear her say it to me now."

For the last year, after getting everything off her chest about her criminal past, Mother Doreen had felt a hundred pounds lighter. She'd been able to completely forgive herself for her actions all those years ago. She'd been able to let go, let all of it go and not hang on to little pieces for souvenir's sake. Prior to that, she'd been like a serial killer when it came to completely letting go of her past; she'd held on to little parts of it for memory's sake. Over the years, she'd seen Christians with that serial-killer mentality when it came to their past. She'd watched them take pieces of it to the grave until the only time their past was truly buried was when it was buried right alongside them in that casket. Mother Doreen had made up her mind that she wasn't going out like that.

Obviously, when she'd called herself handing over to God every souvenir that she had held on to, she'd dropped a few things. The devil must have been right there like a rat, chasing after the crumbs, gathering them up. And now here he was today to present them to her on a silver platter. Satan had reworked the crumbs though, turning them into a whole brand-new tempting delicacy; an attempt to lure Mother Doreen from her rightful place in God to the pits of hell.

It was working. The guilt was beginning to build up in Mother Doreen's heart again. Terrance could see that too. So just like a good little worker being used by the devil, he kept going.

"'Oh, boy, you know your momma loves you,' is what my grandmother used to say to me," Terrance said. "She had to raise me, you know—my grandmother. My momma couldn't take care of herself, let alone a baby. But she was real good with me at first, my grandmother told me. She thought she was living the dream; that God had restored her life, replaced her dead baby with me. So for those first few months after I was born, she was happy. She believed everything he told her; every promise. But he lied. His word wasn't worth nothing. But my grandmother used to tell my momma, 'Once a liar always a liar.'"

"Terrance, I don't know what didn't happen that your mother wanted to happen. I'm sure God has His reasons. But God is not one to lie, so if those things didn't come to pass, then it was for her own good."

Terrance looked at Mother Doreen momentarily, and then started to laugh. "Oh, you thought I was talking about God being the one making promises and all that good stuff? Oh no. Let me be clearer. God's not the liar." An evil grin spread across his lips. "Your husband was."

Chapter Thirty-six

Mother Doreen wouldn't have believed it if she hadn't seen it with her own eyes. After all, Terrance had been rambling on about a lot of stuff. But that journal—that journal had it all in black and white; in Lauren's very own heartfelt words. Reading that journal had been like reading a script to a movie—a very sad movie. But this was real.

For a moment, Mother Doreen was so engrossed in the words she was reading that she forgot Terrance was even standing there. That was, until he spoke.

"That's some deep stuff, huh?" Terrance asked. "You can almost hear her voice rise from the pages. That's the only way I can hear my mother's voice; imagining her speaking those words to me; telling me the story of her life." He smiled. "I just sit and imagine that she's sitting in a rocking chair in front of a blazing fire. I'm kneeling at her feet on a nice soft rug, and we're enjoying cookies and hot chocolate. She's telling me everything about her. The good, the bad, the bliss and the pain.

"Unfortunately, 90 percent of that journal is full of pain. Pain that left my mother speechless. Literally speechless. So much pain that eventually my grandmother had to commit her to a psych ward. So much pain that not even the smiling face of her baby boy could free her mind from the prison it's been confined to. Pain caused by you and your Willie. Y'all did a real

Bonnie-and-Clyde number on her, and I bet you never even knew it, did you?"

Mother Doreen could tell by his tone that it wasn't a rhetorical question. He wanted an answer. So many answers. And Mother Doreen couldn't blame him, because reading the words written by his mother, she wanted answers too.

"In all honesty, I had no idea." Mother Doreen shook her head and closed her eyes. When her lids closed, tears seeped down her face.

"You had no idea what? That you'd caused my mother so much pain, or that your Willie wasn't nothing but a liar?" He walked over and pointed hard at the journal. "Or you had no idea that while you were sitting up in prison, your Willie was still laying up with my mother? While he was probably telling you that everything was going to be all right, he was telling her the same thing. That he loved her. That they still had a chance at sharing a life together."

Mother Doreen's bottom lip began to quiver as she listened to Terrance repeat the words she'd just read. She'd read Lauren's words about how Willie had barely left her bedside after she lost the baby. How once she was released from the hospital, he was at her home almost every minute that he wasn't at work or something. While Mother Doreen was locked up in prison, surviving off of Willie's words that he wouldn't leave her or forsake her and that he'd be waiting on her when she got out—he had been playing house with Lauren the entire time.

"How could he?" Mother Doreen mumbled to herself, once again ignoring Terrance's presence.

"He played you; played you like a fiddle," Terrance laughed. "But he played my momma too. Looks like you got over it. Guess that's because you had Jesus in your life, huh? What's that scripture about being able to do all things through Christ's strength or something like that? Guess somebody should have put my momma up on that one; reminded her about God, Jesus, and all that stuff. My grandmother said Willie became her God and Jesus. When he left her hanging, he pretty much left her for dead. My grandmother did all she could to get my mother back into church and to move on in life. Didn't work then, and it's way too late now." He looked at Doreen. "Maybe instead of beating my momma near death you should have preached the Good Word to her." Terrance began clapping his hands, drawing invisible crosses across his chest and saying, "Hallelujah!"

"God will not be mocked, Mr. Terrance," Mother Doreen said calmly.

"I know He won't," he spat angrily. "Not by my mother anyway, because she can't mock God or anybody else. She can't talk! She can't do anything. She might as well be dead. And you . . ." Terrance pointed at Mother Doreen, "you should still be locked up in jail, because not only did you kill her baby, but you killed her too. My momma ain't never been the same since she came across you and that man. But thank God that Willie met his karma, and now you need to meet yours. And some fairy-tale wedding, and then running off to be first lady just didn't seem like karma to me."

"So do you think your being here, attempting to ruin my life and any chance of happiness I might have, is going to make your mother well? Do you honestly think that's going to make her feel good?"

"No, but it sure is gon' make me feel some kind of good," he admitted. "And who knows? I could leave here and go run and tell Momma all about your wedding day from hell and it might—it just might—make her feel a little better." He held his index finger and thumb just centimeters apart. "Just a wee li'l bit of good.

"I mean, if after losing her baby, sweet-talking Willie could make her feel better, surely that might could. Yeah, I have to give it to that old husband of yours. His words to my momma was like poetry, wasn't it? Go on, read it. Keep reading all those lies your husband was feeding my momma."

Reluctantly, Mother Doreen allowed her eyes to fall back to the pages of the journal and continued to read. Her eyes filled with tears as she read the words of a woman deeply in love. Tears of anger. Tears of jealousy. Tears of anger. What bothered her most was not knowing why all these years later she cared. Willie was gone and buried. It wasn't like she could confront him about it. But there was someone she could confront.

Mother Doreen looked up from the journal at Terrance, wiping her tears away. "I need to go to her," she blurted out. "I need to go see your mother."

Chapter Thirty-seven

"Did you hear me?" Mother Doreen asked after Terrance didn't respond. "I'd like to go see your mother. Do you think that will be possible?"

"You need to go see my mother?" Terrance was in disbelief.

Mother Doreen nodded.

He let out a harrumph. "Why? So you can finish her off?"

"I know you don't trust me, and from what you know about me, you have every reason not to. But that woman you read about in here . . ." Mother Doreen shook the journal. "That woman who did all those awful things to your mother so long ago; well, I'm not her anymore."

"Oh, so you found Jesus and repented while in jail like every other criminal." He thought for a minute. "Oh, wait a minute. That's right. You had supposedly already knew who Jesus was when you did that to my mother. You were a preacher's kid." Terrance nodded and smiled. "I wonder what Mommy and Daddy thought about that—their precious girl committing a crime and getting locked up." Once again, he paused. He then walked over to Mother Doreen and flipped some pages in the journal. He read a few lines, then began snapping his finger. "Ah, that's right, you never told your parents. That was a pact you and Willie had made."

Mother Doreen looked at Terrance surprised.

"Yep, that's right; he told my momma everything. Some of the things you thought was confined to a husband-and-wife relationship only, well, Willie shared with my momma. That's what people in love do—they share everything. And your Willie . . ." Terrance mocked Mother Doreen by crossing his heart with his index finger, ". . . God rest his soul . . ."

Mother Doreen didn't think she could hurt anymore, yet every page in that journal was full of potential hurts. She felt in her heart that if she was going to stop all the pain and all the hurt for good, she needed to see Lauren. She needed to see her now. "Please, Terrance, can you tell me where I can find your mother and arrange for me to see her?"

He looked in Mother Doreen's eyes. "Yous dead serious, aren't you?"

"More serious than you'll ever know." Mother Doreen matched his stare.

Terrance turned his back to her and thought for a minute. After mulling over some things he turned and faced her again. "I, I don't think that would be a good thing. I mean, Momma is bound to see you and really go deep over the edge."

Mother Doreen stepped to him with anxiety. "The deeper the better. With the help of the good Lord, I can cast a pole that will bring her back into the shore of safety, for He has taught me to be a fisher of men."

"So you want me to stand here and believe that you want to go see my mother so you can help her?" Disbelief laced Terrance's voice.

"Yes."

"Ha!" He started laughing. "You Jesus freaks kill me. Y'all really walk around believing that y'all can lay hands on somebody and by the power of the Christ and the Holy Ghost—*bam*—they're healed." He continued laughing. "Then what? You gon' take up an offering?"

"That's not what I'm talking about, but since you asked, yes. I do believe some believers have the power to heal. But the key element is 'believe.' Both the giver and receiver must truly believe in the power of God. There can be no doubt. Because you see, when it comes to the things of God, there is no room for doubt. There is no time for doubt." Mother Doreen held out her hands. "Look at me. I'll be seventy years old before I know it. I'm much older than you, I reckon. But that don't mean a thing. You can walk right out of here and get taken out by a bus." Mother Doreen snapped. "It's over before you know it. Will you be ready for what's to come next, Mr. Terrance?" She stepped in closer to him. "Do *you* believe?"

He nodded his head, but not in affirmation of the question Mother Doreen had posed. "Aah, I get it now. Now, just like the typical Christian, you gon' try to scare me into believing in the works of God. Hell and damnation." He flung his hands up as if he were running scared.

"I'm not trying to scare you, Mr. Terrance. I can think of a whole mess of other ways to make a believer out of you. But scaring you is not one of them. Now please, will you grant me permission to see your mother?"

Terrance was indecisive. "Wha . . . why? I don't get it. There is nothing you have to offer my mother. There is nothing you can do for my mother."

"Maybe not. But there is something she can do for me."

"Her do something for you? What could my mother possibly do for you?"

Mother Doreen looked down at the journal, closed it, then said, "Forgive me—your mother can forgive me." Mother Doreen extended her hands. "Please, will you take me to her?"

"You're going where? With whom?" Bethany looked from Mother Doreen to Terrance. "Reen, have you lost your mind?" Bethany began pacing. "Oh, why am I even asking you that? Of course, you done lost your mind. You done lost your mind if you are thinking about riding all the way to West Virginia with this man. You done *really* lost your mind if you think I'm going to let you."

"I understand it might sound crazy," Mother Doreen told Bethany, "but God sometimes uses the ridiculous to confound the wise."

"Oh, please." Bethany shooed her hand. "I'm not trying to hear that right now. Somebody talk some sense into my sister, please."

Margie stepped up to bat next as they stood in the dressing room. Everything in Mother Doreen wanted to let her pastor know that her words, if she tried to talk her out of visiting Lauren, would be in vain. She'd convinced Terrance to allow her to go see his mother, and that had been no easy feat.

"What's in it for my mother?" he'd asked Mother Doreen. "I mean, I know what's in it for you—you want forgiveness. But I don't see how my mother would benefit out of all this."

"It's hard to explain," Mother Doreen had told him. "But sometimes when you forgive a person, you're not only setting that person free, but yourself as well. Now, imagine if the only thing it's ever taken to set your mother free—to free her mind—wasn't a doctor or any kind of medicine or facility. What if it was just the simple act of forgiveness?" Mother Doreen could see the wheels churning in Terrance's brain. "Wouldn't you give anything, do anything, for your mother?"

"Of course, I would," Terrance was quick to say, almost insulted that Mother Doreen would even think he wouldn't.

"Then do this. Take me to her."

After a few seconds of pondering her words, Terrance had agreed. And now she needed to get to moving before he changed his mind. But she knew that first she had to give her pastor the respect of at least listening to what she had to say.

"Mother Doreen, I understand your wanting to go see Miss Casinoff and your reasons for wanting to go, but you have to use wisdom."

"I'm using wisdom and my spirit of discernment," Mother Doreen told her pastor. "I got a feeling everything is going to be okay. Terrance here is harmless." She nodded over at Terrance and shot him a brief smile—very brief—before turning her attention back to her pastor.

"Harmless? For real, Doreen? For real?" Bethany interrupted. "You *really* believe that? Anybody who comes up in a church, interrupting somebody's wedding ceremony and spitting all kinds of venom is not a person I would call harmless."

Terrance just stood there and allowed the women to talk about him like he wasn't even there.

"Terrance came here for something. He came here for answers. He came here to hear the truth—not just read about it." Doreen gave him a look, letting him know she understood his intentions. She then looked back at Margie and Bethany.

Margie and Bethany looked puzzled, while Terrance knew exactly what Mother Doreen was referring to. He'd read his mother's journal seeking answers. But it hadn't been enough.

"Okay, listen; it sounds like Mother Doreen is hellbent on going all the way to West Virginia to go see this man's mother," Margie said. "Mother Doreen, why don't you ride in my car, and we just follow behind him?"

"Thank you for the offer, Pastor, but I trust riding with Terrance just fine." Mother Doreen looked at him and cracked just a tiny smile. He looked away so that he wouldn't have to acknowledge her smile. Mother Doreen was striving for reciprocity here. She wanted to show Terrance that she trusted him, so he could trust her in return.

Bethany threw her hands up, and then let them smack down to her side. "See? She's lost her mind. We're wasting our breath."

"Wait, wait; I have another idea," Margie interjected. "Mother Doreen, you go ahead and ride with Terrance. We'll just follow behind you guys."

"And I have something I can add to that," Unique, who had been sitting quietly, finally said. "Pastor, you and Bethany follow behind Mother Doreen in your car, and I'll just ride in the backseat with her and Terrance." She shot Terrance the evil eye. "That way, if something pops off . . ." Unique slammed her fist into her palm a couple of times. ". . . I'll have her back."

"No, no, that won't be necessary either," Mother Doreen was quick to say. "Like I said, I'll be just fine riding with Mr. Terrance. Now if you all want to follow behind, then there ain't nothing I can do to stop you. But I'm ready to go." She looked at Terrance. "Shall we?"

"Sure," he nodded, still not 100 percent sure himself if this was a good idea.

"You just gonna leave just like that?" Bethany asked Mother Doreen. "I mean, you haven't even talked to Pastor Frey yet. He's been in that sanctuary on his knees since you left him standing at that altar. Now even Sister Deborah has joined him."

Mother Doreen paused. "Good; leave them there. Because I got a feeling I'm going to need all the prayer I can get." And with that, Mother Doreen followed Terrance out of the church and to his car.

Chapter Thirty-eight

The drive from Ohio to West Virginia was silent, in Terrance's car anyway. Now in Margie's car that followed behind them, that was a different story. Margie and Unique prayed out loud most of the time. Bethany did some praying too, but mostly slept, resting her body. That's the only way her husband, Uriah, finally agreed to allow her to make the trip—if she promised to not be all worked up and rest her body.

Mother Doreen knew her sister and sisters in Christ were praying for her. She could feel it. There was no other explanation for how calm and relaxed her spirit and her mind were. There was no nervousness and no anxiety as she rode the entire time, finishing all but the last twenty pages or so of the journal.

"Well, here we are." Terrance exhaled and threw the car in park after pulling up into the parking lot of the facility where his mother resided.

Mother Doreen admired the well kept lawn. "Wow, what lovely grounds," she complimented. "Look at all the lovely flowers and the beautiful rosebushes."

"Yeah, well, they don't mean much when you can't come outside, take them in, and enjoy them. When you can't do that, well, I guess, they're just like any old plant in the ground." Terrance got out of the car. To Mother Doreen's astonishment, he walked around and opened her door. She looked up at him with surprise. "Spite what you and your church folks think, I am a gentle-man."

Mother Doreen nodded and allowed him to help her out of the car. Just as he closed the door behind her, Bethany, Margie, and Unique came over.

"Whoa, all y'all not coming up in here." Terrance held his hands up.

"The heck if we ain't," Unique spoke up. "No telling what you might do to her behind closed doors."

"Look, if I wanted to do something stupid, I could have easily lost you all on the drive here," Terrance countered.

"Well, we already know you're capable of doing something stupid. You did that back at the church. It's you doing something outright insane that gives me pause," Unique shot back.

"I appreciate you all following along," Mother Doreen interrupted, "but Terrance is right. I don't think all of us going in there is going to be good for his mother. Why don't you all go grab something to eat, or just stay out here or in the lobby or something, and pray?"

"We could have stayed back at the church with Deborah and Pastor Frey to pray." Unique rolled her eyes and crossed her arms. "Or went with Paige to eat."

Paige had stayed back in Malvonia because her blood sugar level had dropped and she needed to eat and get some rest.

"I think Mother Doreen is right." Margie patted Unique on her shoulder to calm her down. "I'm sure this place has security and Mother Doreen will be okay. Let's just go grab a bite, and then come back for Mother Doreen to drive her home." Margie looked from one person to the next. "How does that sound to everybody?"

All nodded in agreement, including Unique—reluctantly.

Each woman gave Mother Doreen a hug and retreated back to the car. Unique was the last to embrace Mother Doreen. After doing so, she cut her eyes at Terrance and reminded him, "Don't forget; I *will* fight a man," then joined the other women at the car.

"Oh, don't pay her no never-mind," Mother Doreen said to Terrance.

"Trust me, I'm not," he assured her.

Terrance led the way up the walkway and into the building. Once inside, Mother Doreen admired the interior décor just as much as she had admired the exterior. A beautiful place indeed it was. Mother Doreen thought in her head how much Terrance must really love his mother in order to provide only the best for her. This place looked to be one of the best.

"Well, hello, Mr. T," the woman at the sign-in desk said to Terrance as soon as she buzzed him through the double doors.

"Hello to you too, Rhoda."

Rhoda looked down at her watch. "It's kind of late for you to be visiting on a Saturday. I didn't think you were going to make it in today."

"Oh, yeah, well, I had some things I had to do today. But I'm here."

"And we are so glad you are here indeed," she blushed.

Mother Doreen stood back and watched the exchange take place between Rhoda and Terrance. It took a moment for Rhoda to take her eyes off of him and even notice that Mother Doreen was there.

"Oh, you brought someone with you?" The smile that had been plastered upon Rhoda's face after seeing

Terrance somewhat faded as her eyes darted back and forth between Mother Doreen and Terrance.

"Yes, I did." Terrance turned to acknowledge Mother Doreen's presence. He also noticed the questioning look on Rhoda's face. "It's okay."

"Are you sure? Miss Casinoff isn't used to any other visitors besides yourself. You know, ever since your grandmother passed, you've been the only one to come visit her."

"Yes, I'm sure, Rhoda. Thanks for your concern, though."

"Well, all right. You know the drill. I just need the two of you to sign is all."

Terrance signed in, then moved to the side so Mother Doreen could do the same. Afterward, Rhoda hit a button. There was a buzzing sound, and another set of double doors opened for them.

"Thanks, Rhoda," Terrance said as he and Mother Doreen made their way through the doors.

"No problem, Mr. Terrance," Rhoda smiled. "No problem at all."

Terrance led the way down the corridor.

"She seems like a fine woman," Mother Doreen spoke, referring to Rhoda.

"Oh, who, Rhoda?" Terrance played it off. "Yeah, she's good peoples. She's been a good friend to me and my mother during all the years my mother has been here."

"She seems nice. And it seems like she wouldn't mind being a little more than just a friend to you."

Terrance shrugged as if he hadn't noticed Rhoda's huge smile toward him and all her blushing.

"And with good reason too. You're not too bad looking of a fellow. Remind me a lot of my Willie back in the day. Oh, the way he could get the girls to go crazy for him without even trying."

Terrance stopped in his track and turned to face Mother Doreen. "Yeah, tell me about it—Drive 'Em Crazy Willie. That should have been his nickname."

Mother Doreen covered her mouth. "Oh goodness. I'm sorry. I didn't mean anything by it."

Her last comment gave Terrance second thoughts. "I'm not sure if this is such a good idea after all. What if you say something in there that pushed my mother away even deeper?" He shook his head. "I'd never forgive myself if—"

Mother Doreen interrupted him, resting her hand on his shoulder. "I promise you, I'll leave my flesh right out here in this hallway. I'll let my every word be directed by the Holy Spirit. What I just said a second ago, I honestly didn't mean anything by it."

"I'm sure you didn't, but—"

Again, Mother Doreen cut him off. She would not allow him to talk himself out of the decision he'd made to allow her to come see his mother. "You said you'd do anything to try to get your mother back right again."

"But the doctors have already tried so much." Doubt laced Terrance's every word and was the only expression on his face.

"Then let me try what they probably have not. Let me try Jesus."

The name of Jesus must have certainly had power, because Terrance turned and continued leading the way. "Well, this is it. This is my mother's room."

Mother Doreen looked up at the door to see the name Lauren Casinoff written on a piece of white stock paper inserted in a slot.

"Are you okay?" Terrance asked with concern after he saw the color drain from Mother Doreen's face as she stared at the door.

At first, Mother Doreen didn't respond. She just held her chest and tried to catch her breath. Finally she was able to compose herself. "Yes, I'm okay. I'm fine."

"Then are you ready to go in?" Terrance asked.

Inhaling a deep breath, Mother Doreen replied, "Yes; as ready as I'll ever be." And on that note, Terrance opened the door, and once again, Mother Doreen found herself walking into room 111 where Lauren Casinoff would once again be on the other side in bed.

Chapter Thirty-nine

"Momma? Momma, it's me, Terrance," he said upon entering the room. He looked over his shoulder and held his hand up for Mother Doreen to stay put where she stood, which was in the doorway. Terrance slowly crept over to his mother.

Mother Doreen couldn't see Lauren's face. She was lying in the bed facing the window opposite the direction of the door. The television was programmed to the Oprah Winfrey Network.

Mother Doreen looked around the quaint little room. She looked everywhere but at Lauren. During her visual tour she concluded that the room was nice and cozy. The bed was queen sized. A nice comfy-looking chair sat on each side of the bed. Over by the window was a couch with a coffee table. Next to the couch was an end table with a lamp on it and a Gideon Bible that in a lot of places served more as décor than a spiritual weapon. The Bible looked as though it had never been touched so Mother Doreen assumed it was for décor. Besides, according to Terrance, his mother probably didn't do much reading.

There was a closet and private bathroom as well. It was quite roomy if Mother Doreen didn't say so herself. She made note of each and every detail in the room. She wasn't big on designing or anything. Her sudden interest in eyeballing every corner of the room was to avoid eyeballing its occupant.

"Momma, there is someone here who would like to see you," Mother Doreen heard Terrance say and knew it was only a matter of seconds before she could avoid eye contact no longer.

An encounter was about to take place; one Mother Doreen never imagined would. She never thought for one moment she'd have the opportunity to ever do what she was about to do today: ask Lauren Casinoff for her forgiveness.

"Is that okay, Momma?" Terrance asked his mother while he simultaneously signaled with his hand for Mother Doreen to step to his mother's bedside.

Mother Doreen took one step toward the bed. It was the hardest step she could ever remember taking. Just hours ago she'd glided down the aisle of her church sanctuary with ease in a failed effort to say, "I do," to being Pastor Frey's wife. Now just taking one step was difficult. It was like she wasn't sure whether she could balance or not. If this was anything like a baby learning to take its first step, Mother Doreen wondered how they ever learned to walk.

Terrance swished his hand to hurry Mother Doreen along as if he wanted to get this over with just as much as she did. Mother Doreen picked up the pace until she finally stood next to him.

"See, Momma, look who's here. Do you know who this woman is?" Terrance asked Lauren.

Lauren's eyes were still fixed on the window. Finally looking at the woman, Mother Doreen could see a longing in her eyes as they stared out the window. They seemed to have such a longing; a longing for what was outside of that window. Fresh air. A blue sky. Green grass. Flowers. Life. Freedom. Yes! That was it. That was what Mother Doreen saw. A longing to be free, for behind Lauren's eyes was such bondage. Mother Doreen knew all about that.

Terrance nodded to Mother Doreen, his eyes asking her to speak words—to say something to his mother.

Mother Doreen cleared her throat. "Hello, uh, hi, Lauren."

There was no response. Lauren just lay there continuing her visual plight on the outside world.

Terrance gently pulled Mother Doreen by the arm and stepped aside so that now Mother Doreen was blocking Lauren's view of the window. Now Lauren had no choice but to look at Mother Doreen.

That moment—the moment Lauren lifted her eyes and they locked with Mother Doreen's, Mother Doreen thought she was going to fall out right then and there and end up being Lauren's neighbor in that place. The energy that generated just from eye contact was overwhelming to Mother Doreen. All the while, Lauren seemed to be unfazed.

"Hi, Lauren," Mother Doreen spoke again. "You, you might not remember me." She swallowed hard. "But my name is Doreen Tucker. I was Willie's wife."

Mother Doreen didn't know if it was the mention of her name or Willie's that made Lauren's eyes light up like a lightbulb. All of a sudden, her hand began to flap up and down. Terrance bumped by Mother Doreen to attend to his mother.

"What? What is it, Momma? Is everything okay?" Terrance asked as his mother continued to flail her hand even faster. He looked at Mother Doreen, then back at his mother. "Is it her? Are you upset?" Still, all Lauren did was flail her hand. Terrance stood up and spoke to Mother Doreen. "I knew this wasn't a good idea. I can't believe I let you talk me into this," he said, his eyes blaming Mother Doreen for upsetting his mother. "I hate that you came all this way, but I think you better find your friends and go."

"Ummph, ummph."

Both Mother Doreen and Terrance looked at Lauren, who was struggling to make moaning sounds.

Terrance rushed back down to her side. "Momma?"

Mother Doreen could see the elation in Terrance's actions. She could tell that this was probably the most reaction he had gotten from his mother in a very long time. Although it wasn't much, he was willing to take it.

"Ummmph, ummph," Lauren continued to moan, now gripping Terrance's fingers on his hand that he'd placed around hers.

Terrance looked at his mother intently as if someone had harmed her. Was she on her last breath and about to tell him who'd done it? "What, Mom? Please."

"Nnnnnn . . ." Lauren swallowed hard and was finally able to say something that both Terrance and Mother Doreen could understand. "No." She then looked from her son to Mother Doreen. "No. Sttttttttttttttttt—stay." She exhaled as if it had taken every breath in her body just to get those words out.

Mother Doreen watched as Terrance's shoulders began to heave up and down. He buried his face in his mother's bed to avoid them seeing the tears fall from his eyes. Hearing his mother speak after all these years—finally hearing her voice—had moved him beyond measure.

"Ohhhhh . . . k-k-k-k-kay." Lauren removed her hand from Terrance's, breathing heavily after forcing that last word out. She rested it on his head. It no longer flailed wildly, but now gently patted his head. "Ohhhhh . . . kah-kay. Iiiit-OK . . . sssssssss-son," she pushed out, which only made Terrance break down now so that he could no longer hide his emotions. His weeping filled the room.

At first, Mother Doreen didn't know what to do. She felt as though she was invading this special mother-son moment. So she did what she knew worked in every situation; she began to pray. Softly, Mother Doreen allowed words of prayer to flow from her lips. Her words could barely be heard. She was sure that the other occupants in the room were so engaged in each other that they didn't even hear her. Didn't notice her. Didn't even recall she was still in the room.

Figuring that perhaps this wasn't the right time to be there, she began to step backward in order to make a quiet exit while still praying. She had barely lifted her foot to take her first step backward when Lauren faintly spoke a word Mother Doreen could not understand. She looked at Terrance to see if he understood what she'd said since he was closer to her.

"She said, 'No,'" Terrance relayed to Mother Doreen, and then looked back at his mother. "No, what?" He wanted to be sure what his mother meant.

"No . . . leeeavve. Puuuhhh . . . puhleaze stay." She swallowed again, out of breath, as if speaking each word was like running a marathon. "Tttttttttt . . ." she struggled. "Need ta . . . ta . . . talk . . . youuuuu."

Terrance wiped his tears and sniffed as he stood up. "Looks like she does want you here—wants to talk to you."

Mother Doreen nodded and reversed her step forward again.

Lauren looked at her son, then back at Mother Doreen again. She then looked back at her son.

"You, you want me to go?" Terrance asked his mother. She immediately replied with a nod. Now Terrance stood there looking the same way Bethany had been looking when Mother Doreen wanted to be alone with Terrance back at the church. "But, Momma . . ." Terrance's words trailed off. This was the first time he'd ever been able to communicate with his mother verbally, and he wasn't about to let it be tainted with back talking. "Okay, Momma, but I'm going to be right outside that door if you need me." He said those words to Lauren but was speaking to Mother Doreen. "And remember, if you need anything, you can always push the nurse's call button," he added, knowing his mother had never used that button before.

Lauren nodded as Terrance reluctantly exited the room. After Terrance left, initially there was silence. Mother Doreen broke that silence by digging into her purse and pulling out the journal she'd read most of the entire ride there. "Oh, by the way, this belongs to you."

Lauren looked at the journal.

"I hope you don't mind, but Terrance thought I should read it." Mother Doreen got no reaction from Lauren. "I'll just go put it over here next to the Bible." She walked over to the end table and placed the journal next to the Bible. She then stared out the window. She pretended to be admiring whatever it was Lauren had been so fixated on, but what she was really doing was taking a quick moment to ask God for direction—to order her steps and her words.

"En . . . End," Lauren said, this time a little more relaxed, as if she was finally getting the hang of this talking thing.

"Huh? Excuse me?" Mother Doreen swiftly turned to face her.

"End." Lauren swallowed, which seemed to help her words come out easier and clearer. "Did y . . . reeeeead end—theeee end?"

"Oh, did I read the end of the journal?" Mother Doreen guessed, and Lauren nodded. "No, but I read most of it. I read enough to know that you were in love with my husband and that he hurt you very mu—"

"Sssssit." Lauren looked at the chair next to her bed. "Si' chair."

"Yes, of course." Mother Doreen walked over to the chair and sat down.

Lauren swallowed twice. "I tell you," Lauren said, now her words much clearer for Mother Doreen to understand. "I'll tell yyyy . . . ou the end." Lauren coughed. Trying to get the words out had nearly choked her. In between coughs she managed to say, "Waaater." She grabbed her throat. "Nur-urse! Waaater!"

Mother Doreen buzzed the nurse. When the nurse replied via the intercom, Doreen asked her if she would bring Lauren a pitcher of water. The nurse brought the water within minutes. She almost jumped for joy, but certainly cried tears of joy when she saw how well Lauren was doing. Before leaving Lauren alone with Mother Doreen, she took her vitals with promises of returning shortly with the doctor.

"This is nothing short of a miracle," the nurse exclaimed. "Wait until your son finds out."

"I think he knows already." Mother Doreen was sure Terrance knew.

"Why that little . . . Wait until I . . ." the nurse flung her hand. "Anyway, Miss Casinoff, I'm calling your doctor pronto. Saturday night or not, I'm sure he's going to want to head right on over and see this for himself and examine you."

The nurse exited the room. Once it was just Mother Doreen and Lauren alone again in the room, Lauren nodded toward the closet. "Shoe box. Closet. Top."

Mother Doreen walked over to the closet and opened the door. On the top shelf was a shoe box. "This?" Mother Doreen asked Lauren over her shoulder. Once Lauren confirmed that's what she needed, Mother Doreen returned to Lauren's bedside with the shoe box in hand. She sat back down in the chair, placing the shoe box on the bed next to Lauren.

Mother Doreen watched Lauren struggle for a moment to get the lid off, then finally assisted her. Lauren fumbled around in the box before finding what she was looking for.

"Yours," Lauren said, holding something out to Mother Doreen.

Mother Doreen opened her hand, and when the cold piece of metal rested in the palm of her hand, her mouth dropped opened. "My ring! My wedding ring. I'd given Willie permission to claim it from the jail property, but when I got out, he said he didn't know where it was. That he had lost it. Honestly, I thought he'd gambled it away or something." Mother Doreen took her eyes off the ring and planted them on Lauren suspiciously. "But you have it."

She slipped the ring on her finger. It still fit just like it did the day Willie slipped it on her finger after saying, "I do." A part of her was glad to know what had really become of the ring. Another part of her wanted to know how Lauren had ended up with it. Within seconds, Mother Doreen would certainly find out. Lauren would tell her in her own words, just as well as she could get them out.

Chapter Forty

Willie felt torn as he sat next to Lauren's hospital bed holding her hand, comforting her; letting her know that everything was going to be okay. He felt torn because perhaps instead of being by his mistress's side, he should have been at his wife's side. She was in jail, a place that would always be thought to be foreign to a preacher's daughter. She'd been raised to dream about heaven; now she was living a nightmare in hell. He was sure most would agree he should have been by Doreen's side telling her that everything was going to be okay. But at the moment, though, Lauren seemed to need him more. After all, the doctors had just made her give birth to a dead baby boy. A baby his wife had killed while it was defenseless in his mistress's womb.

"He's dead. My baby is dead," Lauren said as if she was telling him about the weather. She just looked head-on as if dazed—as if in disbelief. "Willie, our baby is dead." She turned to him, gripping his hand. "Our baby is dead. Your wife killed our baby."

Willie looked into Lauren's eyes and could see for the first time it was registering in her mind exactly what had taken place.

"Shhh," Willie told her. "It's . . . it's okay, baby. It's okay." Willie rubbed Lauren's head. "Don't you worry about a thing, Lauren; everything is going to be all right."

"No, no, no, it's not." Lauren shook her head repeat-edly. "My baby, our baby is dead. What about that nice little area in my bedroom you got together for the baby, with that beautiful bassinet and those teddy bears? And all the diapers, blankets, and little cute outfits? I've gotta go home to that, Willie. I gotta go home with-out my baby. What am I going to do with all that stuff now, huh?"

Lauren began to cry her eyes out as it all began to sink in. Tears streamed out of her swollen black and blue eyes, down her puffy face, and past her bandaged, broken nose and busted, stitched-up lips. "It wasn't supposed to be like this, Willie. You were supposed to tell her about me. You were supposed to tell her about us. You were supposed to leave her and be with me. You were supposed to come here to West Virginia to see about me and the baby—to take care of us. Not bring Doreen with you." Lauren shot back at Willie all the things he'd told her over the past year. Lies they had been—all lies. Obvious lies since Willie had done none of the things he'd told Lauren he would do con-cerning getting out of his marriage.

Guilt consumed Willie. He couldn't help but wonder if this, in fact, was all of his fault. Was he to blame for Doreen's actions? Could God, would God, really hold him accountable for someone else's actions? Now he wished he'd paid more attention in church instead of watching skirts in the choir stand. Now, instead of sneaking away from Doreen from the pew pretending to go to the bathroom, all the while sneaking in the back choir room with Lauren, he wished he'd sat his tail right there in that sanctuary and listened to the Word. After today's unforeseen catastrophe, he wished he'd just stayed his behind in Kentucky and never went to West Virginia in the first place.

What on God's green earth made him pick up and do something so stupid? So selfish? He looked down at Lauren and pictured the beauty that lay behind her swollen, distorted face. Those pretty brown eyes with batting lashes, delicately arched eyebrows, that perfect nose and full lips. The body—good Lord, that body. He had to admit, Doreen had a nice li'l figure on her too, but she didn't work it like Lauren worked hers.

Willie shook his head and reminded himself, *That's why—that's why I did it.* Yes, they may have been shallow reasons, very shallow reasons, but they were his reasons nonetheless.

"You didn't leave her, Willie," Lauren said, jerking Willie from his own selfish thoughts. "Guess you gon' leave me now, huh? Guess you gon' leave me here like this and go running to see about her . . . the woman who murdered your own flesh and blood. You gon' go see about her, huh, Willie? Are you?"

"Lauren, honey, I know this hurts. I'm hurting too."

"Oh really?" She sounded doubtful. "You're probably glad the baby died. You were probably only being bothered with me because of the baby. Now that there's no baby, there's no me and you." Lauren began to break down. "Please tell me that ain't so, Willie. I already done lost the baby; I can't imagine losing you too. I'll have no reason to live. No reason to breathe."

Willie buried his face in his hands. He didn't know what to do or what to say. This was all too much. He never meant to hurt anybody. He never meant for no woman to get hurt; not Doreen, not Lauren, or the other one-night and one-month stands he'd had in addition to them. Doreen was his wife. He loved her above all. She was a part of him. The one-night and one-month stands—they meant nothing. Lauren, on the other hand, had grown on him. Even before she turned up pregnant, there was something about her Willie was drawn to. She was just this young, innocent church girl who knew very little, if anything, about the world. If he wanted to be honest with himself, she reminded him of Doreen. And just like Doreen, she had a singing voice that could put him to sleep at night, and it did—on many occasions.

"So are you? Are you gon' leave me here like this, Willie?" Lauren asked. "Or are you going to be a man of your word and still be with me? Leave Doreen and make me your wife?"

Willie was in the hot seat now. These weren't just rhetorical questions Lauren was throwing at him. She wanted answers, and she wanted answers now. But Willie didn't have all the answers. He didn't have any answers. It didn't take long for Lauren to begin to help him make up his mind.

"She's gon' probably spend the rest of her life in jail anyway, so you might as well be with me. What can she do for you in jail? Nothing. But me, Willie, you and me got a chance."

Willie just stared down at the hospital floor. Could Lauren perhaps be right? At this point, Doreen hadn't been to trial yet, let alone sentenced. She'd mentioned to Willie something about a plea bargain her lawyer had said was on the table. But Doreen had been adamant about not taking it. Said she wasn't gonna admit to something that would make the world think she was a monster. No telling how long she could be locked up—maybe forever, just like Lauren was suggesting.

As painful as it was, Lauren scooted up in the bed and lifted Willie's face up toward her. "You and me, Willie, we still have a chance. I'm out here free as a bird. God's gon' give us another chance. All we have to do is repent. God can give us our baby back. We can make another one." Lauren sniffed as tears fell from her eyes. "I want my baby back. I want our baby. We can do this, Willie. We can."

Lauren wiped her sad tears away and almost instantly filled with excitement. "Her—your wife—being in jail is like abandonment. It's like she left you. No judge in their right mind will refuse you a divorce. Then it will be just you and me, Willie." She touched her now empty womb. "Just you and me and the baby we can still have." Lauren stared at Willie while waiting on a response. "So what do you say, Willie, huh?"

Willie thought for a minute. Some of what Lauren had said made sense. Most likely Doreen would have to serve some time in jail. How long, he didn't know. But in jail or not, she was his wife and he loved her. He'd always loved her. He would always love her. But there was nothing he could do for her while she was incarcerated. There was nothing she could do for him. But like Lauren had stated, she was out here with him free as a bird. And she was so fragile right now, he could only imagine how much more it would devastate her if he was to tell her what he was really feeling in his heart.

Lauren was a bird, a free bird, but she was broken right now. She was a bird with a broken wing. She couldn't fly right now—not without his help. So perhaps he could just be there for her until her wing healed and he could set her to flight . . . without him. But for now, he would tell her all the things he thought would make her better, not knowing in the end, they would only make her worse.

Chapter Forty-one

From the hospital room, to the courtroom, to the jailhouse, not to mention his job—Willie was spreading it thin. In two weeks alone he'd lost several pounds. Half the time he didn't know if he was coming or going—or where he was coming or going. One day, in the midst of all the back and forth, he lost his set of keys. He couldn't drive, get into the house, or anything.

Unfortunately, he didn't have enough money to pay a locksmith to help him get into his vehicle or house. He'd paid Lauren's hospital bill once she was released. That's the least he could have done considering his wife was the reason she'd been in there anyway. He was also paying the bills and putting money on Doreen's books. He was always left with just enough for bill money and plenty of alcohol to drown his troubles in. That meant there was no money for emergencies, and needing to get into his house and vehicle was an emergency. The only other person who had keys was Doreen, but the jail had taken all her personal effects when she'd been arrested.

With the help of Doreen's attorney and her signing an affidavit, they released Doreen's belongings into Willie's custody. Even with the keys to his car and house now in hand, he still felt locked out; locked out of his own life. He was living for everybody else; trying to make everybody else happy in their circumstances. Guilt was a mutha, that was for sure. Along with guilt came the feeling of obligation. That meant never being able to tell that person who he felt obligated to the word "no."

It was official. Willie was a "yes-man."

"Yes," Willie said to Lauren's question. He hadn't even really heard her clearly. But he knew from her tone that a question had been posed which required a response. So he said what he always said.

"Oh my God, Willie, for real?" Lauren got up off the couch from where the two had been sitting watching TV. She jumped up and down. "Oh, Willie, I love you so much." She went and flung her arms around his neck and began planting an array of kisses all over his face. "I can't wait to be your wife!"

Now *that,* Willie heard—loud and clear. "Huh? What?" He gently pushed Lauren off of him until she was seated next to him, his hands around her wrists. "What are you talking about?"

"Boy, quit playing," Lauren laughed. "I'm talking about you just saying yes to wanting to marry me." She wriggled her wrists from Willie's hands and threw her hands around his neck again.

Willie sat there in a daze. What on God's green earth had he gotten himself into now? "Well, wait a minute now, Lauren. Yes, I want to marry you, but you know I'm already married."

"Then we'll just have to take care of that then, won't we? Brother Carl over at the church is a lawyer. I'm sure he'll be glad to help for a small love offering," Lauren said. "Why, it shouldn't take long to finalize the divorce at all. I mean, heck, your wife's in jail so she can't really fight it. And besides that, you love me. You've been with me almost every day."

Willie sat frozen. Was this really happening to him? Was it really?

"Oooh, I can just see it now. Us standing before the preacher man vowing to love, honor, and obey. Me in a pretty gown and you slipping a beautiful ring on my finger." Lauren jumped up and down with her hands clasped together. "I can't wait! I can't wait! And I'm going to make you the happiest man in the world. I'm gonna be more woman than that Doreen ever could have been. No way are you ever gonna want to stray away from me for another woman. Because not only do I love you more than anything in the world, but I know deep in my heart you love me more than anything too. Otherwise, you wouldn't even be here with me. Ain't that right, Willie?"

He was in too much of a state of confusion to even respond.

"Willie?" Lauren went and sat back down next to him on the couch. "You do love me, Willie? Don't you?" She turned Willie's face to face her. "Do you love me? Do you love me, William Tucker?"

"I . . . I do," Willie had stammered, first on the couch when Lauren had asked him if he loved her. And now he was stammering those same exact words in front of the judge who was asking him if he took Lauren to be his wife.

"And I do too!" Lauren exclaimed. The two witnesses down at the courthouse chuckled at Lauren's outburst.

"Then I now pronounce you man and wife," the judge said. "You may kiss the bride."

Lauren eagerly laid a huge smacker on Willie's lips. He just took it all in. He took it in with the hugest lump ever in the pit of his stomach. What had he done? What in the world had he done? That was one question. But the bigger one was how, if at all possible, could he undo it.

***

"It's been almost a week. Where you been?" Doreen asked Willie during his visitation to her at the jail. "Oh, shoot . . ." she thumped herself on the forehead. "Over-time, huh? You been working overtime in order to pre-pare for when I get out of this place, haven't you? Sure, you have, and I appreciate it so much. I hate not being able to talk with you. But I know you're just doing what you have to do." Doreen squirmed uncomfortably in her seat. All she wanted Willie to do was agree—to af-firm what she'd said with a nod. Whether or not it was true, Doreen had learned that hearing the truth was sometimes far more than she could possibly bear.

Being the yes-man that he was, Willie simply nod-ded, followed by a soft, lying, "Yes." What else could he have told her? That he'd been on a honeymoon with his new bride? The bride that he was legally able to marry because he'd legally divorced Doreen. He divorced her without her even knowing. Thanks to Brother Carl, he learned that getting a divorce was as simple as one spouse filing and alleging that they didn't know the whereabouts of the other. Since they didn't know the other's whereabouts, they couldn't serve them divorce papers. What they could do, though, was list it publicly in the newspaper and hope and pray that the defendant didn't see it and respond, or worse, contest it.

Obviously, all Willie's hope and prayers had paid off, because Doreen was none the wiser that she was no longer legally Willie's wife.

"I'm counting the days, Willie," Doreen said. "I'm counting the days when I can get out of here and live as husband and wife with you again."

Willie thought he was about to turn beet red. Was Doreen messing with his mind? Did she know some-thing? She always did have what he referred to as women's intuition, but what she referred to as a spirit of discernment.

"I, I, I can't wait either," Willie stuttered before their conversation was plagued with heavy silence.

"Well, you been thinking about where you want to move to when I get out of this place?" Doreen picked back up the conversation.

"Uh, well, uh, you know with all the work I've been doing, guess I just didn't have the time to stop and think about nothing."

"That's all right, because I have." Doreen's eyes lit up. "I heard about some little town in Ohio called Malvonia."

Willie scrunched his nose up. "Malvonia? I ain't never heard of that place before."

"Right! And neither had I. That means probably nobody else has either. And even better, if we ain't heard of Malvonia, then it probably ain't never heard of us. And that's just what we need in order to be able to do this thing right. So what do you say, Willie? Why don't you start looking into things and setting up shop? Even if you've got to go without me and be away for a while, I don't care." Doreen began to sound desperate—look desperate. "I just want to start fresh again, just like you promised."

Willie smiled on the outside, but on the inside he felt sick. He'd made a lot of promises lately; some to Lauren and some to Doreen. His only dilemma was which ones he was going to keep . . . and with whom.

Chapter Forty-two

"Arrrre, are, okayyyy. Youuuuu okay?" Lauren asked Mother Doreen.

"No." Mother Doreen was being honest. "Actually, I'm not okay." She looked down at her wedding ring that rested on her trembling hands.

"You not know. Didn't know?" Lauren figured as much by the expression on Mother Doreen's face and the way she'd paused as if she'd swallowed a frog when she heard about Lauren and Willie's nuptials. "He never told you he divorced you and married me, huh?" Although she'd stuttered and stammered some, Lauren's words were becoming clearer.

All Mother Doreen could do was shake her head. "I had no idea. No idea." She paused for a moment. "That means that the first year we were in Malvonia together, we were living in sin."

"You mean the entire time y'all was living in Malvonia together it was in sin. He wasn't married to you. He was married to me," Lauren corrected.

"No, no, because he married me. Willie married me again. Well, he said it was just the renewing of our vows. But now I know it was something more than that. It was him marrying me all over again because he knew we weren't. That son of a devil's bride." Mother Doreen chuckled bitterly. "Heck, I guess you could say I was the devil's bride, 'cause I'm really starting to feel like for all those years that's exactly what I had done—married the devil."

Mother Doreen just sat there shaking her head for a minute. The longer she sat there, the more the words she'd read and had heard Lauren speak sank in. And the more they started to puncture her heart, and those puncture wounds hurt . . . like crazy. Before she knew it, her eyes began to water. But right as Mother Doreen was about to start her woe-is-me campaign, she looked at Lauren. It was clear that Willie's lies had done far much more damage in Lauren's life than it had in hers.

"Oh my," Mother Doreen said, covering her mouth. "Here I am about to cry a river that's long been drained, and look at you."

Lauren stared at Mother Doreen puzzled.

"I mean, I dealt with it. The good Lord, who is an all-knowing God, knew exactly what I needed to know and what I didn't. God knew I would not have been able to bear knowing Willie had divorced me and was married up with you. I would have lost my mind. Just like—" Mother Doreen swallowed her words.

"Go ahead and say it," Lauren urged. "Just like me? That is what you were going to say, wasn't it? That you would have lost your mind just like me?" Mother Doreen's eyes confirmed it. "Well, go on ahead and say it, because it's the truth. That's exactly what happened. When I woke up that Saturday morning to find Willie gone—not just from my bed but just gone period—words can't describe how I felt." Lauren looked over at the journal Mother Doreen had laid beside the Bible. "Well, actually, maybe words can describe." She nodded toward the journal, and then said to Mother Doreen. "Get it. I want you to finish reading it. I want you to read the end."

Hesitantly, Mother Doreen stood up and went to re-
trieve the journal from beside the Bible. She returned
to the chair, and then looked down at the journal. She
opened it to the page where she had left off. She continued to read the last few pages of the journal, which
would be the last reflections of Lauren with a sane
mind. But after reading the final installment, Mother
Doreen had no idea just how sane she could remain.

Lauren ran into her house that looked as though a
cyclone had hit it. She'd torn that house up looking for
Willie. Looking for Willie or anything that belonged to
him. Just something—something to show that he was
coming back. Something he'd left that she knew he
would come back for, but there was nothing. Not even
his toothbrush. She even went to the old place he and
Doreen used to share before she was carted off to jail.
It had been sold and was bone empty. That's where she
was just coming back from. Her own home might as
well have been empty as well without Willie there.

"He's gone. Oh God, he's really gone." Lauren wrapped
her arms around her stomach and began to caress herself.
She caressed herself like she would have wanted Willie
to—like he'd done for so many nights.

"This can't be. This just can't be." Lauren jumped
up off the couch and started pacing. "Maybe he's gone
back to visit his peoples in Kentucky. Yeah, that's it.
He said his momma hadn't been feeling well lately.
Yes, that's where he's gone; to see about his momma.
And that's a good thing, right?" Now Lauren was talking to herself and expecting answers. "A girl wants a
man who's gonna look after they momma. That means
he's gonna look after her too. So it's all right that Willie done went to see about his momma. I'll just wait

here. I'll wait right here until he gets back. I'm not even gonna go chasing after him like that ex-wife of his used to do. No. I'ma trust my man to come back to me."

Lauren looked around the house. "Oh no, but Willie can't come back to this mess. No. What man wants to come home to a filthy house? None. Girl, you betta get this place together, and fast, if you want your man to come back."

Lauren began cleaning the house like never before. For three days straight, without taking a rest, without food and without water, she cleaned that house spotless. She stripped the floors. She bleached down the walls, every doorknob, every light switch, and every electrical outlet. She cleaned the refrigerator and stove. She cleaned out closets, threw out clutter, and cleaned the basement. Everything sparkled—the windows, the mirrors, and the countertops. She'd taken all the curtains down, cleaned them, pressed them, and rehung them. By the time Lauren finished with that house, it could have appeared on the cover of a *Better Homes and Gardens* magazine. Lauren had cleaned and cleaned until she couldn't find a dirty thing in that house. Unfortunately, though, after three days, she still didn't find Willie either.

On day four, Lauren sat on her couch waiting—just waiting to hear Willie's key turning in the lock. Waiting to hear the phone ring and Willie on the other end saying he was coming home. By day five, Lauren was up and down off the couch every five minutes running to the picture window in the living room. She wanted to see if she could spot Willie coming up the drive. She never saw him. By day six, she was picking up the phone every five minutes to make sure it still had a dial tone. But the phone worked just fine. At least every time Lauren's mother called to check on her it was working.

"Ma, I can't talk right now. I'm 'spectin' Willie to call. I can't be tying up the line talking nothing with you." Before her mother could protest, Lauren had slammed the phone down in her ear.

On day seven, Lauren's mother couldn't even get her to pick up the phone anymore. That's when she broke down, pulled out her walker, and had her neighbor's son drive her over to the house. She knocked and knocked and knocked, but there was no answer.

"Oh, dear God, I ain't got a good feeling about this," Lauren's mother had moaned after five minutes of knocking.

"You want me to get inside and see if there's any foul play or anything going on?" the neighbor's son offered.

"Naw, you ain't gon' be able to. Her doors are locked. I done tried 'em."

He cleared his throat. "Ma'am, uh, if you want me to get in there, I can." His eyes cast downward.

"And just how do you plan on getting in a locked house?" Lauren's mother asked as she watched as her neighbor's son looked everywhere but at her, and then began to whistle. "Oh, you youngins always up to no good." She sucked her teeth and shook her head. "Well, go on, then. Use that evil trade of yours for somethin' good."

"Yes, ma'am." And on that note, he went to the trunk of his car, came back with a bag of tools, and went to work like a pro until he got Lauren's front door opened in less than three minutes flat. "There you are, ma'am." Still, he couldn't look the old woman in the eyes.

Lauren's mother tightened her lips. Balancing on her walker with one hand, she took the other and slapped the twenty-two-year-old boy upside the head. "And don't you even think about doing something like this to my house. I'm telling you now, before my husband died he left me a mound of bills. But he also left me a shooting gun that will split a man's wig, if you know what I'm saying."

"Ye . . ., yes, ma'am. I knows what you saying."

"Now help me on into my daughter's house."

"Yes, ma'am." He helped the old woman into the house.

"Lauren," she called out, thinking she'd have to cart around the house in search for her only child, but that wasn't the case. Lauren lay right there on the couch, sleeping, looking like an angel in her spick-and-span clean house. Nothing looked out of the ordinary—except for the blood surrounding Lauren all over the couch.

Chapter Forty-three

Mother Doreen dropped the journal. Or it slid from her hands. She wasn't sure. All she knew is that it was no longer in her hands, and she felt as though she was no longer in her right mind. This was all just a nightmare, and she was going to wake up any minute now.

She was going to wake up, and she was going to be walking toward the altar back at the New Day Temple of Faith sanctuary. At the altar her future husband would be waiting. Their ceremony would go on as planned and there would be no interruptions. Nuptials would be exchanged, and she would become Mrs. Wallace Frey.

"Arrrre . . . you okay? Do you want me to call the nurse?" Lauren pushed her water toward Mother Doreen. "Would you like some water?"

Mother Doreen shook her head in the negative. She didn't dare speak. If she did, she knew her voice would crack like an egg left boiling with no water in the pan; and then just explode.

It took a couple of minutes, but Mother Doreen managed to get herself back together. "Oh dear, I'm sorry," she said about the journal that lay splat on the ground. She bent over, picked it up, then extended it to Lauren.

"But you're not finished," Lauren said, slowly taking the journal.

"I, I can't read anymore. I mean, what's left to read anyway? Your boy told me all about how Willie and me changed the course of your life. And I can see here for myself that he wasn't lying. I don't need this journal to tell me the wrong I've done and that I owe you an apology." Mother Doreen took in a deep breath. "Matter of fact, that's why I'm here anyway."

Mother Doreen leaned in and extended her hands to Lauren. "Lauren, this is long overdue, and it doesn't even seem sufficient, but dear God, I'm so sorry. I'm so sorry for what I did to you at that motel room all those years ago. I'm sorry for what I did to your baby. Now I know this doesn't change things, but I promise you I had no idea you were with child at the time. If I could take back what I did, I surely would. But I can't. For years, I didn't even want to face the wrong I'd done to you. It was like a part of me I wish never existed; a part of me I wish I'd never known. I made sure that no one else ever knew that part of me again.

"Not too long ago, I finally shared the truth with some folks I trust. God's forgiven me, and I've forgiven myself. But in order to put complete closure on this thing, for me, anyway, I need your forgiveness," Mother Doreen pleaded her case. "Can you find it in your heart to ever forgive me? Even if it's not right now, not at this moment, to just know that one day God will put it on your heart to forgive me is all I can ask. So will you? Will you forgive me?"

Lauren looked down at Mother Doreen's hands while Mother Doreen waited with bated breath for Lauren to respond. Finally Lauren shook her head. "I . . . I can't."

A gasp came out of Mother Doreen's mouth as if she were a balloon that someone had just let the air out of. She dropped her hands, and they began to tremble as her eyes moistened.

"I can't forgive you," Lauren started, "unless you can forgive me too."

Tears dropped from Mother Doreen's eyes as she looked at Lauren stunned. "Huh? What?"

"I need your forgiveness too, for what I put you through. I had some wrong in all this too," Lauren admitted. "I had no business sleeping with a married man in the first place, but there was just something about Willie. I don't have to tell you that, though. I'm sure whatever it was that had me tailing after a married man was the same thing that had you to marry him in the first place. It was like an addiction; an obsession that I couldn't let go of."

"I know how you feel. Willie had what these young folks call swag—swagger—something like that. But it's still no excuse for how I acted."

"And it's no excuse for me clutching to him like he was an available man." There was a few seconds of silence, and then Lauren spoke again. "So, what we gon' do here? We gonna forgive each other or not?" Lauren extended her hands.

Mother Doreen looked down and smiled as she grasped Lauren's hands. "I'm sorry, and I forgive you."

"I'm sorry, and I forgive you."

At that moment, Mother Doreen could have sworn she felt and heard shackles and chains dropping off of her body and on to the floor. It was loud. Even after all the weight had been shed, she continued to hear the sound of chains hitting the floor. Those must have been the ones that had Lauren held in bondage for all these years.

Mother Doreen couldn't help it; the next thing she knew she'd released Lauren's hands, jumped up out of that chair, and got her Holy Ghost dance on, lifting her hands and her voice, giving praises unto God.

Lauren sat up in the bed clapping and smiling at Mother Doreen's display. "That's right, girl. You go on and praise Him for me too."

After a few minutes, out of breath, Mother Doreen plopped back down in the chair. "Whew, child, I'm too old for this."

Lauren cracked up laughing. "No, you're never too old to praise the Lord. I might have turned my face away from Him all these years, maybe even stopped believing. But I reckon it's never too late to send up praises to Him."

"Yeah, I know that's right." Mother Doreen took a deep breath. "Child, I think I will take some of that water after all."

"Help yourself," Lauren told her.

Mother Doreen helped herself to one of the several Styrofoam cups the nurse had brought in. She then filled the cup with some water from the pitcher the nurse had brought in as well. She gulped it down and felt refreshed. "Thank you, I needed that."

"No, I needed that." Lauren shook her head. "Look at us; once two young foolish girls, now old wise women breaking the chains of the past. Hallelujah!"

"Glory to His name," Mother Doreen cosigned.

Lauren stared off for a minute, and then spoke. "I could kick myself for giving up on life all these years. But when Willie left me, I just felt dead, so I just gave up on life. I felt that I couldn't breathe without that man. That I couldn't live without him."

"Is that why you tried to kill yourself?" Mother Doreen asked.

"Kill myself?" Lauren was confused.

"Yes, that day your mother and her neighbor's son found you lying in blood, what had you done? Slit your wrist or something?"

Lauren stared at Mother Doreen for a moment, and then burst out laughing. "Now Willie was all that and then some, but not worth killing myself over, that's for sure."

Mother Doreen waited for Lauren to settle down from laughing before she asked, "Then if you hadn't tried to kill yourself, what was all the blood about? What happened?"

Lauren stared at Mother Doreen for a minute. "You really have no idea, do you?" Mother Doreen shrugged. "Here, honey," Lauren nodded toward the journal for a final time. "I really think you better read that last page."

Chapter Forty-four

"Oh, Lord, in the name of Jesus! Call 911! Call 911!" Lauren's mother shouted.

The neighbor's son did as he was instructed, and within minutes, the ambulance arrived at Lauren's house.

"Can someone tell me what's going on?" one of the three EMTs entering the house asked.

"It's my daughter," Lauren's mother cried. "She's pregnant. Blood's everywhere. Her baby . . ." she said frantically.

"Okay, just calm down. Calm down, ma'am," one of the other EMTs told her. "You don't want us to have to take you too. Let us see about your daughter. Everything is going to be okay."

The neighbor's son helped Lauren's mother sit down in a chair next to the couch while the EMTs tended to Lauren.

"Oh, God, in Jesus' name, not again . . . not again." Lauren's mother rocked back and forth. "She can't lose not another baby. Her mind won't be able to take it. It just won't." She began to pray as the EMTs worked on Lauren, and then transferred her into the back of the ambulance. They allowed her mother to ride with them, and she sat there with her eyes closed, praying the entire ride to the hospital.

Ten minutes later, the ambulance pulled up to the ER. They helped Lauren's mother to the waiting room while Lauren was taken on a stretcher to the back.

"We've got a young female in her twenties," one of the EMTs began shouting off as they rolled Lauren through the hospital. "She's full term. Looks like she went into labor but didn't call for help. She has a pulse."

"What about the baby?" a nurse asked as she speed walked alongside of the stretcher.

"You can see its head. It wants to come out, but it's like something kept it in there or someone. I mean, she's fully dilated. Her water has already broken. I'm surprised the baby hadn't just popped out already. We're stumped on this one. We made the call not to begin delivery since we were only ten minutes away from the hospital. Figured both baby and mother would have a better chance with hospital equipment and technology."

"I guess the baby thought so too," the EMT at the foot of the stretcher added, "because the baby's head is out now!"

It was like someone hit the fast-forward button and everything began to speed up. Lauren was taken into a room where doctors and nurses were moving well above the normal speed limit in order to get the baby delivered.

"Lilah, Lilah, can you hear me?" a doctor said.

"Lauren; it's Lauren," a nurse said. "I'm sure that's what one of the EMTs told us her name was. Her mother's out there in the waiting room. They said she rode along."

"Lauren, Lauren, sweetie. You with us?" the doctor asked.

"She's still got a pulse, but her heart rate is dropping," another nurse said.

"You're going to be okay, Lauren. You're going to be just fine," the doctor said as she proceeded to deliver the baby, without Lauren's assistance. It was difficult because they didn't have enough time to do a C-section and Lauren was not helping to push. But they had to get that baby out of her. Dead or alive, they had to remove the baby . . . and fast.

"Lauren, Lauren, honey." Her mother stood over her bedside rubbing her hair back with her hand. "Lauren, it's me, Ma."

Lauren moaned, fluttered her eyes, and then tried to move. "Ohhhhh," she groaned in pain.

"Just lie still. Don't try to move. The doctors said you'd be in a lot of pain. Just take it easy, baby. Take it easy."

Lauren moaned and groaned a little more, and then her eyes fell shut again. Her hands, initially at her side, rose to rest on her belly. That's when her eyelids snapped open. "Baby! The baby. Where's the baby? It can't be born yet. Willie needs to be here to see it be born. I can't let the baby out. Willie has to be here to see his baby born."

"Calm down. Please calm down," her mother insisted.

"No! No! Momma, please tell me they didn't let my baby be born. Not without Willie. Not without Willie. It wanted to come out. It kept trying to come, but I told it no. I told it no, no, no. It had to wait for its daddy to get here. I held it in there. I pushed it with every ounce of strength I had left. Please don't tell me they let my baby be born. Please," Lauren cried.

Tears began to fall from her mother's eyes. It hurt her to see her daughter like this. She'd seen it before, almost a year to the day when Lauren's first baby didn't survive the beating the angry wife had dished out to the pregnant mistress. She remembered praying and fasting; pushing away her plate for the pure sanity of her daughter's mind. She would have hoped that it was her earnest plea to God that had gotten Lauren back on her feet, but she knew deep in her soul it was Willie and all his promises that had pulled her out of her funk.

Now there was no Willie and no promises for him to make. Lauren's mother feared praying and fasting alone might not do the trick this time.

"Has the new mommy come to yet?" a nurse whispered as she entered the room, pushing a rolling bassinet in front of her.

Lauren's mother brushed the falling tears from her eyes. No, Willie was no longer here, but he'd left behind a part of him that just might do the trick. "Oh, looky here. Look at the beautiful baby," the doting grandmother exclaimed. "And guess what, Lauren, honey? It's a boy. It's a boy, and you can name him Willie Jr. if you'd like. It will be just like Willie is here after all." She did everything but cross her fingers and hope to die that seeing the baby would pull her daughter back into reality; the reality that Willie was gone, but she still had a baby to raise.

"And one beautiful baby boy he is," the nurse complimented, parking the bassinet right next to Lauren's bed.

Lauren fixed her eyes on the baby. Both her mother and the nurse waited on a reaction, but they got none. When Lauren finally did react, it wasn't exactly what the two women, who were mothers themselves, had been expecting. After staring at the baby for a few moments, Lauren turned her back completely to the baby, pulled the covers up to her neck, and then stared off.

Embarrassed, Lauren's mother looked at the nurse. "It's okay. My daughter's just not feeling well. Why don't you just go ahead and leave the baby with me?"

The nurse smiled pleasantly, then exited the room, leaving the baby boy for his grandmother to tend to. And sadly, she would be the one to tend to him permanently.

Chapter Forty-five

Mother Doreen stood to her feet. "Terrance . . . Terrance is Willie's boy?"

"Terrance is Willie's boy," Lauren confirmed.

With her hand over her mouth, Mother Doreen began to pace. "You mean to tell me when Willie and I moved to Ohio, he left knowing you were with child? With his child?"

"Yes. And it devastated me to no end." Lauren looked around the room. "As you can see."

"But, why? How? I . . ." Mother Doreen couldn't even put her words together. She was too floored. Everything—this entire day—needed to sink in. So much was beginning to register in her mind, right back to the day she got released from jail.

Willie had been so antsy and jittery that day. Mother Doreen had thought it was because he'd been so excited about getting to be with her again. Now she knew different.

"Baby, you're free! You're free!" Willie had said as Doreen was released from jail. "No more jail and no more West Virginia."

"Yes, I know, baby. I know!" Doreen was just as excited. She went to hug Willie, but he was too busy ushering her to the car as if he'd planted a bomb in the jail and it was about to blow. "Will you slow down a minute?" Doreen chuckled. "I know you're trying to hurry and get

me home and all so we can . . . you know . . ." Doreen
flirted.

"Actually, I'm not."

Doreen stopped in her tracks—offended. "Excuse
me?"

Willie had kept it moving and now stood by the car,
holding the passenger door open for Doreen. He noticed Doreen's demeanor. "Oh no, baby, I didn't mean
it like that. It's just that, I'm trying to get you home, but
not the home you think. You see, I done already sold
our house here. Sold your car too. We all set up in a
nice little spot in Malvonia, just like I promised."

Doreen's heart fluttered. "Willie, you kept your
promise." She began walking toward her husband.
"You really did." She placed a hand on each side of his
face and kissed him more passionately than she had on
their wedding day. "I love you, William Tucker, and I
always will. I'll never be away from you like this again,
and that's a promise. It's a promise I'm going to keep."

Doreen kept her promise all right. As difficult as it
might have been, she stayed with him. For the first year
it wasn't too hard, but once Willie got comfortable in
his new town, he turned back to some of his old ways;
most of his old ways. Eventually, all of his old ways.

"There's a hundred dollars missing from the bill
money," Doreen had complained one night as soon as
Willie hit the door. It was two o'clock in the morning,
and she'd been angrily pacing the floor of their two-
bedroom home in Malvonia, Ohio. She'd been waiting
for Willie to show his face through the door so she
could question him about the missing money. This was
the third time she'd noticed this much money missing. There had probably been other times, but she just
hadn't paid that much attention until recently. "You
gambling our money away, Willie? You promised—you

promised you'd stopped gambling. Matter of fact, you swore on a stack of Bibles." With hands on hips, Doreen waited for Willie to respond.

Closing the door behind him, he stumbled and removed his hat from his head. "Oh, woman, ain't no money missing. You probably just miscounted or something. Or, matter of fact, didn't I see you in a new pretty dress last week 'fore you went to church? Maybe that's where the money went."

"Don't you play with me, Willie," Doreen pointed. "You know I ain't never bought or even owned no hundred-dollar dress in my life."

"Then I don't know where the money run off to then." He scratched his head, then shooed his hand, brushing her off.

"So you acting like it's no big deal? Let's see if you're acting that way when you sitting in the dark because I can't pay the electric bill."

Willie squinted his eyes and shook his head as if he was trying to shake off a headache. "Looky here; I got an idea. Why don't you go ask that pastor of yours for some help in paying the bills? All the money you done put in that offering plate since we been here, I'm sure the church can help out a little."

"It is not New Day Temple of Faith's responsibility to pay our bills. It's yours, Willie, and I won't embarrass myself by going down to that church asking for money when I have a healthy able body of a husband to provide for me."

Willie jerked to catch his balance, and then stared at Doreen. "Embarrassment? Oh, is that what I am to you now? An embarrassment?" So much anger and resentment filled Willie's eyes. "Woman, if you only knew." He turned his back to walk away.

"If I only knew what, Willie? If I only knew what?" Willie continued walking away. Doreen went after him, grabbing him by the shoulder to stop him. "Please tell me, because I want to know." Tears began to fill her eyes. "I want to know what's going on with you. Why you find more pleasure in being out there in the streets gambling, drinking, and carrying on, then lying about it, instead of just being here with me. What's wrong with me, Willie? Is it because of . . ." Doreen choked on a few tears. ". . . is it because I ain't a whole woman no more and can't give you no babies?"

"Dang it, woman!" Willie slammed his fist through the wall, scaring the living daylights out of Doreen, for she'd never before seen a violent, angry bone in his body. Not even the day she . . . the day she . . . "Didn't I tell you I ain't care about no babies? I don't care about that stuff no more, Reen. Besides . . ." He paused. He looked at Doreen as if he was holding something back. As much as she wanted to pull it out of him, her gut feeling told her it was better off left inside Willie. It was a demon he'd have to live with within; not one she needed to pull out of him and have to fight. No siree; that battle was not hers.

"I'm sorry, Willie," Doreen apologized. "Perhaps you're right. Maybe I did miscount, miscalculate, or something. I don't know." She threw her hands up and let it go. "Anyway, you want some dinner? I was too mad to cook earlier, but I can whip you up one of those cold cut sandwiches you like," Doreen smiled.

"Naw, you do enough," Willie smiled back.

"You sure?"

Willie nodded.

"Well, all right, then. I guess I'll just go set you a bath. You look like you've had a long day." Doreen walked by Willie toward the bathroom, kissing him on the cheek as she walked past him. The next thing she knew Willie had grabbed her by the arm. "What, Willie? What is it?" Again, he looked as though there was something deep within him that he wanted to let go.

"I, I just wanted to tell you that . . ." Willie paused and swallowed hard. "That I love you. Glad God gave you to me. Lord knows I don't deserve you, but I sure am glad He gave you to me anyway."

"Then why don't you join me at church this Sunday so you can thank God personally for your lovely wife," Doreen blushed. "You ain't been in a couple of Sundays."

Willie chuckled, smiled, and blushed himself. "Why don't you just go ahead and tell Him for me? I'm sure He listens to you much more than He listens to me anyway."

Doreen shook her head. "Oh no, you don't. There's a whole lot I don't mind doing for you, because you're my husband and I love you. But there are some things a man just ought to do for himself; talking to God is one of them. I'm sure pastor will be glad to see you on Sunday." Doreen winked, then headed off to run Willie a bath, leaving him alone . . . with his demons.

Chapter Forty-six

"I knew it! I knew it!" Doreen yelled after she burst into her bedroom to find Willie lying up with some floozy. "Those women thought I had lost my mind when I told the driver taking us to the women's retreat to stop that bus and let me off. They thought I was crazy to want to walk almost ten miles back home. But my spirit was telling me something wasn't right, and my spirit is never wrong—never!"

"Doreen, honey, if you just let me explain." Willie had his hands up in surrender while the woman next to him gripped the covers, fearing for her life.

"Explain *what?* I might have been a virgin when we got married, but trust me, what you two doing—and in my bed no less—don't need no explanation." Doreen was fuming. At this moment she had nothing but complete disgust for her husband. She couldn't even look at him, so she didn't. Her eyes landed on the girl next to him. "Shanna! Shanna, is that you? Sister Farmer's baby girl?"

"Ye, ye, yes, ma'am," Shanna stuttered as fear put tears in her eyes. She had no idea of Doreen's past. Nobody in Malvonia did. So she had no idea of just how much danger she could have been in if Doreen had decided to beat her down like she had the last chick she'd caught with her man.

"You're just a girl. Right out of high school," Doreen said.

"Ye, yes, ma'am. Just had my eighteenth birthday last week." Tears fell from Shanna's eyes. "And please, ma'am—please let me live to see my nineteenth. Please don't tell my mama. She'll kill me. She'll kill me dead."

It was clear that Shanna wasn't the least bit worried about Doreen doing damage to her. It was her mother she was in fear of. Still, seeing the fear in her eyes reminded Doreen of the fear she had seen in Lauren's eyes. She looked at Willie, and for the first time ever, she could even see fear in his eyes. She could tell that it wasn't just fear that she would run off and leave him. He feared that there was about to be another repeat of what happened inside motel room 111. What really worried Doreen at the time was that she was in fear too. She feared that once again she would lose control.

Was God testing her again? Was the devil tempting her? She held her head in confusion. She really didn't know what to do. Should she do what she should have done years ago and just walk away? Walk away from what? Willie? The situation? Both?

If she didn't walk away—if she did what her flesh really wanted to do and wring both Shanna and Willie's necks, she knew the consequences. Could she stand being locked up again away from society? Away from her family? After all, she'd just gone home and visited her family for the first time since she'd been thrown in jail.

"Girl, we were all worried sick about you just jumping up and leaving West Virginia," Sarina had said when Doreen showed up on her parents' doorstep.

"Speak for yourself," Doreen's mother had said. "I prayed to God that He'd look after you no matter where you was at; that whatever was going on that was keeping you from us, He'd have His hand on."

"Good," Sarina spat, "'cause somebody needs to put they hands on Willie, because we all know *that's* what's been keeping her from us. All she's been doing is chasing that fool and his women around town; same thing she was doing when she was here. Too worried about that fool to even pick up the phone and see about your family. What did we get? A letter once every blue moon. And those letters were the only things that kept us from filing missing persons on your tail."

Doreen hadn't lashed back at her little sister's comments. She felt it was better not to. Just as long as her family thought those were the reasons for her being gone, they would never know the truth. But would they believe that a second time around? If she laid a hand on this young girl and got locked up again for another year, or even more, what would her family think?

In all honesty, she didn't care what her family thought. Looking at the scared young girl who was just getting a start on life—lying next to a grown man buck naked; not just any grown man, but Doreen's husband . . . Doreen couldn't resist the urge.

Glaring at the girl the entire time, Doreen slowly walked over to the nightstand that sat beside her and Willie's bed. Once there, she gently slid the top drawer open and reached in.

"Oh, God, no," Shanna began to whimper. "Please God, no."

"Doreen, honey . . ." Willie held his hands up in surrender. "What you doing over there, Reen?"

With her hand still in the drawer, Doreen stopped and looked at Willie. "What's the matter, Willie? Is this feeling a little like déjà vu? Well, don't worry. This time it will be different. This time I got something for both of you." And on that note Doreen pulled her hand out of the drawer, which now had something black and hard in it. It was trimmed in silver. And it was about to change everybody's life in that room.

***

"Thou shall not commit adultery. Thou shall not for-nicate . . ." Doreen found every scripture she possibly could in relation to the situation at hand. And for the past hour she'd sat there going over the scriptures with both Shanna and Willie.

Doreen was the only one dressed. When she had ordered Willie and Shanna to sit on each side of her while she opened the black hardback Bible with pages trimmed in silver, they'd tried to get dress first.

"No need to get dressed," Doreen had told them sternly. "God's already pulled the covers off of you and seen your naked selves. No use trying to cover up now."

Glad that what Doreen had pulled out of the night-stand drawer was a Bible and not a gun, the two obliged. Strangely enough, after about a half hour, each of them had almost forgotten the circumstances which had led to a mini-Bible Study session.

"You know, they shouldn't be so scared to teach us this stuff in youth church," Shanna said. "I wish I'd learned all this before—just what it means to present my body to God as a living sacrifice—holy and accept-able." She looked down in shame. "Now it's too late."

Doreen was quick to tell Shanna, "Child, it's never too late. It's never too late to repent to God and give yourself to Him. To Him . . ." She looked over at Wil-lie, rolled her eyes, then turned her attention back to Shanna. ". . . not some man who ain't even your hus-band—who's somebody else's husband."

"Really?" Shanna asked Doreen, looking a little un-sure.

Doreen nodded. "Really. Trust me. I know. Just say a prayer of repentance."

"That's all?" Still, Shanna looked unsure.

"That's all," Doreen assured her.

The girl swallowed, lifted her hands, and closed her eyes. Her mouth opened to form the first words of her prayer, but then Doreen stopped her.

"One more thing, though," Doreen said. "You have to mean it in your heart."

"Oh, I mean it," Shanna said, as she assumed the position and began a prayer of repentance to God.

Willie sat as still as a statue on the other side of Doreen while Doreen herself watched the tears flow from Shanna's eyes as she repented to God. She not only repented for the act of fornication and adultery, but for several other things as well. She was so into her words to God that she forgot Doreen and Willie were even in the room. Once she was finished, Doreen shocked herself and everybody else in the room when she threw her arms around the weeping teen and told her that everything was going to be all right—that from this day forward she was renewed in Christ and that God was giving her another chance.

Doreen closed the Bible and stood from the bed. She picked the girl's clothes up off the floor and threw them in her lap. "Get dressed and get home," Doreen told her.

Shanna didn't have to be told twice as she quickly followed orders and got dressed. Once she was dressed she stood there, making sure Doreen was finished with her.

"You know your way out," Doreen told her.

Shanna scurried toward the door before Doreen changed her mind and pulled something else up out of that nightstand drawer. Doreen stared down at the floor and didn't look up. But she did hear Shanna's feet stop in her tracks once she made it to the bedroom door. She then heard her say. "I'm sorry, Ms. Doreen. I'm sorry this had to happen. But I'm glad it did."

Doreen looked up sharply, and Shanna quickly explained herself.

"Because had it not happened, no telling what would have become of my life. So I thank you, Ms. Doreen. Thank you." She turned to leave again, but as if having another sudden thought, she stopped and turned around again to speak, but Doreen cut her off.

"No, Shanna. No, I'm not going to tell your momma."

Shanna nodded, half-smiled, and then was gone.

There was silence before Willie spoke. "I don't know what just happened here, Reen, but I feel like a changed man. Just sitting here seeing you—I mean, I know it was nothing . . . it was nobody but God. It had to be God in you doing all that. I mean, 'cuz I've seen what the flesh in you can do." Willie had slipped on his boxers and now stood. "Baby, I'm so sorry, and I promise . . . I swear on everything breathing I will never cheat on you again. I'm sorry, baby, for real. I'll make it up to you. I'll make everything up to you. Just tell me what to do. What do you want me to do for you, Doreen?"

Doreen looked at her husband knowing that what he was shooting off right now was nothing but talk. Yeah, he'd been moved by what had just taken place the last hour. He wanted to change, but she knew he wouldn't—not really. This move of God would have an affect on him for about a week; two at the most. He'd join her for church a few consecutive Sundays, go down to the altar to get prayer and hands laid on him. But then he'd be back to his old self. Not because God couldn't change him, but because deep down inside he didn't want God to change him. And Doreen could hardly fault Willie for that. She knew firsthand what it felt like to not want change . . . to fear change. Perhaps a fear of change was exactly what was keeping her by Willie's side. Willie was the only man she'd ever been with. Life without Willie would mean a big change for Doreen. She couldn't even envision her life without him. And on top of that, she'd made some poor decisions too, and Willie had stood by her. Heck, perhaps the two were made for each other. At least those were the reasons that would get Doreen through her years with Willie.

Perhaps this wouldn't be the last time she'd catch Willie with another woman, had to pray, pull out the Bible to read scripture, and even get a couple of his mistresses saved. Keeping that pushed in the back of her mind, Doreen knew not to ask of Willie more than he was capable of doing. Otherwise she'd be setting herself up to fail.

"Please, Reen, tell me. What can I do?"

Doreen took a deep breath. She looked down at their bed her husband had just defiled with another woman and said, "You can wash my sheets," then exited the room.

Chapter Forty-seven

"I should have left him," Mother Doreen said to herself as her mind returned to the present day. "I would have left him," Mother Doreen said somberly to Lauren. "Had I known he'd left you back in West Virginia with a child to tend to, I'd left him." Mother Doreen didn't know if those words were true, if she was just saying them now that Willie was gone and she didn't have a choice but to picture life without him, or if she was just saying it to make Lauren feel better. She was saying them nonetheless. After all, Mother Doreen wasn't the same woman today as she was years ago.

"What decent woman would stay with a man who she knows abandoned his own child?" Mother Doreen continued. "Who she knows isn't taking care of his child? How could she stand to be with him?" Mother Doreen began to rub her arms as if she had the heebie-jeebies. "How could she stand to lie up with somebody, have them buy her food and keep a roof over her head, and he won't even do it for his own helpless child?" Mother Doreen shook her head.

"Not that I'm defending Willie or anything," Lauren said, "but Willie did take care of his responsibilities with Terrance; moneywise, anyway." She shrugged and continued. "No, he wasn't there for him in the physical like a boy needs a daddy to be. But every month like clockwork, he sent my mother a check." Lauren stared off. "'Willie done sent more money to take care of the boy,' my mother would tell me on her visits. 'Still no return address,' she'd add."

"So Willie was sending money for Terrance?" Mother Doreen couldn't believe what she was hearing.

"Yep. When the first envelope of money ever came, my mother said it had a note in it saying he was sorry, but he'd be a man and send money for his child until the day he died." Lauren sighed. "Well, when the money stopped coming, we knew then Willie had died. I mean, he didn't keep good on all his promises . . . but the one that counted most I guess . . ."

Mother Doreen's mouth dropped open at the epiphany that had just landed on her. "So that's where all the missing money was going. He wasn't gambling. He was sending the money here to West Virginia to take care of his son."

"Cash too—every time. I guess so there was no way of tracing it," Lauren said.

"Oh, Willie," Mother Doreen said, "why didn't you just tell me? Why didn't you just tell me, you old fool?"

"'Cause just like you said, you would have left him. Heck, even I knew that. A thousand times I thought of just finding you and telling you myself. I knew he'd leave you and come back to me." A sad expression covered Lauren's face. "But at the same time, I knew he'd only be coming back to me because he couldn't be with you anymore. And I . . . well, I didn't want him that way. A part of me did. But it was that feeling of him wanting to be with me, not settling for me, that drove me. That made me feel alive. And so when I didn't feel alive anymore, I just died. I just lay down and died." Tears flowed from Lauren's eyes and her nose began to run.

Mother Doreen handed her a tissue.

After wiping her nose and a few tears away, Lauren confessed, "Do you know I never even held my baby boy?" The tears came harder, and Lauren's shoulders began to heave up and down. "I couldn't do it. He reminded me of everything that hurt. He reminded me of everything painful. He reminded me of everything bad." She sniffed, and then calmed down a little. "He felt like an Ishmael in a weird sort of way. Like God was giving me a sign when I lost the first baby with Willie; then I run off and had to have another one. It was all my will and not God's at all. And my poor baby had to suffer for it. My poor baby."

Once again, Lauren's shoulders began to heave up and down as she cried hard. Mother Doreen went and placed her hand on Lauren's shoulder. After a few seconds, Lauren looked at Mother Doreen's hand, and then placed hers on top of it. Then the two women looked into each other's eyes but never said a word. Their eyes did all the talking for them. This was it. This was the moment each woman had needed in her life in order to be set free.

As painful as it had been to learn the truth for Mother Doreen, it had set her free indeed. She and Lauren apologizing and forgiving each other had, figuratively speaking, loosened the cap on the jar that once held the butterfly. Now the lid had been lifted and the butterfly was free—for Mother Doreen anyway. But she knew for Lauren, there was still a little more untightening of the cap that needed to be done, and just as if God had read her mind, the door cracked open.

"Momma, it's been awhile." Terrance peeked his head in. "Are you okay?" He walked all the way in. "The doctor is out here, Momma . . . and the nurse. Can we come in?"

Lauren looked at her son and shook her head. "Not yet."

Terrance nodded and went to close the door.

"Just you," Lauren stopped him. "Just you come in. Because there's something I need to give you. And then there's something I need from you." Lauren looked at Mother Doreen, who smiled and nodded, knowing that what Lauren needed to give and get from her son was exactly what Mother Doreen had needed to give and get from Lauren.

"What? What is it, Mother?" Terrance hurried over to his mother's bedside. That was Mother Doreen's cue to give mother and son time alone. She made sure she had all of her belongings, then headed to the door. Before exiting she looked over at the pair, knowing that in just a few moments, the room would be full of beautiful butterflies . . . flying free.

Chapter Forty-eight

"If Sister Deborah was here to hear that story you just told us, Mother Doreen," Unique said in disbelief, "she'd write a book about it."

"A *New York Times* bestseller indeed," Bethany said in just as much awe as Unique and Margie were in after hearing the details Mother Doreen had shared with them on their drive back from West Virginia to Malvonia.

"What about Terrance?" Bethany asked. "I mean, you and Lauren are all squared away and cool, but how does he feel about all this?" Bethany shook her head in disbelief and said under her breath, "Ol' Willie had a kid—wow."

"I think Terrance will be okay," Mother Doreen said hopeful.

"You sure about that?" Unique asked. "I mean, that was one angry brother right there; straight hood. And take it from me—I know hood when I see hood."

A couple of the women laughed, and Mother Doreen replied, "Yeah, I think so. I mean, we really didn't get to say too much more after Lauren and I talked, but he knows where to find me. He knows he can reach out to me," Mother Doreen replied. "I still got a few things of Willie's stored in that old shed behind my house. When I moved back to Kentucky, I was going to throw the stuff out or give it to charity. But now I know just what to do with it." Mother Doreen smiled and looked upward. "Thank you, God!"

"Amen," Bethany cosigned. "Amen."

"Well, that's good to hear," Margie stated. "I'm glad you know what to do with Willie's things. But can I ask you one question?"

"Sure; go right ahead," Mother Doreen replied.

"What in the world are you going to do about Pastor Frey?"

"Thank you, Lord. Thank you, Jesus."

As Mother Doreen, Bethany, Margie, and Unique entered the church, they could hear someone praying. They'd come back to the church because that's where the women's cars were parked. There were still a few cars in the parking lot. Considering it was just a shadow away from midnight, they all went inside together.

"Yes, God. Thank you, God."

That prayer came from another person. It was a man and a woman and the voices were coming from the sanctuary.

They heard a third voice. "We thank you in advance, God." It also belonged to a woman.

All four women looked at one another.

"Um, uh, it can't be," Unique said, and was the first one to go barging through the sanctuary doors. "Well, I'll be . . ." Her mouth dropped. She was in awe as she saw that Pastor Frey and Sister Deborah were still pretty much in the same position they had been in hours ago when the foursome had headed to West Virginia. And Paige had obviously joined them after grabbing a bite, because she was in there praying up a storm too. Sister Deborah was sitting on the church pew with folded hands praying. Pastor Frey was on his knees at the altar.

"But it's been how many hours? And they are still . . ." Unique shook her head.

All Mother Doreen could do was stand there and weep at the sight of Pastor Frey praying like he was praying down the walls of Jericho. Deborah was the first to look up and see that her friends had returned. She stood up from the pew and walked toward her sisters in Christ. Sensing the movement, Paige followed behind Deborah. Once Paige and Deborah reached the women, no words were spoken. All the women just simply embraced.

"God is good, Sister Deborah," Mother Doreen whispered in Deborah's ear. "God is good."

Deborah pulled herself from the embrace. "And so is that man right there." She looked over her shoulder at Pastor Frey.

Mother Doreen exhaled. "Oh, Sister Deborah, you don't have to tell me that." She excused herself from the women and made her way down the altar to Pastor Frey. She managed to kneel down beside him and place her hand on his back. Like he knew her touch, he just began to weep. Before anyone knew it, the two were embraced weeping like two children who had dropped their ice-cream cones on a hot summer day; and the cones had been their only hope of keeping cool.

"I prayed He'd send you back to me," Pastor Frey said through tears. "I told Him I wasn't gonna let go of this prayer until He answered it. I told Him I wasn't gonna let go of this prayer until He brought you back to me." Pastor Frey pulled away from Mother Doreen and looked her in the eyes. "So did He? Did God bring you back to me, Doreen? Because if so, I still want to be your husband. Do you still want to be my wife?"

***

"I do," Mother Doreen replied.

"Then I pronounce you Mr. and Mrs. Pastor Wallace Frey," Margie said as Paige, Bethany, Unique, and Deborah cheered.

It wasn't quite the wedding Mother Doreen had planned, but it was a wedding nonetheless. Margie had performed the ceremony with the other four women and God as witnesses.

"Pastor Frey," Margie continued, "you may kiss your bride."

Pastor Frey put both hands behind Mother Doreen's head and pulled her into a big juicy kiss. The onlookers cheered even more.

"I love you, Mrs. Frey," Pastor Frey said, looking into Mother Doreen's eyes.

"And I love you too, Mr. Frey," Mother Doreen said back. "You know, for years, I've been waiting for God to tell me, 'It is finished,' and mean it. Well, guess what? He did say it some time ago, and He meant it too. I'm the one who had to let everything go, though. But guess what? I finally did." Mother Doreen smiled a huge smile. "I let it go, all of it, everything. My past; it is so finished." She looked at Pastor Frey like she thought she'd never look at another man—with nothing but deep love and passion. "But me and you . . ." she pointed from her chest to her new husband's. "Honey, me and you . . ." Mother Doreen planted a kiss on Pastor Frey that would have made a sinner blush. ". . . we are just getting started."

The End

About the Author

BLESSED selling author E.N. Joy is the author of *Me, Myself and Him,* which was her debut work into the Christian Fiction genre. Formerly a secular author writing under the names Joylynn M. Jossel and JOY, when she decided to fully dedicate her life to Christ, that meant she had to fully dedicate her work as well. She made a conscious decision that whatever she penned from that point on had to glorify God and His kingdom.

The "Still Divas" series is a continuance of the "New Day Divas" series, which was incited by her publisher, Carl Weber, but birthed by the Holy Spirit. God used Mr. Weber to pitch the idea to E.N. Joy; sort of plant the seed in her spirit, of which she prayed on and eventually the seed was watered and grew into a phenomenal series of books that she is sure will touch readers across the world.

"My goal and prayer with the 'New Day Divas' and the 'Still Divas' series is to put an end to the Church Fiction/Drama versus Christian Fiction dilemma," E.N. Joy states, "and find a divine medium that pleases both God and the readers."

With the success of the "New Day Divas" and the "Still Divas" series thus far, it is safe to say that readers agree this project is one that definitely glorifies God in every aspect, but still manages to display in a godly manner that there are "Church Folks" (church fiction), and then there are "Christian Folks" (Christian fiction), and come Sunday morning, they all end up in the same place.

E.N. Joy currently resides in Reynoldsburg, Ohio, where she is working on book three of the "Still Divas" series titled *The Sunday-Only Christian*.

You can visit the author at: www.enjoywrites.com or e-mail her at: enjoywrites@aol.com to share with her any feedback from the story as well as any subject matter you might want to see addressed in future Divas books.

Coming December 2012
The Sunday-Only Christian
Book Three of the "Still Divas" Series

What kind of woman wants a man so badly that she'd be willing to lie to get him? What if that lie includes denying the fact that she has a child?

Deborah Lewis is that woman. The suave, debonair Lynox Chase is the man Deborah wants. He's the man Deborah has wanted for years, almost had, but decided to give her ex a try, leaving Lynox hanging. With her ex no longer in the picture, Deborah is willing to eat crow and go claim Lynox. She can't help but worry if he will be forgiving and take her back, but figures after two years, he's had time to get over it.

Readers' Group Guide Questions

1. Do you think Mother Doreen owed it to the entire congregation to share her past?

2. Do you think Terrance had a right to approach Mother Doreen regarding her past that involved his mother?

3. Do you think Mother Doreen wanted to visit West Virginia for selfish reasons?

4. Did Mother Doreen owe it to Pastor Frey to let him know one way or another if she was going to marry him before she even went to West Virginia? Did she not owe her current situation closer versus her past situation?

5. Mother Doreen stayed with Willie regardless of his continued faults? Do you think that made her a good woman or so called Ride or Die Chick? Why or why not?

6. How do you feel about the advice Mrs. Tucker gave Doreen as a young bride?

7. Put yourself in Mother Doreen's shoes. Had you seen Willie's car at that motel, would you have turned your car around and gone back to check

things out? How would you have handled the situation?

8. If you found out the things Mother Doreen found out about her deceased husband, how would that make you feel?

9. Do you think, after what Mother Doreen had been through with Willie and in addition the new things she learned about him, she'll be able to fully trust a man? Or do you think ultimately Pastor Frey will pay for Willie's sins?

10. Most of my readers of the "New Day Divas" series always saw Mother Doreen as the perfect Christian. Did you? How do you feel about her now after learning her entire testimony?

UC HIS GLORY BOOK CLUB!

www.uchisglorybookclub.net

UC His Glory Book Club is the spirit-inspired brain-child of Joylynn Jossel, Author and Acquisitions Editor of Urban Christian, and Kendra Norman-Bellamy, Author for Urban Christian. This is an online book club that hosts authors of Urban Christian. We welcome as members all men and women who have a passion for reading Christian-based fiction.

UC His Glory Book Club pledges our commitment to provide support, positive feedback, encouragement, and a forum whereby members can openly discuss and review the literary works of Urban Christian authors.

There is no membership fee associated with UC His Glory Book Club; however, we do ask that you support the authors through purchasing, encouraging, providing book reviews, and of course, your prayers. We also ask that you respect our beliefs and follow the guidelines of the book club. We hope to receive your valuable input, opinions, and reviews that build up, rather than tear down our authors.

WHAT WE BELIEVE:

—We believe that Jesus is the Christ, Son of the Living God.

—We believe the Bible is the true, living Word of God

—We believe all Urban Christian authors should use their God-given writing abilities to honor God and share the message of the written word God has given to each of them uniquely.

—We believe in supporting Urban Christian authors in their literary endeavors by reading, purchasing and sharing their titles with our online community.

—We believe that in everything we do in our literary arena should be done in a manner that will lead to God being glorified and honored.

—We look forward to the online fellowship with you. Please visit us often at www.uchisglorybookclub.net.

Many Blessing to You!

Shelia E. Lipsey,
President, UC His Glory Book Club